To Chris my

otl

Table of Contents:

1. Black and Blue

The navigation beacon of the Super Space Destroyer Missile threw a pulsating cast of blue light onto the ground and the burnt oniony tang of hot dogs wafted down to him from a circle of onlookers. His own hot dog wasn't far away but the contents were moulded into a footprint and the bread roll lay agape by the brim of a plastic boater.

'Had enough then funny boy?' asked a voice from above.

He nodded. Yes, three our four seconds had been enough, he didn't usually change his mind so quickly.

The voice seemed dissatisfied.

'Maybe you didn't hear funny boy,' it said more distinctly. 'I said have you had enough?'

He nodded again and added an 'Mmmning,' sound.

Things weren't going to plan. Pimple had always been conscious of having 'something extra' - something that set him apart from individuals like David Carter and Godfrey Smith, but it didn't seem to be working at the moment. Whatever it was, he hoped would develop in its own way rather than being helped out by the boots which occupied most of his vision.

One of the boots slid under his chin and levered it upwards until he had a watery perspective of two leathered leggings towering into a zippered jacket.

'He's had enough!' said the voice. A change in tone implied that this information was being relayed to some colleagues nearby. The boot jerked upwards and his teeth chinked together sounding off a roundelay of harmonics above the eyebrows.

'Quite sure?'

He made a longer 'Mmmming' sound.

'He's quite sure' confirmed the voice.

'Ask him what we're supposed to watch?' said another voice.

'I've been asked,' continued the first voice, 'to ask you what we are supposed to watch?'

A rivulet of blood trickled over the toe of the boot and soaked into the bread roll

'Well funny boy?' The voice acquired an impatient edge. 'What are we supposed to watch?'

'Nothing really,' said Pimple.

'What was that?' I didn't quite catch that,' said the voice, 'I thought you said 'nothing'?'

'We thought he said 'nothing' as well,' confirmed the other voices.

'He might have said 'nothing',' speculated the first voice. 'Shall I ask him again?'

'Yes ask him again!' chorused the other voices.

'My friends think it would be appropriate if I might make so bold as to ask you again.' The question was not repeated.

He thought desperately. It was a difficult question. How could he explain 'Watch it!' There had been nothing obvious to watch when he had muttered the warning so clearly the 'it' had to be him. That being so he needed no further watching, but it required explanation.

Being careful to stress that in his opinion the danger had passed, he apologized for offering the warning in the first place.

'He says he's sorry,' said the voice. 'Do we accept his humble apology?'

'Finish him off!' yelled someone in the crowd. 'We want a good laugh.'

'Yeah-why make half a job of it?' sniggered someone else.

The boot stayed where it was while the crowd settled to an indecisive buzz. Then a no-nonsense contributor broke through.

'Come on now lads, fair's fair! There's no need to make a meal of it!'

A group of children speculated excitedly as the suggestion was being considered. At last a murmur in favour of leniency seemed to come from the crowd and conceding to the general mood the voice said: 'It seems that the jury has given their verdict. I presume they are honest men and true?'

The boot rose from sight then came hard down on the plastic boater. Seconds later two ring encrusted hands clamped onto the folds of his bomber jacket and hoicked him upwards until he was level with a face that matched the voice.

'On account of your age we accept your humble apology,' it growled. 'But on footcher occasions me and my friends here suggest you listen to mummy and keep your cheeky mouth shut – OK?'

The hands released him with just enough force to send him skittering back to earth, then, turning their backs on him the Old

Rockers continued in search of more memorabilia from their youth.

'Just like old times Stevie,' one remarked as they loped away.

'Yeah - brings you back don't it?' Stevie slid his comb through a preened crop of greyish hair. 'Had a twinge of arthritis though.'

Given hindsight Pimple would have known that this was one of those defining moments that celebrities often recall when choosing their favourite recordings. He might also have known that mere chance played no part in deciding the Carshalton Brotherhood of Old Rockers to take a nostalgic stroll in one of their favourite haunts just as he was emerging from the pier bar with Godfrey Smith. Armed with such knowledge he might have declined Godfrey's request to cross over to the giant rabbit seeking their custom from the other side of the road. But he was not armed with such knowledge, and neither was he to know that the moment they stepped into Funlands he would be recruited into a scheme so brilliantly masterminded in advance that his place was guaranteed even before his birth.

Shakily scouting round for items that had flown from his pockets during his rapid descent, he retrieved the backdoor key and some small change. The photo taken on the pier with Rose Freeman and Godfrey Smith was scuffed over with mud, but it would be worth keeping if he trimmed off Godfrey Smith.

Behind came the sound of thudding footsteps, then something hazy with speed swooped onto his mobile phone and holding it aloft, a boy whooped triumphantly back to his friends. It wasn't worth much, but the laughing together with the indifferent stares he received from the crowd as it fanned past him to alternative amusements only boosted his desire to be isolated from the rest of humankind.

There had been previous occasions when he felt at odds with the circumstances of his own life, and the wallop just received had raised this quandary to an even higher level. Behind lay a muddle of experiences pointing to nowhere in particular and ahead? Well, that was anyone's guess. Yet the moment was familiar. The bright lights, the garish faces on the House of Horrors - even his state of mind were all repeats of some past crisis which lay just beyond recollection. Stronger still was the anticipation of more to come, but lacking detail it arrived as a mere flavour with no hint as to what it might be.

At first there was nothing unusual about the gowned figure, except there was no obvious reason why she should have been heading straight for him.

Stopping a few paces ahead, she nodded as if confirming some previous notion about his appearance, then came in closer to peer at his lip.

He acknowledged her with an uneasy grimace.

'I've just been thumped.'

'Then come and beget patched up.' She spoke with authority and without question he followed her back the way she had come.

They walked briskly and he tried to assess her age and appearance against the flashing lights, but as he later discovered, it was difficult to judge her appearance in any light. Skirting behind the Killer Car Race Track and past a line of rumbling diesel generators they arrived at a small tent pitched in the open some distance away from the main attractions. Above the entrance, and harshly lit by a sodium lamp a plain board announced: Madame Zelda Adlez. 'Destiny Consultant.''

She drew aside the entrance flap, and bidding him to: 'Enter and beget seated,' went to the rear of the tent through a black velvet drape. The only illumination was provided by an oil lamp on a squat table, and the flickering light was picked up by reflective discs attached to the inside of the tent in fair imitation of a night sky. Feeling his way to the chair, he waited for his eyes get accustomed to the gloom. A third chair; an eight-armed statuette and a tea trolley completed the furnishings. More unexpectedly was the bottle of antiseptic and first aid box ready for use on the table by the lamp.

She emerged from the drape bearing a bowl of water and flannel. Placing the bowl and flannel on the table she instructed him to: 'Washeth thoroughly while the medicants are prepared.'

Gingerly wiping his face with the flannel he looked up from the bowl and watched her soak a ball of cotton wool in the antiseptic. It was done with religious solemnity, and putting herself between him and the lamp she held out the ball of cotton wool for him to take.

'Now dabeth where it hurteth.'

He dabbed, and again tried to gain some idea of her appearance, but it was just as difficult. A faceted broach beneath her chin threw the light back into his eyes, and her outline was confused by a black headscarf which merged with the drape leaving only a floating portion of her face open to inspection. The wrinkles and black eyebrows were plain enough though, and coupled with her peculiar way of speaking he decided she was a Romany.

'My mither was Swedish,' she announced piously, 'and I am an international destiny consultant.' Pressing the sticking plaster onto his top lip and thumbing the edges smooth she stood back to examine the result. 'It is done, but remaineth here while I return the medicants.'

She ferried the bowl and first aid box behind the drape, returning moments later with a framed picture that she placed beside the lamp.

'He is my best pupil so far.' A young Asian faced him mid-blink against a background of mountains. 'He will be receiving his third eye soon.'

'That's pretty good.'

'But with you it is lips.'

She moved clairvoyantly over the lamp and he felt for the loose change in his pocket.

She peered into the lamplight.

'You must soon prepare yourself for a long journey. The way will be fraught with impedimenta until the vernal equinox, after which an even longer journey will await you. Temptation will abound and fame will jostle with despair. But standeth firm for your lips will sustain you throughwith until you are called again.'

'Do I have to come here?'

She gazed upwards for an answer, but the tent flap parted, and the intimacy of the consultation expired in a triangular pool of sodium light. The silhouetted form of the intruder hesitated just long enough to be recognised.

'Oh! I didn't realise you had someone with you... sorry.' The tent flap closed.

'Entereth!' commanded Madame Zelda.

The tent flap opened again and Rose Freeman stood awkwardly at the entrance.

'I don't want to interrupt anything.' She noticed him. 'But Pimple, fancy you being here!'

'You are acquainted?' asked Madame Zelda.

'Yes,' began Rose.

'Then entereth.' repeated Madame Zelda.

'But Pimple was here first. It doesn't seem fair.'

'Entereth!' Madame Zelda palmed her into silence and produced two white cards. 'You were both expected, so beget seated, and pray complete these while I seek more astral guidance.'

Rose frowned at her card.

'I can never remember my national insurance number.'

'It mattereth not.'

Madam Zelda took the cards behind the drape where the unmistakable sound of a filing cabinet drawer being opened and closed was followed by a hollow clatter. She returned holding a long white bone pointedly labelled 'Tibetan Monks Shinbone'.

Rose giggled and prodded Pimple.

The bone was placed on the table and Madam Zelda waved her hands above it. 'Already it beginneth,' she intoned. 'It is indeed a propitious moment and for a while you will share unbounded happiness. But a foreign gentleman will intrudeth and casteth over you a shadow that will darken your travels. Yet faltereth not.' She fanned her hands while turning her gaze to both of them in turn. 'The wheel of fortune is spinning and love is just around the corner.'

A kettle gurgled from the tea trolley and Madame Zelda breathed the sigh of a job well done.

'Well, after that lets have a cuppa shall we?'

'But I'm not even going out with Pimple!' protested Rose.

'It surpriseth me not,' parried Madame Zelda, 'More water has yet to speedeth under the bridge...Sugar?'

'No thanks,' said Rose.

'Two for me please,' said Pimple.

Two tiny cups were put before them, and as she leaned over the lamp to reach the teapot, some blond curls could be glimpsed beneath Madame Zelda's headscarf. It was also clear that heavy make up rather than age accounted for her wrinkled features. She settled back with undisguised satisfaction.

'Nothing like a nice cuppa after a hard days work.'

'Have you finished then?' asked Rose. 'I mean, well - surely you expect more customers before Funlands closes?'

'I choose who I see.' Madame Zelda spoke imperiously. 'Only exceptional destinies are my concern.'

'But,' Rose was puzzled. 'Surely our fortunes are just ordinary - you know? I mean foreign gentlemen and long journeys. There's nothing unusual about that sort of thing is there?'

'Much dependeth on the gentlemen and where the road leadeth.'

Madame Zelda studied the cups and took them behind the drape. Again the drawers of the filing cabinet were opened, and returning with a carbon pad she tore off two receipts.

'That will be eight pounds and fifty pence each including VAT.'

'The Old Fake!' exclaimed Rose as they stepped outside. 'She charged us just the same as if we'd been seen separately. And did you notice? She only used that silly way of speaking when she was telling our fortunes. 'A foreign gentlemen will intrudeth and casteth over you a shadow.' indeed! And the way she pretended to read our teacups? There weren't any tea leaves in mine at all. I don't think she cared whether we believed her or not!'

She turned to him.

'Anyway why were you there? I didn't think you would be interested in having your fortune told.'

He pointed to his lip.

'She took me inside to patch this up.'

'You mean she just found you?' Rose was curious.

'Yes.'

'Where?'

'Near the Super Space Destroyer Missile.'

'It sounds all very peculiar to me.' She seemed unconvinced. 'I won't ask you what happened in case it's too embarrassing. Does it hurt?'

'A bit.' The fist shaped ache was sending exploratory feelers to his ears.

'Well, the change in temperature won't help it. It's quite chilly now.'

They had stopped just beyond the lamplight. Assorted pieces of litter skittered across the open patch of ground.

'Yes, and the wind's getting up as well,' he observed. 'I reckon we could be in for some rain soon.' Words didn't come easily to him and he lamented his lacklustre response.

'Yes, and if we stay here much longer it might rain on us.' She inclined her head at him. 'Mightn't it?'

'Yes it might.' He sensed that something more was being demanded from him. 'Do you fancy a coffee or something like that?'

'Well, what a good idea, I thought you'd never ask.'

'The trouble is I've run out of money.'

'Hmm,' she compressed her lips. 'I wonder why?'

'It's just that...'

'It's just that you spent most of your money in the pier bar with Godfrey Smith. Anyway I'm paying. Women are allowed to pay these days you know.'

She led the way through Funlands and along the promenade until they came to the hull of a boat suspended by chains above the entrance to a restaurant.

'The Ship Café. This will do.' she said decisively.

Once inside he remembered to take her coat, and later, on the way back to their table with the coffee he caught a reflection of himself in a long decorative mirror. He didn't look so bad really. The sticky plaster might have been better placed on his forehead, but a trace of ruggedness peeked out from the rigging of a sailboat etched into the glass.

He sat down with more confidence.

'I'm starting at Rilltots on Monday,' he announced.

She shuffled through her handbag. It was large and well furnished with pockets and zippers.

'I thought you were doing a course at Crantree Foundation?'

'I'm leaving it.' He spoke as if he had a choice.

She frowned as she withdrew her purse.

'Are you sure you'll like it at Rilltots? My Dad couldn't leave fast enough when he got a job at Shore & Toop.'

'It'll be alright.' He leaned back casually. 'It'll be better than the Foundation anyway.'

'You could have got a qualification at the Foundation couldn't you?'

'Yes, but I'll be earning a fair bit at Rilltots.' He tried to sound offhand. 'So I'll be able to take you out next week.'

She widened her eyes in mock surprise.

'Are you asking me to go out with you then?'

'Well,' his composure faded, 'if you're not doing anything special one night.'

'Only one night?' The corners of her mouth flickered upwards.

'More than one night if you like.' He sought refuge in the coffee cup.

She spoke quietly.

'Have you ever been out with a girl before Pimple?'

'Well, yes.' He hoped the grim episode with Maureen McDuncan had passed unnoticed in Bleak Leigh.

Her voice dropped to a whisper.

'Look at me.'

Two hazel miniatures of him stared back from her eyes which by now had become intensely personal. It was hard to believe he was the object of such uncompromising attention.

'You go shy very easily don't you?'

An edge of the sticking plaster popped away from his lip.

'Sometimes.' he mumbled.

'Well, why don't you say so you silly thing? You wouldn't be half so vulnerable if you did.'

She pressed the sticky plaster in place with her forefinger.

'You've got to stop pretending that you're something you're not.'

'It's a bit difficult.'

'It shouldn't be. You're not ashamed of what you are, are you?'

'No?'

'Then promise me that you will try to be yourself.' She searched his face for any insincerity.'

'Alright,' he spoke into the cup. 'I promise.'

Her forefinger moved to his chin and raised it up.

'Do you really mean it?'

'Yes.'

'In that case,' she kissed him lightly on the forehead. 'Could you please ask me again, and I might say yes.'

He asked her again and she said yes.

2.Muddy Water.

The hedged drive led to a quadrangle of flat roofed buildings and temporary classrooms which housed the Crantree Foundation. Once a youth training centre it had become an extension of the new Crantree University College and offered a range of vocational qualifications tailored to the needs of local industry. It was here that Pimple's parents had enrolled him for an additional year of study. Nestling on the only green patch of ground at the bottom of Spring Hill, the Foundation provided a chance for some ex Pin Lane High pupils to achieve something. For his parents, it meant another year of old carpets, but they decided it was worth the sacrifice.

In one direction the Bleak Leigh to Crantree road dipped into industrialized countryside, and in the other, the tallest brick structure in eastern England cast a possessive shadow over the study blocks. Once part of a coal fired power station, the huge central chimney stack proclaimed: 'Rilltot Fabrications' in vertical white lettering, and below it in the old turbine hall, hundreds of operatives worked furiously to produce windows and metal construction components for the vast housing and infrastructure programmes in the forthcoming years.

The rumble of machinery penetrated the thin walls of the classrooms like the sound of close battle; providing a constant reminder to those inside of the consequences should they fail to acquire the basic skills needed for electrical and mechanical engineering. Time and time again a dedicated team of instructors preached the truths expounded by Hook, Young, Ohm and Newton until every student had a rough understanding that a body in motion will continue in a straight line until acted upon by external forces, and that stress is directly proportional to strain - providing of course, that it is within the elastic limit. Proof of these truths were provided by fractured steel bars, a meteorite, and a bullet mushroomed by impact with something hard.

For a while, Pimple believed that the Foundation would rescue him from the tedium of a Rilltot production line, and that his studies might even lead him into an intimate world of fits and clearances offered by Shore and Toop Precision Control

Systems. But this was not to be, and it fell upon Mr Dowdsett - himself a veteran of 'Shore and Toop' to advise the Principal that Pimple would be unlikely to benefit from continuing on the course.

Mr Dowdsett had the responsibility of maintaining a workshop crammed with equipment donated to the Foundation by local industry. A variety of metal shaping machines were installed in lines down the shop, and over his objections, a gas welding plant was later added to the only uncluttered corner. He alone had the responsibility of ensuring that the powerful forces so enthusiastically described by his colleagues in the safety of their classrooms were unleashed in a way that would be least likely to cause injury to himself and his students. The first aid cupboard was positioned beside a black and yellow striped emergency button which triggered the trip relay of the main fuse box, and the office freezer contained an icebox big enough to take a foot.

Before untrained hands were permitted to touch anything remotely mechanical he lectured each new intake on safe workshop practice, and mindful that words were no substitute for reality, he readily exposed his own person to stress the vulnerability of important organs. Both the bold and squeamish were compelled to visualize his kidneys following a butting from the planing machine, or his groin after a scorching from the welding torch, and further insurance against short memories was provided by a gruesome display of safety posters.

But the most grisly outcome of workshop laxity was reserved for the first day of practical work when each class had to parade before Mr Dowdsett for inspection. Long hair had to be netted, overalls buttoned to the neck, and dangly ornaments removed. Any objections were soon quashed once Mr Dowdsett recounted the horrible experience of an early student called Moss.

Intent on clamping a steel rod accurately into the chuck of his lathe, Moss also clamped some loose fibres of his necktie into the chuck and promptly fed himself into the rotating jaws. But for the prompt action of Mr Dowdsett by the emergency button and some messy mouth to mouth resuscitation, Moss would have been no more. As it turned out, skilful surgery, and many visits to the dentist restored his features to something like their original condition, but for years afterwards he had to put up with close scrutiny from curious students.

Moss retained top position on Mr Dowdsett's list of unwanted memories, but Pimple came a close second the moment he decided to machine finish the base of his brass pen stand on the 'Dickensian Grinder'.

The properties of non-ferrous metals might have been better explained to him. Neither was he to know that Dickensian Ltd had included design improvements in their later models, but the moment he placed the magnetic clamp and his work on the wrong side of the grinding wheel Moss had a soul-mate to share his notoriety.

Compressing it's overload spring, the burst-proof grinding wheel screeched over the base of the pen stand at many thousands of revolutions per minute, and with no equal and opposite force to keep it where it was, the base instantly obeyed the laws relating to mass and acceleration and left the magnetic clamp without delay. The trip relay popped out and the Machine Shop sighed to a halt.

Mr Dowdsett stood bolt upright. The hairs on his arms stuck out like toothbrush bristles and various glands squirted out strange chemicals. He hadn't heard a sound like that since the army. Flicking his eyes around for signs of carnage he noticed Pimple gazing ashen faced but still intact at the bare surface of the clamp.

'It's gone,' he said.

'What has?' squeaked Mr Dowdsett.

'My pen stand.'

Noticing the brassy streak on the grinding wheel Mr Dowdsett roughly assessed the kinetic energy contained in six ounces of brass moving at about one hundred meters per second and stooped to look along the surface of the grinder bed. In line of sight through a neat oblong hole in the office door, a fragment of his silver jubilee mug lay in a puddle of tea on the desktop. Beyond that a shaft of dusty sunlight shone through a second oblong hole to a third oblong hole in the partition separating the workshop from the catering school. He straightened up, and in defiance of fire regulations lit his pipe and sucked deeply.

Somewhere outside a door slammed shut, and clearly audible in the silence of the workshop came the sound of hurried footsteps crunching along the access path. Moments later a chubby man with eyes like bilberry tarts bore down on him.

'For heavens sake Dowdsett!' he exclaimed. 'What was that?'

The following day his parents received a sympathetic letter from the Principal offering an excellent character reference, but advising them that their son would be unlikely to benefit from further attendance at the Foundation.

He sighed regretfully, and turning his gaze from the drive, rummaged through his haversack for the letter from Rilltot's human resources department. The hooter on the central chimney stack had already rallied the day shift, and the rush of traffic to the east entrance of the site had dwindled to just a few bleary eyed stragglers. Glowing red in the morning light, terraced rows of houses sloped upwards like coarse mountain scree to the gaunt north wing of the building. It was a forbidding sight, and presented a gloomy prospect for the future.

Stowing his bike in a rack beside the huge car park he climbed a broad flight of steps to the arrival hall. Facing him was a semicircle of clocking in machines, each one displaying a warning about the consequence of their misuse. He followed an arrow directing new employees to the human resources department, and announcing his arrival at an open window, gave his letter to a receptionist. Soon he was met by a senior assistant to the human resources under manager who led him to a line of sliding steel doors.

'I'll have to shout!' yelled the assistant. 'But don't worry, you'll get used to the noise after a while!'

The centre aisle of the production shop stretched away into a bluish haze towards the west wall of the building. High above, suspended in grids from roof girders, lights shone down onto the parallel lines of machinery below. Ranks of auto riveters, jig benders, and hydraulic presses furiously discharged window frames and metal construction components onto conveyor belts while roof mounted gantries slowly traversed the centre aisle dangling various loads from steel cables.

Assorted bangs, hisses, and whirring noises came from every direction and he gained the impression he was walking keeled over backwards.

The assistant grabbed his arm. 'Newcomers sometimes think they are walking keeled over backwards. Don't worry, you'll get used to it after a while.'

A Bleak Leigh resident glanced screw-faced at him from a pile of rough cast window handles and further along he recognized an ex Pin Lane High pupil pushing an open trolley stencilled 'Ferrous Scrap'.

Stopping before one of the overhead gantries they watched a working party manoeuvre a large machine over studs set into the floor.

'Programmable cutters,' shouted the assistant. 'Cost a quarter of a million each. Made in Japan. Only one operator needed. Our 'Greenline' range of aluminium greenhouses.'

The centre aisle continued through a series of partitioned enclosures occupied by electric welding operatives. Their projected silhouettes jumped among decorative iron gates.

'Bespoke fabrication shop,' yelled the assistant. 'Special orders only. Council parks, cemeteries, country houses - all skilled work.'

Increasing his pace, the assistant entered a windowless block shaped building connected to the outside wall by a stainless steel duct. Seen through a porthole set into a sealed door hundreds of silvery window frames and lintels glinted beneath the surface of a sunken tank. Above them, suspended in glittering racks, hundreds more awaited the same process.

'Galvanising Plant. Working at half capacity until the extractor system is fixed. Union blacking of fan blades in Manchester.' He shook his head in exasperation.

The partitioned enclosures multiplied into a suburban sprawl of mobile offices on both sides of the centre aisle. It was a much quieter area, and inhabited, or so it seemed, by more genteel staff in suits and white dustcoats who frowned tolerantly at each other over computers and charts.

'Fleet Street. The assistant dropped his voice deferentially; 'Statisticians, production planners, research and development. This is where all the thinking is done - permanent staff of course.'

The screeches and bangings coming from behind suggested greater crudity of purpose by those employed on the production lines, and he hoped that his job in Receipt and Despatch -

whatever that was, would keep him to the Fleet Street end of the production shop.

Stopping for a moment, the assistant looked up to the lighted offices in the west wall of the building. Tiny figures could be seen scurrying along corridors, and others at the higher levels, stood with their backs to the windows in apparent discussion with unseen colleagues. One figure was very noticeable. He was perched on the topmost fire escape balcony, and in the glare of the overhead lights could be seen scanning the floor below with binoculars.

The assistant clicked his tongue irritably, and moving off at speed, wheeled round at right angles to the centre aisle and descended a concrete ramp into a subway.

'Sorry to hurry you along lad.' He spoke breathlessly. 'But I'm needed elsewhere.'

They covered a distance roughly equivalent to half the width of the floor above and came to an open hatch through which could be seen lines of storage racks. The assistant pushed a bell button.

'Receipt and Despatch. You'll be working for Mr Moss but I'll have to leave him to explain things to you.'

A man with unruly hair and a misshapen nose appeared at the hatch.

'Can't stop I'm afraid Dave,' said the assistant. 'This is the lad you were expecting but you'll have to introduce yourselves, Tranmere's on the lookout.'

'Is it binoculars from the balcony?'

The assistant walked backwards as he spoke. 'It's going to be binoculars from the balcony from now on until that extractor system is fixed.'

Dave Moss slid a bolt, and grinning knowingly at Pimple as he opened the lower door of the hatch said: 'I've heard about you. Pray entereth and survey your future niche in life.'

They shook hands, and Pimple stepped into his first place of work.

Once inside, he could see that the storage racks extended forward to an elongated window overlooking a concrete loading ramp stacked with loaded pallets. The window was divided into hatches similar to the one he had just entered, and deep counters at each hatch supported filing cabinets marked: 'Receipts',

'Bondhaven', 'Isby' and 'Various'. Space between the racks formed corridors for easy access to plastic trays stencilled with reference numbers for items needed in the production shop. A section of racking had been cleared for an electric kettle, a teapot, some mugs and a packet of chocolate biscuits. The kettle was boiling, and a carton of milk and open bag of sugar waited beside the mugs.

'Is everything sent out from here?' he asked.

'Aye,' said Dave. 'And if you can spell Receipt & Despatch and use a calculator that's about all you need to know.'

He felt relieved.

'Mind you,' Dave passed the biscuits. 'It gets difficult sometimes. Let's take extractor fans for instance.'

'I was told about them.'

Dave grinned again and pointed to a large sheet of plywood leaning against a wall.

'Take a peek behind that.'

Pimple walked over to the plywood and pulled it away from the wall. Behind it were three large aluminium blades sealed in clear plastic transportation bags. He felt something was expected of him.

'Are they the wrong ones then?'

'No.' Dave moved to the kettle.

'Are there some bits missing?'

'Nothing missing when they arrived.' Dave filled the teapot.

'Why can't they use them?'

'Fan blades are tricky things at the moment.' Dave stirred the teapot. 'But there again.' He spoke offhandedly. 'It's not what you know, but who you know.'

3. <u>The Glory of Love</u>

Rose leaned over the style at the bottom of Pipers Lane and gazed across Mill Meadow. A light breeze stirred up the grass and it shimmered towards them in waves.

'It makes me think of the sea and all those places I'll never have the chance to visit,' she sighed.

By now he had become accustomed to her changes of mood, but this was an abrupt change. She had been pushing grass inside his shirt only a few seconds ago, but in the time it had taken him to chase her to the style she had become whimsical.

'Madame Zelda reckoned you'd go on a long journey,' he said.

'She probably says that to everyone.' She spoke dreamily. 'It would be nice to go somewhere different though.'

'Like Africa you mean?'

'Maybe.' She scraped the style post with a fingernail and lapsed into silence.

He studied her. She wasn't strikingly pretty. Her appeal was more subtle than that. The mass of freckles which bloomed in warmer weather camouflaged her beauty so that it came as a revelation only to the discerning beholder, and she was able to hint at hidden depths by a series of natural expressions. The half-smile and quizzical tilt of the head could have been nurtured by the experience of greater years, but they were natural to Rose, and emphasised her uniqueness to such an extent that he never thought of using a general term of endearment in place of her name.

She turned to him.

'Wouldn't you like to get away from here and do something exciting?'

'I wouldn't mind, but it would cost a bit wouldn't it?'

'Well, just if you could. I don't mean a holiday, I mean a complete change.' She turned again to the style post. 'More like an adventure.'

'I don't know.'

'You wouldn't want to stay here if you had the chance, would you?'

He tried to work up some enthusiasm for the idea.

'America would be alright I suppose.'

'You don't sound very keen?' She seemed disappointed.

'Well things aren't too bad at the moment'

He recognized the blandness of his reply, but the job at Receipt and Despatch had turned out much better than expected, and outside of work Rose was all he needed.

'Maybe,' she persisted. 'But don't you think you could do much better if you had the chance to prove it?'

Something inside fidgeted uncomfortably. 'I suppose so.' He moved uncertainly towards her. 'But I wouldn't want to leave here without you.' It was the first time he had openly proclaimed his affection for her and she blushed.

'I really don't know what to say.' She returned her attention to the style post.' Would you really miss me?'

'Yes I would.' He hesitated. 'Would you miss me?' Aching with apprehension, he looked down and missed the flicker of concern that she bestowed on the post.

'Of course I would you silly thing.' She swiftly became playful again and tweaked his nose with her thumb and forefinger. 'I would miss you very much.'

Crossing the meadow they arrived at the Leigh to Antwitam road in time to hear the approaching thud thud of a bass boomer. Seconds later a car came over the hill and aimed itself at a family of ducks. The cargo of youths shouted things at them and an empty can clattered alongside a cloud of feathers.

Rose rushed to an injured duckling as it fluttered against the verge and screamed at the car as it sped toward the extending fingers of Cowgrass Estate.

'I hate you! I hate you! You stinking rubbish! Oh Pimple I hate them so much. I want to kill them and their stinking parents - or whatever!'

She cupped the duckling in both hands; it pecked weakly at her thumb. Then she cried openly and loudly.

'Stinking rubbish and there are thousands of them. All doing cruel horrible things, and all breeding more stinking rubbish!'

She snorted as she caught her breath. 'I hate this place. Oh Pimple I want to leave so much!'

He stared helplessly at the duckling. Beyond it on the roadside another duckling paddled round in circles. He sought her permission.

'I'll have to finish it off.'

She turned away.

'Just do it. I won't watch.'

He walked over and stamped hard on the duckling - it died with a pop.

'It's dead now.' he announced flatly.

'I hate them! I hate them so much! Stinking rubbish from stinking rubbish!'

The duckling in her hand flipped its head round like a periscope then raised two eyelids on the last images it would see in a brief life.

'This one is dying.'

She sobbed and snorted as the bird went limp.

'Why are they so evil? Please let them die. Why should they live?'

He hated them just as much, but there was nothing he could do, they were tough and had all the power on the estate - no one dared do anything.

'They get noticed if they are cruel and hard,' he said.

'Then why aren't nice people noticed?'

'They're just ordinary, like us. A bit boring I suppose.'

She laid the duckling under a hedge and they walked in silence, letting the episode weigh down their moods.

At last she said: 'Why should they ruin our afternoon, that's just what they want. I still hate them but I'm going to wait so I can hate them properly later.'

He tried to do the same, but the nastiness of the incident persisted and they walked in silence to the Antwitam crossroads.

She stopped.

'Look, we've got to
make ourselves concentrate on something else. So let's be different today and go to Parkers Knoll.' She pulled him towards Antwitam. 'It's not much further and we can follow the stream from the water mill.'

He went reluctantly. Already they were in sight of Godfrey Smith's cottage, and a wheelbarrow full of hedge cuttings told them someone was at home. Perched on the brow of Mill Hill and facing aloofly away from the estate, the Smiths enjoyed an unhindered view of the Antwitam Valley. He wasn't keen for Godfrey to come out and present himself in a much better environment than Rose could ever hope to enjoy at No76.

'It's a pretty cottage,' she said. 'Godfrey invited me in once but he just kept on and on about his new motorbike.' She chided herself. 'But I mustn't talk about your friends like that.'

'It doesn't matter.' He still felt let down by Godfrey's disappearance in the face of trouble at 'Funlands'. 'He's always going on about his motorbike.'

But Rose had already skipped ahead to the millpond and leaning over the handrail was tossing her head from side to side in the rush of cool air from the waterfall.

Set against the dark trees she was easily the most colourful object around, and her movements were wild, as if in those few seconds alone she was shaking off the previous episode. He joined her and tentatively took her hand. Water swooped over the ledge in a glassy curve and crashed into the millpond creating a small rainbow in the spray. It was too noisy for natural conversation, so together they watched the continuous display of watery energy dissipate in semi-circular ripples to the outgoing stream. There was just enough variation in the eddy currents to hold the attention, and pleasantly mesmerised he lost sense of time.

It could have been minutes or even hours afterwards when he became conscious that his state of mind had completely changed, and that he was now viewing the scene with considerable anxiety. For no apparent reason the flow of water and location of dry land around it had become very important, and Rose, who had been foremost in his thoughts was now merely a painful recollection. It was as if he had been dumped into a future segment of his life without the intermediate events. Close to panic he blinked and turned to see if the hand he was holding belonged to Rose. She met his gaze with concern.

'What's wrong? You look, well - almost frightened.'

'I don't know.' He hadn't the word power to explain. It was hard enough for him to describe simple events, let alone something as intangible as a peculiar sensation. 'I had a funny feeling, that's all.'

'Hmm,' she pressed her chin diagnostically. 'Do you feel dizzy?'

'No.'

'Not queasy, anything like that?'

'No.'

'Well what sort of feeling was it? You must know.'

He struggled to explain.

'A bit like a dream, but not quite.'

'Then you were hypnotised by the waterfall.' She spoke decisively. 'Waterfalls have that effect on some people. I heard about it on the radio.'

She pulled him away from the handrail.

'Come on, let's follow the stream. If we start walking again it will help to get you over it.'

Only partly convinced by her explanation, he crossed the road and followed her along a narrow path beside the mill house to the old miller's garden.

She gripped his hand excitedly.

'I hope no one else is here, I love this place.'

The garden had been left to nature long ago. Nettles competed with ground elder and hollyhocks in previously cultivated patches, and some vandalised relics hinted at the lifestyle of a generation he'd read about in some schoolboy annuals left by his granddad. An upended wooden trailer still displayed part of the millers name in faded gold lettering, and the remains of a mangle; its wooden rollers bleached white from countless starched collars, stood amid the rubble of an outside washroom.

Still taking the lead, she motioned him over to the remnants of a summerhouse then skipped down the steps to a sunken lawn, part of which had been laid out for tennis. She ran her fingers along the top seam of a tattered net still strung up for play.

'It must have been fun on days like this. I wonder who played the last game.'

'I shouldn't think it was the miller, he was about ninety when he died.'

'Well, he would have been watching from the summerhouse then.' She placed him in position with her forefinger. 'From that corner of the veranda I would say. His wife would have been on the other side, and their friends and family would be sitting between them. If I concentrate hard enough I can bring them back to life.' She closed her eyes to simulate the event. 'Yes they are watching us play, I can picture them exactly. Go on see if you can.'

He wasn't sure that venturing into the past would be sensible so soon after an unintentional leap into the future, but he closed his eyes and tried to imagine the scene she had described.

'I think I can.'

'Good, are you ready then?'

She was already miming a serve from her side of the net when he opened his eyes.

'Come on we'll have to hurry this set, tea is nearly ready and you know how mother hates to be kept waiting.'

'Oh, does she?' He hadn't expected a command to play.

'Yes,' insisted Rose 'And it's no good expecting grandpa to approve if you don't like tennis. He was several times champion of Bleak Leigh.'

'I didn't know that?'

Feeling foolish, he waved her serve back hoping it would be a brief set, but she responded by darting between the weeds and returning ever more energetic volleys. It seemed to go on forever. Not only did she provide a running commentary on the state of play, she also extended her flight of fancy to the spectators on the veranda who shouted so much advice and criticism that he was chivvied into playing with more enthusiasm.

'My game!' she gasped at last, and still maintaining close contact with the family gathering, led him breathlessly up the steps to grandpa.

'Grandpa is a stickler for good manners,' she warned, 'so you'll have to speak up. He can't hear very well these days.'

'How do you do grandpa? Nice day isn't?' He cringed at his lack of inventiveness.

She nudged him. 'Grandpa is holding his hand out to you.'

'Oh, is he?' He shook hands before an aerosoled expletive.

'He's been a dreadful grump this week. We've had to stop him driving the pony and trap because it makes him giddy.'

She guided him to the other corner of the veranda.

'Grandma has just taken her pills. Are you awake grandma?'

'Doesn't look like it.' He was eager for formalities to be completed.

'No…well, I'll just have to introduce you later. But you must meet the Brigadier. He was shouting all that advice to you.' She ushered Pimple forward. 'What do you think of my new boyfriend Brigadier?'

He dutifully shook hands.

'He says you need a good haircut. But that's the trouble with retired army officers isn't it? They expect everyone to behave like soldiers. Mind you, he needs holding down when he's been at the brandy.' She glanced sideways. 'Don't you Brig? You naughty thing.'

Pimple resented the Brigadiers forwardness and was thankful to be moved onto Leonard and Susan who stood expectantly in the splintered entrance to the summerhouse.

'Pleased to meet you.' His voice resonated tonelessly onto some protective plywood.

'No one really knows what Leonard does. Banking or films… well, something like that, but he's fun to have around.'

'What about Susan?'

'Yes, well.' She pulled him away from Susan. 'Susan is complicated, but Leonard understands her which is all that matters.' She clapped her hands.

'But look, here comes mother with the tea.'

'Good.' He speeded up the pretence of helping himself to a cup. 'Just what I fancy.'

Rose angled her head into the telling off position.

'Really Pimple, I can't take you anywhere.'

'Why what's wrong?'

'You should know that Grandpa always comes first in our family. Then it's Grandma if she's awake, and after Grandma it's aunts and uncles. Children always come last.'

She allowed a smattering of haughtiness to enter her voice.

'I am family of course. Even so, I know my place, and boyfriends are certainly not expected to just grab things whenever they come along.' She pulled her lips down and shook her head slowly from side to side. 'I'm afraid you've failed. I'm sorry but you just wouldn't fit into our way of life.'

'Why not?'

'I'll have to be quite blunt with you. You simply don't have the breeding, and it shows.' She patted him patronisingly on the head. 'It's not your fault of course, but nothing can be done about it, so you'll just have to come back to reality.'

'Oh.'

Feeling aggrieved and uncouth, but thankful to be released from the miller's social gathering, he waited for Rose to emerge from her flight of fancy. She sighed herself into the present with greater reluctance.

'I wonder what life was really like for them. I bet they were never bored.'

He drew on his mediocre knowledge of rural history.

'It was rough for some.'

'I suppose so.' She encompassed the derelict garden with a wave of the hand as they returned to the path. 'But it still feels friendly and safe, like my real grandma's front room with all her china and pictures. I bet they took more trouble to make things nice in those days.'

A wooden footbridge forded the stream between Parkers Knoll and a clump of beeches. She stopped, and removing her shoes and stockings sat on the side of the bridge and patted the board beside her.

'I still like paddling my feet in the water. Come on, there's plenty of time left.'

He removed his shoes and socks and sat beside her but avoided staring at the water. She leaned her head on his shoulder.

'Has that peculiar feeling gone away?'

'Just about.' The sensation still lingered but this was no time for diversions. The moment at hand was far more important. He put his arm round her waist and she lolled her head round to him.

'I enjoy our walks together. How many have we had so far do you think?'

'About six I reckon.' He nestled squarely against her.

'That's lots of walks, but I've never been bored because something different could happen each time.'

She rolled her eyes at him. 'Do you know what I mean?'

'Yes.' He wasn't sure at all.

'Nothing really exciting of course.' She leaned back against his arm. 'We watched that big American plane going to land at Wendlesfield Aerodrome. Then you were stung by something, and now it's spring so...well, anything could happen, couldn't it?'

'I suppose it could.' His arm ached.

'And we really should make the most of the nice weather.'

'Yes we should.'

The pressure on his arm became unbearable, and they tipped backwards onto the bridge. A freckled leg rose high into the air and she draped her stockings round his neck.

'I'll race you to the top of the knoll - no trainers allowed.'

They grabbed their trainers, and Rose cheated by running before her own count of three. He managed to catch her up and they arrived roughly together at the crest of the knoll. It was the highest point on that side of the valley and gradually the restlessness of the surroundings overcame the sound of their own breathing.

Overhead, the tinny buzz of a microlight mingled with the electronic jingle of the 'Mr Frostcream' van seeking business on the estate.

Suffering an agony of indecision he lay still for some time, then, laying her stockings on the grass closed up to her and kissing her lightly on the lips told her that he loved her.

4.Undecided

Mr Tranmere's Personal Assistant looked up from her computer and smiled.

'Good morning Pimple, this is your first interview with Mr Tranmere I believe?'

'Yes, I've only seen him on the fire escape.'

'With his binoculars?' She took out a folder from one of several filing cabinets.

'That's right.'

He waited expectantly while she clipped a white card onto the folder.

'Well there's nothing to be apprehensive about. Mr Tranmere makes it his business to meet new employees.' She spoke to a microphone on her desktop. 'Pimple here to see you Mr Tranmere'

'Good, send him through Mrs Humblestone. Personal file as well please.'

She led him to a panelled door and knocked lightly.

'Just go straight through.' She smiled again. 'And do you prefer tea or coffee?'

'Tea please.'

Pleasantly surprised by the use of his first name, he opened the door and entered. Mr Tranmere rose from his desk and greeted him with enthusiasm.

'Pimple, we have met at last, and my apologies for taking so long about it.' He took the folder and pointed to a chair. 'Make yourself comfortable while I update myself on a few details.'

At close quarters Mr Tranmere looked exactly as expected. Tall and slim with black hair parted centrally back from the forehead, he would have been convincing behind any desk of importance. It was as if someone just like him had been waiting to offer encouragement and advice whenever needed, and here he was in person. Yet it was strange that he should have conveyed such a reassuring impression so quickly. Only the large divers watch protruding untidily from a shirt-cuff seemed at odds with his general appearance.

He placed his elbows flat on the open folder with his chin just above the desktop.

'Welcome to Rilltots. It's always a pleasure to meet employees who have been commended to me so soon after starting with us.'

Pimple crossed his hands and sat upright. Mr Tranmere flicked his eyes down approvingly.

'In large industrial concerns such as this, it is sometimes difficult for individuals to recognise their contribution to the total productive effort, and this applies especially to those engaged on repetitious tasks.'

He inched upwards.

'Occupational indifference goes hand in hand with modern production methods I'm afraid, and all too often this leads to amorality beyond the factory gates.

He pressed both hands hard on the desk and looked directly at Pimple.

'It is my contention that industry, and this company in particular, owes more to the general populace than to release hoards of disgruntled workers onto the streets of Britain every day and night.'

'I can see that.'

'I'm sure you can, so you will understand why I am anxious to impress upon all of our staff how highly I value their contribution at whatever level.'

He inched further upwards.

'The 'Luddites' were motivated to preserve the dignity of their labour just as much as their pay packets. An arguable point for some perhaps, but it is certainly true that the gradual dividing and sub-dividing of labour through the years has presented us with a technological caste system more finely graded than even that of old India.'

Pimple turned his toes inwards.

'Occupational indifference has too often been treated as a minor hindrance to productivity - something which can be easily countered by piped music or one of many iniquitous inducements such as team payment. Indeed, I have even heard it suggested that occupational indifference can be an asset in extremely mundane operations because workers achieve a trancelike state of mind while their reflexes take care of the assigned tasks.'

The elapsed time bezel of the divers watch came hard down on the desktop as Mr Tranmere again flattened himself over the folder.

'Quite dreadful!'

He levered himself upwards with his elbows.

'And I am fearful that some of the measures our directors are so keen to introduce will challenge the self-esteem of our workforce to such an extent that only the most extreme forms of self expression will suffice as an antidote.'

From somewhere below the screech of rending metal intruded into their conversation.

He lowered his voice.

'Boredom is rarely discussed in boardrooms and sadly our own board is no exception to this, so something has to be done.'

He leaned even closer.

'It is my ambition to harness and develop the creative energy of our workforce before it stagnates in a pool of unfulfilled aspirations.'

'That's not a bad idea,'

'It is a formidable undertaking of course, but early results are encouraging. The Paint Dip Surrealist Group now hold weekly meetings to satisfy increased membership, and the Jig Benders Pottery Club have already submitted two entries for the 'Doubleday' amateur ceramics award. It's only a start of course, but I'm sure you will be pleasantly surprised by some of the uplifting activities available to you here.'

'Oh Good.'

There was a light knock on the door and his personal assistant arrived with the tea. She placed the tray on the desk and with a questioning glance handed him a slip of paper. 'It doesn't tally with our records.'

'A typing error perhaps Mrs Humblestone?'

'No,' she tucked in her chin. 'I've made extensive checks.'

'Strange?' He raised his eyebrows. 'I've never known her to be wrong on a matter like this before.'

They eyed Pimple uncertainly.

At last Mr Tranmere said, 'We seem to have a discrepancy in our records Pimple. Can you tell us your exact date of birth?'

'Mum said it was midnight on Saturday because Big Ben was chiming when I came out.'

They smiled in unison.

'I think that resolves the difficulty Mrs Humblestone.' Mr Tranmere screwed up the slip and dropped it into a wastepaper basket. 'She really is amazing don't you think?'

'Very impressive, very impressive indeed.' Mrs Humblestone beamed and left.

He returned to the folder.

'You have been with Mr Moss in Receipt and Despatch for some time now, so how do you feel about your work with us so far?'

'It's alright. I like working with Mr Moss.'

'A fine man Moss and a 'Foundation' student as well I believe. But tell me, how do you see your progression in the company? Do you think you would be able to do even better if you were given the opportunity?'

He hesitated. Rose had asked him a similar question during one of their walks and she seemed disappointed with his answer. He didn't want to give Mr Tranmere the impression he lacked ambition.

'I reckon I could.' He tried to sound keen.

'Let me put it this way.'

Mr Tranmere closed the folder.

'We are all presented with a myriad of occupations to choose from when we are too young to sensibly decide. A few lucky individuals perceive their vocation early in life while others can rely on a residue of family wealth to make good several false starts. For most of us though, this choice is defined neither by preference or ability, but by the simple need to earn a living.'

He looked keenly at Pimple.

'So wouldn't it be remarkable if your position in Receipt and Despatch even roughly coincided with your aspirations?'

Pimple took a chance. 'I suppose so.'

'Exactly.' Mr Tranmere again inched upwards.

'I have seen so much discontent from this side of my desk that I listen with doubt when an employee expresses enthusiasm for his work. In truth we are offered a mass of specialisms, many of which reduce us to the level of trained chimpanzees, while others leave us wondering about the point of it all. A few rebellious spirits hop from one occupation to another searching for their niche in life, and those who do find it are rarely able to resist the perverse temptation to promote themselves out of it. Even those who have the courage to stick to what they enjoy usually have it distorted by the demands of distant superiors who feel compelled to devise measures of performance to justify their own positions.'

He rose from the chair and strode over to one of several glass fronted cabinets from which he removed a large steel cylinder and a set of brass scales. Placing the scales on top of the cabinet, he held up the steel cylinder.

'This is our programmable locking pin for industrial security systems.' He placed the steel cylinder on the scales. 'It weighs four kilo's, and this.' He obtained a stack of forms from another cabinet and laid them on the other side of the scales. 'This is the internal paperwork required for each of these units.'

The locking pin rose sharply and clearing the scales fell noisily onto the cabinet top.

He stroked the shiny surface of the pin.

'This is four kilos of ingenuity, and this.' He picked up the stack of forms. 'This is six kilo's of senseless accountability.'

He shook the stack of paper.

'Measurements of compliance''. The latest in a series of miserable devices conceived by those barely able to recognise a locking pin let alone produce one!'

The exhibits and scales were thrust back into the cabinet and he returned to his seat.

'Every task, no matter how small, has to be timed and costed. But it doesn't stop there. We now have a 'Production Facility Senior under Accountant' who has devised a 'Key stage production analysis' for each component so that any fluctuations in production can be investigated and corrected. Everything we do has to be converted into codes to be read by a suite of computers, which, even as I speak are being replaced by even more sophisticated machines. My senior supervisors now use a language which is utterly incomprehensible to me. A language consisting largely of computer acronyms which I am expected to understand and instantly convert into intelligible meaning.'

He again inched upwards.

'Accountability is the new oppressor. It has elbowed out trust and smothered job satisfaction, yet when I ask why, I am told it is to promote efficiency and growth.' He dropped onto the desktop again. 'Growth for what?'

Pimple jumped.

'Hard to say I suppose.'

'Very hard.'

He gripped the front edge of his desk.

'During a fact finding study of production methods in Tokyo I came across a party of school children eagerly taking photographs inside a huge camera factory. So who knows? We may yet be able to park inside the mighty motor works of Britain and celebrate getting our own back at the countries who sell their cars over here.'

His knuckles whitened.

'And when the last patch of wilderness has been levelled for intensive agriculture, are we also to rejoice while consuming the end product in a revolving restaurant high above a never ending London?'

'That's difficult as well.'

'Very difficult. I have asked myself these questions over and over again. I have asked my colleagues, I have asked the sales manager from Shore and Toop. I have asked Bishop Pocklington and I have even asked my wife. None of them were able to assuage my fears by reasonable discussion. Most of them prefer to avoid me on public occasions, and without exception, all of them including my wife, vehemently maintain that without continuous growth, chaos and mayhem will follow. So what am I to do?'

He released his hands from the desk then raised them in a gesture of helplessness.

'I have almost been driven from my home by growth. We have four high definition televisions and I have no idea how many computers and games centres litter our rooms. My daughter has her own web site and is now pestering me to buy her the very latest mobile phone so she can hold silly conversations with her friends in three dimensions. Is this really the paradise we seek?'

He cleared his throat.

'I am a weak man with my family. A fleeting indiscretion many years ago has left my wife with the indelible impression that I am something of a gad-about, and this misdemeanour is ruthlessly exploited whenever I question her insatiable appetite for material possessions. Unfortunately my salary provides us with a purchasing power far in excess of our needs. At one time I could seek solace in the garden, but the squash court and a recent garage extension for my oldest daughter's sports car has reduced my refuge to just a few trees.'

'That's a shame.'

'Even so, I don't wish to mislead you into thinking that I cannot escape the tension and turmoil of my personal circumstances.'

Mr Tranmere fiddled with the elapsed time bezel on the divers watch. The action appeared to generate an inner serenity that gradually surfaced as a smile.

'I believe it was Albert Einstein who said he found great satisfaction in contemplation of the 'It' but very little in the 'I' and the 'We'.'

He pressed his thumbs together and gazed upwards.

'In that respect I am very fortunate because I will soon have access to a spot where I can disregard the enormity of human affairs and ponder the majesty of nature.'

He smiled briefly at Pimple.

'Only my closest acquaintances will know about it, but one day I hope to share it with you.'

'Thanks.'

'He rose from his desk and walked across to the fire doors. 'Are you afraid of heights?'

'No.'

'Good, then let me show you something.'

He pressed the fire bar and swung the doors open. The acrid smell of corrosive liquids and hot metal mingled with the scented air of the office. They stepped onto a small balcony and shielded their eyes against the glare of the roof lights.

Below, and seen through a bluish haze thickening with distance, the separate stages of production were clearly laid out on the huge floor area. It was easy to follow the progress of items through the machine lines and down the centre aisle to the wooden pallets waiting for despatch. Chargehands in white dustcoats moved between operatives in blue overalls and suited administrative staff who conveyed forms and documents to and from the departments in Fleet Street. The figures moved predictably within their allotted zones, and from such a commanding viewpoint the activities of machines and workers combined to produce a satisfying motional pattern.

Mr Tranmere turned to Pimple and dropped a hand from his eyes as if returning the salute from a junior officer on the bridge of a battleship.

'Well, what do you make of it?'

'It looks easy to be in charge from here.'

'Well perceived.' Mr Tranmere ushered him back through the fire doors. 'And that; or rather a related matter is what I now wish to discuss with you.'

They returned to their seats.

'You may be aware that we have two smaller branches. One is at Bondhaven in Sussex, and the other is at Isby-Le-Fen in the north. Both were established to cater for regional development programmes in the1960's and 70's. Bondhaven has a manufacturing capability which we are upgrading to cater for a new estuary eco -town, and Isby-Le-Fen is now a distributive centre for the new housing and port complex at Tillingham. We only have a small staff at Isby, but a vacancy will arise there soon and I would like you to give it serious consideration.'

He looked keenly at Pimple.

'Promising employees should have the means to advance their careers within the company, and this position would, I am sure, be ideally suited to your abilities.'

'Would I still be in Receipt and Despatch?'

'At first, but when my plans for the branch are completed, an altogether more attractive post will be available.'

Mr Tranmere leaned back in his chair.

'You will of course need time before making your decision, and there may be some good reasons why you would prefer to remain here, but it is surprising how quickly circumstances can change.'

It seemed a good offer, and he would be unwise to refuse it, but he was happy working with Dave Moss in Receipt and Despatch and most of all he didn't want to leave Rose.

'Is it a long way from here?'

'Roughly one hundred and twenty miles by road.'

Mr Tranmere glanced at his watch.

'You will need more details of course. But your salary would be effectively raised because of the lower cost of living in the north, and you will receive the rail fare and a lodging allowance.'

'That's not bad.'

Mr Tranmere lowered his voice.

'But please treat this conversation with the utmost discretion. I have very good reasons for not wanting my plans to become common knowledge at this stage.'

He stood up and walked over to the door of his office.

'I must say that I have enjoyed our first meeting enormously. It is so rewarding to go beyond undemanding concepts when talking to junior staff.'

They shook hands.

'Do think over our discussion, and remember my door is always open.'

The door closed, and lost in thought, Pimple walked across the lobby to the lift.

From her desk Mrs Humbleston viewed him with undisguised approval, and waiting until he had entered the lift, spoke excitedly to the intercom.

'Mr Tranmere?'

'Yes Mrs Humblestone?'

'He's the one.'

'Are you quite sure?'

'Yes, quite sure; everything fits into place.'

'We can only await developments Mrs Humbleston. I'm afraid the next stage is currently beyond our control.'

'I know, but have faith Mr Tranmere.'

'We must have faith Mrs Humblestone. So much depends on it.'

5.Trouble in Mind.

The shock came on Friday morning.

He had sorted the paperwork in preparation for the next transporter, and noticing that the stock of one by two 'Vistavacs' had become critical he jotted down the total so that Dave could alert Production Control.

Friday mornings were enjoyable.

The weekend lay ahead, and while Dave was scouring the production shop for the ideal 'Industrial League' darts team it was left to him to ensure that the department ran smoothly. He had coped well during his short time in Receipt and Despatch and this had been recognised by Mr Tranmere, but now he was in an awkward position. If he refused the offer of a better job in the north it would look as if he didn't want promotion. But he couldn't move away from Rose. It was bad enough that he couldn't see her over the weekend because she was still suffering from flu. He would just have to think of some way to tell Mr Tranmere that he couldn't take the job.

He plugged in the kettle and settled down with the Crantree and Antwitam Gazette.

Then the shock came.

At first he didn't recognise Rose. It was a black and white photo and the harsh newsprint coarsened her features, but it was Rose all right. So, why was she in the Gazette?

He stared in disbelief.

Was that a veil she was wearing? And who was that American airman beside her? It looked like Barney Rockyman. No, it couldn't be - could it? It was Barney Rockyman though. Anyone who had been to Klub Nitro couldn't mistake that face.

He angled the paper to the light.

Rose and Barney Rockyman? She wouldn't do a thing like that - would she? She'd never been to Klub Nitro - had she? And surely that wasn't a wedding cake they were cutting together - was it? A big wedding cake ringed round with union jacks and stars and stripes. She didn't have time - did she?

His eyes jumped to a smaller photograph of Rose and Barney in the cockpit of a jet fighter while the Base Commander toasted them from the ground. It had to be a mistake. She was suffering with flu - wasn't she?

He slumped against the wall.

There had to be a simple explanation. Perhaps she'd agreed to take part in a promotion for hired dresses and wedding cakes? He searched the column for any tell tale clues but the hope soon faded.

Headed: 'Wendlesfield Celebrates Five Hundred Anglo/US Weddings' the report explained that it had been a lightning romance because Barney was due to leave the USAF and on arrival in Los Angeles would take over the family business: Bronco Aerodynamic Enterprises Inc.

The kettle chattered.

It wasn't as if he had quarrelled with Rose. They were booked for the company disco dinner next week and she didn't object when he cuddled her on their last walk together.

He wiped his face in the growing humidity.

Anyone else would have been bad enough, but Barney Rockyman? How could she do that to him? Even Marion Moorhen had been forbidden to go out with him. Rose wasn't that sort of girl - was she?

Grim doubt clutched at him from the sagging paper. Perhaps Rose wasn't that sort of girl but it hadn't taken her long to drop him in favour of Barney had it? He shuddered involuntarily then Dave came in and turned off the kettle.

Dave listened to his tale of woe through descending clouds of steam.

'Well, you can't win them all,' he surmised. 'Like as not there'll be another door open now this one's closed.' He thumbed through his 'Industrial League' fixtures book. 'We're one short…fancy throwing a few arrers in the club tonight?'

'Might as well.' Pimple stared vacantly at the floor. 'There's not much else for me to do

6.<u>Wild Man Blues.</u>

Lake and Rilltot Social Centre was housed in the upper floor of a narrow building which had once been used as a tarpaulin repair shop for the previous fleet of lorries. A covered iron walkway led to the entrance door which was overhung by a large roller winch and its supporting girders. All the exposed metalwork had been painted Rilltot blue to maintain corporate identity, and once inside, a row of video games and fruit machines divided the floor-space into roughly two halves. One half was taken up by chairs and tables facing a small stage which supported bingo and karaoke equipment, and the other half was devoted to darts, snooker and pool. A substantial bar occupied most of the far wall.

Two girls in matching green trouser suits were operating one of the fruit machines. The tall one usually managed to pinch him on the rump whenever he went to the packaging department, and on seeing him she nudged her friend and giggled. Avoiding them by squeezing between the nearest machines he made straight for the dartboards, and arrived at the centre board where Dave was playing the Machine Shop Supervisor.

Poised on one foot and making dainty rowing motions with his free arm, the Machine Shop Supervisor placed his dart barely a wires width above treble nineteen. A man with prominent red ears chalked up the score.

'Six microns lower and you'll be inside the fence Len.'

'Then its ballast I'm needin'!' exclaimed the Machine Shop Supervisor. He took an uninhibited gulp from a pewter tankard and noticing Pimple said: 'Your new lad's here Dave.'

Dave handed Pimple a glass and an open bottle of Pointers Special then took his place on the rubber marker mat. 'Time to reap and sow.' he declared.

'Aye, weather permitting,' rejoined the Machine Shop Supervisor.

Two darts hung precariously from treble twenty.

'Twenty two needed.' announced Red Ears.

'And don't anyone breath out.' chuckled the Machine Shop Supervisor. 'Farmer Moss is relyin' on calm weather.'

Motionless except for his wrist and forearm Dave sighted up double eleven through the flights of his dart. A few false motions later he released it and it loped into double eleven where it hung slightly less precariously than the others.

'Arrer!' exclaimed Red Ears.

Pimple was impressed. It was better than anything he had seen in the Bleak Leigh Arms.

'Aye, canny throwing right enough,' conceded the Machine Shop Supervisor. He scooped up the empty glasses. 'I suppose it's my round, unless there's someone here wantin' to stop me spendin' the housekeepin' money.'

Red Ears mimed a drinking motion. 'Get that down you lad, you've arrived at a rare moment, and stick with him in case he can't make it back with all those heavy mugs.'

Pimple followed the Machine Shop Supervisor to the bar.

'It's another Special for you is it lad?' The Machine Shop Supervisor scattered a handful of pound coins and assorted bolts on the bar top.

'Yes please.' He noted the label on the bottle. It wasn't bad stuff at all. Already there was the beginning of a pleasant calming sensation below the hairline, but the effect was dulled by the sight of the Bottom Pincher sidling along the bar towards them. She eyed him with amusement then closed up to the Machine Shop Supervisor who promptly lifted her up by the waist.

'You can stop that an' all Len Beggs!' she protested, 'Especially now you're too good for the packaging department!'

The Machine Shop Supervisor simulated bafflement.

'Now what's Uncle Len done to upset his little darlings this time?'

The Pincher twisted her head away from him and spoke loudly to her friend.

'Lookin' down at us from a great height weren't he Diane?'

'Like royalty,' confirmed her friend.

'Cups and saucers as well,' continued the Pincher. 'Mrs Humblestone makes tea in a proper pot don't she. Wouldn't be right havin' to slum it with tea bags while viewin' the 'Hoi Poloi' over the balcony would it?'

'Course not.' The Pinchers friend preened herself in the bottle shelf mirror. 'Mugs wouldn't do at all. Tranmere couldn't have his ding dongs stooping that low could he?'

'Not at all fitting Diane.' The Pincher smoothed bubble gum over the tip of her tongue. 'We'd better get rid of that dirty old mug. They can't be doing with mugs in such high circles.'

The Machine Shop Supervisor appealed to Pimple.

'An' there I was saying all those complimentary things to Tranmere about the packaging department lad. Not much gratitude about is there?'

Pimple tried to grin.

'Even broke into the cocoa tin so I could treat them to a Baby Sparkly,' continued the Machine Shop Supervisor. The latter part of his appeal was extended to the barman who dutifully shook his head at the contrariness of human nature.

'Never know who your friends are these days Len,' he commiserated.

'He don't speak very clearly do he Diane?' said the Pincher. 'All I heard was 'Baby Sparkly'.'

The Pinchers friend blew on her nails.

'He didn't say much else worth listenin' to.'

The Machine Shop Supervisor turned reproachfully to the Pincher. 'And I thought something beautiful was happening to us?'

'Be a bit one-sided wouldn't it?' chirped the Pinchers friend.

'Hurtful aren't they lad?' The Machine Shop Supervisor again appealed to Pimple, 'Just when I had something special to tell them.'

'We're listening,' said the Pincher.

'Well lets be havin' you closer then.' The Machine Shop Supervisor patted the bar top. 'I'm not tellin' everyone.'

The Pincher moved warily towards him.

'You watch him Gloria,' warned her friend. 'We know all about his specials.'

Screwing her face up impatiently the Pincher turned an ear to the Machine Shop Supervisor. 'Well let's be hearing it.'

Pimple moved along the bar to distance himself from them. He didn't want to be part of the conversation, especially if he'd been noticed on the fire escape with Mr Tranmere. He looked straight ahead into the bottle shelf mirror but then caught sight of the Pincher. She was staring straight at him with an expression strangely out of character with what had gone before. He wouldn't have thought she was capable of an expression like that, but in a fraction of a second it was changed to one of injured innocence, and jumping back from the Machine Shop Supervisor she exclaimed: 'You just wait Len Beggs, I'll tell your Missus - see if I don't!'

Giggling, they returned to the fruit machines with their Baby Sparkly's while Pimple helped the Machine Shop Supervisor take the drinks back to Dave and Red Ears.

The Machine Shop Supervisor nodded towards the fruit machines.

'A laugh a minute are those two.'

'Aye, we could see you were making a meal of it,' observed Red Ears. 'A right pair of cards they are lad. You ought to get in there I'm thinking.'

An image of Rose instantly appeared in protest at the suggestion. It hovered between Red Ears and the dartboard, and when, like patterns seen through closed eyelids it dissolved, all that remained looked dull and alien. He took a large gulp of Pointers Special.

'Right then,' said Dave decisively. 'It's Larry and the lad.' He gave his darts to Pimple.

'I'm not much good,' said Pimple.

'As long as you're good enough for the next round don't fret,' said the Machine Shop Supervisor.

Red Ears unsheathed his darts and announcing 'Middle for diddle,' bobbed up and down before the board. His dart arced into the bulls-eye.

'Arrer!' exclaimed Dave and the Machine Shop Supervisor in unison.

Pimple took his place.

'Room for one more lad,' ventured Dave.

'Still is,' observed the Machine Shop Supervisor following Pimple's dart to treble three.

'OK. It's Larry for off,' said Dave.

Red Ears scored double twenty.

'Nice dart, and it's still open for lodgers,' said the Machine Shop Supervisor.

Red Ears scored double thirteen with his second dart.

'Right line wrong station,' intoned Dave.

Red Ears grimaced in self-depreciation then scored treble nineteen with his third dart.

'Fair bombing Larry,' observed the Machine Shop Supervisor.

Pimple threw with as much enthusiasm as he could muster. He was well into his second bottle of Special and the shock of the morning was fading by degrees. He felt slightly uplifted, and items he would have ordinarily considered commonplace now vied for his attention. There were the incandescent particles of chalk floating beneath the dartboard light; the deep redness of Red Ears ears and the spiders-web of glinting wire set into the dartboard. Linked to this was the cosy assurance of being at one in a man's world. It was as if masculine alternatives were being attractively presented to him in the wake of Rose's departure.

Quite by chance his darts arrived at respectable destinations.

'Cheeky arrers,' grinned Dave.

'Come you now Larry,' chided the Machine Shop Supervisor. 'We should be havin' some class darts from you. It's the Industrial Cup we're after.'

Red Ears scratched his head in exasperation after his second dart followed the first onto the mat.

'They're just not going in for me tonight,' he complained.

'Just need more help than you're givin' them,' grunted the Machine Shop Supervisor.

'Wire trouble, sixty scored,' announced Dave.

Acquiring a radiance not entirely due to the dartboard light, Red Ears chastised himself as he gathered up his darts.

'Take it easy lad,' advised Dave, 'he's not dead yet.'

Pimple stepped forward, and to the right and left of him, players on adjoining dartboards advanced with him in line abreast like ill-armed yeomanry.

He scored one hundred and twenty.

'Useful darts,' said Dave.

Red Ears faced the board with fanatical determination. His first two darts found treble nineteen.

'Twice two,' advised Dave chalking a cross on the slate.

Red Ears shadow boxed the board; flicking his head from side to side in a ranging motion.

'Trespassers will be prosecuted,' warned the Machine Shop Supervisor.

Red Ears threw his dart and froze on tiptoe as he followed it into double two.

'Nice one Larry!' chorused Dave and the Machine Shop Supervisor.

Red Ears retrieved his darts and drained his mug in one single continuous motion.

'You had me worried there lad.' He pressed the handle of his mug into Pimple's hand. 'That's a Belchards when you get round to it.'

'Yes, it's time for another bevvy I'm thinking.' agreed the Machine Shop Supervisor. 'And being the lad's on Specials we'd better get to the bar while he can still pull money out of his pocket.'

Pimple ordered the drinks. The Pincher and her friend were nowhere to be seen and hoping their absence would be permanent, his thoughts returned to Rose.

She was probably drinking cocktails with Barney Rockyman beside their swimming pool in Los Angeles. He pictured the scene. There would be palm trees and waiters with top ups, and lots of rich friends and probably film stars. He became resentful. But why should he think of her? He could be pretty certain she wasn't thinking of him. She might even have done him a favour. At least he wouldn't have to worry about her if he went for that job in the north.

What was it that Mr Tranmere had said during their meeting? *'You may have some very good reasons for wishing to stay here but it is surprising how quickly circumstances can change.'...* Well, he was right there.

Red Ears reached for his pint and faced the Machine Shop Supervisor.

'So what's all this about you hob-nobbin' with the hierarchy Len?'

The Machine Shop Supervisor placed his darts and case on the bar top.

'Something's afoot Larry. Don't ask me what, but Tranmere made a good job of tellin' me nothin' for an hour. I went away with my ears ringin' and wonderin' why I'd been called up there in the first place.'

'Did you get the balcony treatment?'

'Aye, and the Humblestone tea. Last time I had them was when he lumbered us with the cold presses.'

'Maybe its Bondhaven, he might be opening up a new line there.'

'What for Larry?' The Machine Shop Supervisor unscrewed the flights from his darts.

'What about greenhouses?'

'Never, it's all tower blocks there; mainly vandal replacements, two by two sliders and Vistavacs. We don't even know how greenhouses will go here yet.'

Red Ears looked thoughtful. 'That only leaves Isby.'

'Right, and we've been stockpiling for Isby since August.' He turned to Dave. 'True Dave?'

'True,' agreed Dave.

'Alright, so it's Isby.' Red Ears jabbed at the air with his throwing hand. 'You're not tellin' me that Tranmere intends starting a line of greenhouses at Isby with Agriframe just down the road?'

'It's you who's keepin' on about greenhouses Larry.' The Machine Shop Supervisor slotted his darts into the case. 'I'm more interested in the stacks of plasterboard which have been clogging up the despatch lane these past few weeks.'

'On pallets?'

'Aye, except you might be forgiven for thinking they were Ecotherms if you didn't know what tarpaulins to look under.'

'How do you know?'

'I'm not sayin' how I know Larry. But it wasn't Tranmere who told me, and it wasn't Tranmere who told me they were goin' to be joined by fifty rolls of carpeting either.' He rattled his glass. 'Now if you told me that filing cabinets were there as well I'd say offices, but that would be dafter than greenhouses.'

'Filing cabinets are on the way,' announced Dave. 'Acoustic panels are coming soon.'

The Machine Shop Supervisor looked at Dave mid-gulp. 'You've been mustering all this stuff then?'

Dave grinned.

'So it's offices. Don't tell me he's moving Fleet Street to Isby?'

'Tricky question,' Dave shrugged his shoulders. 'But with all the wisdom assembled here I was hoping for enlightenment.'

'Well I'll tell you this much.' The Machine Shop Supervisor lowered his voice and waved his darts case between Red Ears and Dave. 'There's been plenty of comin's and goin's to Tranmere's office lately, and he's makin' no secret about who he's invited up there either. I'm sayin' no more than that.'

Pimple fidgeted uncomfortably. So he must have been noticed on the fire balcony with Mr Tranmere. Should he come clean about his interview as an act of kinship with the others? Or should he keep the trust placed on him by Mr Tranmere and say nothing?

He felt their eyes on him and came close to revealing all, but suddenly the air reverberated with loud rock music.

Chewing open mouthed with their arms locked stiffly downwards, the Pincher and her friend were jerking spasmodically to each other on the small stage. It was like watching two monstrous puppets.

Red Ears leaned back with his elbows on the bar top. 'Now there's a couple of beauties I wouldn't mind splittin' up.'

'Likewise I'm thinkin' Larry.' The Machine Shop Supervisor grinned approvingly, 'But I've taken on a deal of cargo since courtin' the missus and those two are smart on their pins.'

The Pinchers friend threw a contemptuous glance at them.

'What you all lookin' at?'

'Hard to tell from here!' bellowed the Machine Shop Supervisor. 'Can't see who's pullin' the strings!'

Red Ears nudged Pimple.

'Right couple of cards they are lad. You ought to be gettin' in there.'

'Go on get in there lad.' urged the Machine Shop Supervisor. 'A faint heart never won a fair lady.'

Pimple reddened and spoke to the bar top. It rose and fell disconcertingly.

'Can't dance,' he murmured.

'Nor can they from where I'm lookin'.' observed the Machine Shop Supervisor. 'Get in there lad!' It was more of a command than a request.

Pimple turned to Dave in the hope of some diversion, but Dave and his pint had vanished.

'Go on lad,' persisted Red Ears.

Panic stirred among the Specials, but the music stopped, and settling to rest the Pincher and her friend scowled at the bar.

'Put on somethin' slow!' yelled the Machine Shop Supervisor. 'There's a lad here wants some dancin' tuition!'

The Pincher looked icily at Pimple.

'He got a voice ain't he?'

'Bashful that's all!'

The Pincher blew a bubble and sucked it back.

'Now's your chance lad,' urged Red Ears.

Desperation took over.

'I reckon' I've had a few too many.'

A queasiness down below told him that this wasn't just pretence, and an experimental step forward told him that it wasn't pretence at all.

The Pinchers Friend observed him with disdain.

'Looks like he's dancin' already!'

'Had a few that's all.' explained the Machine Shop Supervisor.

The Pincher moved centre stage and shouted: 'You got another thing comin' if you think I'm havin' sick over my suit!'

The Machine Shop Supervisor and Red Ears studied Pimple. 'He's had a few right enough,' agreed Red Ears.

'Aye,' The Machine Shop Supervisor nodded towards the exit. 'Better get him outside before he explodes.'

Red Ears marshalled Pimple to the door.

'Pity about that lad.You've missed out on a good thing with those two.' He opened the door to the walkway. 'Careful down the steps and don't get tangled up with those beer crates at the bottom.'

Gripping both handrails Pimple arrived at the bottom step just as a shadowy figure darted behind the corner of the building. Above him the door closed, then quickly opened again.

'Now you take it easy lad!' Red Ears paused to listen to someone inside the club. 'Yes, and mind the road works down Spring Hill!'

He located his mountain bike and fumbled with the combination on the wheel lock then sank slowly to his knees. Suddenly he was very tired. Everything seemed pointless. Rose wasn't in Bleak Leigh, and if he went north she wouldn't be there either. From now on Rose wouldn't be part of his life, so why bother to go anywhere or do anything? It just wasn't worth the trouble.

Shifting to relieve the pressure of the spokes against his forehead, he rolled sideways onto the ground and began to dream of travelling through outer space.

Soon he was experiencing trouble with his spaceship, and attributing the noise of smashing glass to an emergency landing on Mars, he continued to doze until the danger had passed. Neither was he aware of the protectors who had rushed down the walkway to encircle him until his safety was assured. Yet the amplified hissing that followed was intrusive enough to goad him into a sitting position.

From somewhere close by came the sound of music. The piece was slow and sorrowful, punctuated by the deep boom of a bass drum and the mournful interweaving of a trumpet, trombone, and clarinet. Like words from a consoling voice each note sought out every hurt and offered solace. It was as if someone once, had also known what it was like to be wretched and unwanted, and through the ages, had found a way to express it in a way he could understand.

He didn't know it then, but that someone was Blue Gums Foster.

A long time had passed since Blue Gums had raised his trumpet to a microphone in far off New Orleans. His woman had left him; he had no place to go, and a life of over-indulgence had played havoc with his liver. All that lay between him and the cemetery was a bottle of bourbon and a head-full of crotchets and quavers which were soon to be translated into a mournful synopsis of a ruined life.

As usual he was the last to shuffle into the recording studio to join the band, but when the master disc whirred to a stop a young Slidebone Walker expressed his admiration.

'Gums, you said it all that time!'

'There ain't nothin' more I can say boy,' wheezed Blue Gums. 'Cos I ain't got nothing else left worth sayin'.'

Silently handing his trumpet to the young man, he picked up his hat from a nearby chair and without looking back, shuffled into a balmy New Orleans night for the last time.

As the sound of that trumpet spanned the years to saturate the air around him Pimple stood up, and eyes streaming, shared a few minutes of inspired melancholia with someone from a previous age. Blue Gums had long gone, but his trumpet had rallied a soul mate who understood Pimple better than any of his so called friends. Suddenly he had a companion, a strange sort of companion admittedly. But why shouldn't a tune be a companion? Maybe he couldn't touch or see it, but it had done more for him in that short time than any person he knew.

The music came to a scratchy stop and, above him at the top of the walkway, the door to the Social Centre opened a few inches as he mounted his bike and pedalled onto Spring Hill. He tried to recall the tune as he dodged the traffic cones and broken glass scattered over the road, but the 'whoop whoop!' of a police siren broke his concentration and flashes of blue light tracked ahead of him along an adjacent street. Crude shouted taunts and jeers cut through the rush of wind as he sped to the bottom of the hill and onto the Bleak Leigh road.

There had been lots of trouble in Crantree and it was getting worse. Even his parents had bought a security light after a neighbour's shed had been set alight.

Perhaps he should see Mr Tranmere and ask for that job in Isby-Le-Fen. Life in Bleak Leigh wasn't going to be much fun now that Rose had gone. After all what had he got to lose?

He made a decision.

Yes, he would see Mr Tranmere first thing Monday morning and ask for the job at Isby-Le-Fen.

7.Bye Bye Blues.

Peterborough continued as a boring succession of railway sidings and warehouse backyards.

It had been snowing ever since his parents had seen him onto the early train at Wenthem, and dawn, now two hours old, had come more as an increase in contrast than as a bright start to a new day. He propped his head against the seatback and stared indifferently through the carriage window. After several false starts, the countryside at last broke free from the grubby tentacles of a huge site clearance operation, and escaped onto a flat plain which extended to the limits of vision in all directions. It was a cold bleak scene unrelieved by anything more interesting than a tilting church spire. Deep drainage ditches portioned the land into huge squares and oblongs. Farm buildings stood out like ships stranded in a frozen sea, and on their own, or huddled together in small black copses, trees leaned resolutely west as if yearning for the impossible.

Lumpy black lines connected by pylons and high tension cables grew predictably into huddles of gaunt slated houses proclaiming their ancestry on small rail stations with names like 'Shreekby', 'Freeze Enderby', and 'Bogdyke'. A black line, thicker and lumpier than its predecessors, hove into view, and for the first time since leaving Peterborough, the train pulled round in a slow circle.

'Well I reckon this is it,' he thought, and retrieving his case from between the seats, waited at the carriage doors. A large tractor on an adjacent road pulled ahead of the train and turned off to make a beeline to the horizon alongside a huge dyke, then the view was obscured by acres of greenhouses fronted by stacks of wooden crates. As the train came to a stop, he pulled on the balaclava knitted specially by his mother and, adjusting the eye-slit, stepped onto the platform. A few passengers waited for the train but he was the only arrival.

A spindrift-laden wind greeted him outside the station, and getting colder by the second he hurried to the junction of a long wide street. Aptly named Straight Street it consisted mainly of small shops and houses, most of which backed onto open farmland. A church at one end and a boarded up cinema opposite appeared to be the most notable buildings. There was very little activity; just a few shopkeepers clearing snow from doorways and some muffled pedestrians inclined at angles to the wind.

Following the directions given by Mrs Humblestone he located the chimney. It was some distance away at the other end of the street and a replica of the huge Crantree stack. Resting his case every so often to swap hands, he continued past the Agriframe factory to a line of advertisement hoardings flanking the security fence at the bottom of Rilltot's yard. As he approached, three loaded transporters rumbled out of the entrance and turned towards the greenhouses he had passed earlier. The yard was huge, and walking towards the main building he could see that it was a Lilliputian version of the Crantree production shop.

A man in a white dustcoat emerged from the building and made towards a company van parked outside, but on seeing him changed tack and came down the yard to meet him.

'Don't tell me, let me guess.'

He pressed the edge of a clipboard against his chin.

'You're looking for the 'Holiday Inn'?'

'No.'

'You're a parachutist?'

'No.' Pimple reached for the letter given to him by the human resources department.

'You're a terrorist?' The man spoke in short staccato bursts.

'No.'

'Don't tell me you're the lad I'm expecting from Crantree?'

'That's right.'

'You're the first to get this far. They usually catch the next train back.'

'Oh...' It wasn't quite the reception he had expected.

'What made you come here - torture?'

'No.'

'You didn't volunteer did you?'

'Well yes.'

He was regarded with curiosity.

'It takes all types I suppose. I'm only here because the wife owns a potato field.' He extended his hand. 'I'm Jack Benson by the way.'

They walked to the entrance. It was diminutive compared with the Crantree arrival hall and housed only one clocking in machine. Mr Benson pointed to the floor.

'You might as well leave your case here. We'll be back for it once I've sorted a few things out.'

They continued down the centre aisle of the warehouse between pallets of window frames arranged in rows according to type. Overhead, two chain winches dangled from steel girders and a few gridded lights shone down from the roof. In everything but size and noise the Isby depot was identical to the Crantree production shop. Even the office doors opened onto a fire balcony overlooking the warehouse floor. But once inside all similarity with Mr Tranmere's office ended. Two large workbenches stacked with computers and electronic equipment in varying stages of repair took up most of the floor space, and there was just enough room for a small desk tucked into a corner beside a filing cabinet. Clearly Mr Benson had a very different style of management.

He drew up a packing case for Pimple to sit on.

'Right…' he produced a company claim form from the filing cabinet. 'You can claim eight hours shift premium for the journey here, then twelve pounds for supper and breakfast, plus thirty pounds disturbance allowance.'

'I didn't have supper or breakfast.'

'Look at it as compensation for being hungry then.'

Mr Benson countersigned the completed form with a pen from his dustcoat pocket.

'Next we have to fix you up with somewhere to stay. But let's see what this says first.' He opened the letter from the human resources department. 'Did you know they'd already booked you into lodgings?' He looked puzzled.

'No.'

'Well they have.'

'Mr Tranmere said they would pay me an allowance.'

'That's right, but it says here you have to stay with Beth Barnes in Church Street for the first month. Do you know her?'

'No. Is it very far away?'

'About as far as you can get in Isby.' Mr Benson thumbed through the telephone directory. 'Let's see if she knows you're coming.'

He keyed in a number and someone answered. 'Beth? It's Jack Benson...Yes the holiday season's over at this end of town as well. Look, are you expecting a lodger today...That's right, when did they book him up with you then...No I didn't know, but I'm only the manager.'

He cupped his hand over the mouthpiece. 'You were booked in with Beth three months back.'

Pimple was mystified. That was even before his first meeting with Mr Tranmere.

Mr Benson kept his eyes on him.

'What he like? Well, blondish, shortish and a bit pasty-faced...No, that's just shock - he's seen Isby...Don't worry he can't escape...OK we'll be round in a few minutes.'

'Mr Tranmere only told me about the job a month ago.'

'Well, he'd decided you were coming here before then. Did he give you any idea what you were supposed to do?'

'He said he might give me a better job when he had completed his plans for Isby.'

'When he had completed his plans for Isby?' Mr Benson repeated the words slowly, and with feeling.

'That's right.'

Mr Benson spoke to the ceiling.

'He's going through one of his nutty phases again. Pass me that calendar lad.'

He consulted the calendar and again spoke to the ceiling.

'Stroll on! We're due a full eclipse of the Sun in February. Has he sprouted a moustache yet, a sort of handlebar job, not clipped like mine?'

'No'

'He will.' Mr Benson spoke with conviction. 'Last time he nearly caused a revolution with his cold presses and that was only a partial eclipse.'

Pimple thought back to his interview with Mr Tranmere.

'He seemed a bit peculiar, but I thought he was always like that.'

'He is, with Tranmere it's just a matter of degree. Did you get any idea what sort of havoc he had in mind?'

'The Machine Shop Supervisor thought it might be offices.'

'Not dramatic enough. He'll do better than that with a full eclipse.'

Mr Benson selected a marker pen from his dustcoat pocket and ringed round the date on the calendar.

'Remember that date lad. Believe me he'll have driven us all bananas before then.' He pressed the cap of the pen into his chin, and speaking slowly once again, looked quizzically at Pimple. '...And something tells me he's started already.'

They left the office and walked along the centre aisle to the entrance hall. Mr Benson gave him a set of keys.

'Will you be able to drag yourself here by seven tomorrow morning?'

'I reckon so.'

'Good. We've only one early load for Tillingham so there's no point in us both turning out. The hooter button is just inside the door to the office, give it three blasts at eight sharp - Isby depends on it. After that, put on the kettle. Black coffee with two sugars for me OK?'

They reached the van, and Pimple squeezed beside a computer monitor in the passenger seat. Turning left outside the yard they followed a tractor and trailer to the end of Straight Street, then forked right at the church into a narrower street past a pub and antique shop. Mr Benson pointed out a small wooden building with a shallow pitched roof.

'That's Beth's fish and chippery. You'll have cod or haddock with mushy peas every other night and scampi on Saturdays if you're lucky. You might even have to help her out sometimes. She runs it herself since her husband was killed.'

'When was that?'

'About a year ago, her son was killed as well, and it left her with a bad limp.'

'Oh.'

'No need to feel awkward about it, she'll tell you in her own way, but don't ask me why Crantree singled her out as your landlady.'

They pulled up at the first in a line of small terraced houses and a short blonde woman in her early forties opened the door to greet them as they came up the path.

'In you come, we're all a mess, but you'll have to take me as you find me.'

She shuffled lopsidedly from the step to give them room to enter and held Pimple at arms length as they crowded into the small hallway.

'Gracious! You put me in mind of my nephew. He looked just like you before he emigrated to Australia.'

'It was either that or a fortnight in Isby.' Mr Benson glanced quickly from one to the other. '...Don't tell me its love at first sight?'

'Of course it is.' agreed Beth. 'We're going to get on famously aren't we Ducks?'

'Well - Yes.'

He hesitated, not through doubt, but by surprise that he should feel such an instant kinship towards Beth. She could have been a favourite aunt if he'd had one.

Mr Benson made an exaggerated move to the doorway.

'Enough said.' He flicked his eyebrows up and down. 'No introductions needed...won't be a gooseberry... better leave you to it. Remember lad, sound the hooter at eight sharp.'

Within minutes Pimple was in an armchair after a late breakfast of toast and scrambled eggs. Above him, some muffled bumps and scrapes penetrated through the ceiling as Beth prepared his bedroom. He was under strict instructions to stay where he was. She held the view that it would be wrong for her first paying guest to help out so soon after arriving. It would get her into bad habits and she wanted to be sure she could manage. She might not feel so awkward about it later.

He glanced round the living room. It contained an amiable jumble of possessions that she and her late family had accumulated through the years. A drop leaf table under the window was scattered with magazines. Facing him on the sideboard by a roughly turned wooden bowl, the head and shoulders of a man in army uniform stared severely over a smaller photo of a schoolboy inset into the same frame. Behind him on the piano top was a cartridge case fashioned into a lighter, and closer to hand, a rumpled sheepskin rug sent hairy breakers over the hearth surround. On the seat opposite beneath a pair of scissors, lay some cooking recipes cut from the magazines. A large television on a wheeled stand was angled directly towards the chair.

The bumps moved across the ceiling towards the landing, and Beth called down to him. 'It's ready for you now Ducks if you'd like to get sorted out!'

He took his case upstairs and was shown into a freshly decorated bedroom overlooking the back of a tractor sales yard. There was a strong smell of mothballs and emulsion paint.

'This used to be Malcolm's room.' She spoke without reticence. 'When the hospital finished with me I set to and re-decorated it. Jack Benson told you about our car crash did he?'

'Yes.'

'I don't mind talking about it. It happened, and that's that. I'll just have to wait a bit longer before seeing them again.' She straightened a painting on the wall. 'Don did that when we came back from our last holiday in Cornwall.'

He studied the painting. It was a seascape at sunrise. A coil of rope lay in the foreground and a flock of pterodactyls wheeled over a cliff-top.

'It's very nice,' he said.

'I was going to put it away,' she continued, 'but having their things around doesn't upset me now, and it goes nicely with the wallpaper.' She moved to the door. 'Just as long as you feel at home here, that's the main thing.'

He laid his case on the bed and went to the window. Below in the yard, a mechanic with a bobble hat stretched tightly over his ears was probing with something beneath an open tractor bonnet, and beyond, the white open fields merged with the sky to seal up the horizon. He gazed at the scene for some time before opening his case and starting to unpack.

'Well I'm here,' he mused. 'I wonder what happens next.'

8. That Old Feeling.

A flicker of gold caught his attention as he unlocked the entrance gates. It came from the top of the chimney and sparkled brightly in the morning light, but the sky had clouded over by the time the last load had started off for Tillingham.

It was later in the office when he saw Mr Bensons message hanging from the hooter button. It read: 'The hooter's kaput. See if you can fix it but don't do anything daft!'

From the button a pipeline went up through a hole in the ceiling, and another went down through a hole in the wall to an air compressor on the warehouse floor. Perhaps the compressor wasn't working? He pushed the button and heard a prolonged wheeze from high up outside, then the compressor started to make up the pressure loss. He went outside. The pipe emerged from the building at about roof level and bridged a short gap where it followed a metal access ladder to the top of the chimney.

Could it be that the light from the chimney had something to do with the hooter malfunction? He glanced at his watch. The hooter was due to sound in twenty minutes time. Should he try to fix it?

He tested the ladder. It seemed firm enough, and climbing the first few rungs he looked upwards. The blotchy clouds skated overhead giving the impression that the chimney was continually falling onto him. But curiosity overcame timidity and he climbed to roof level. Testing the pipe for security he kept going until he was well above the warehouse roof, and daring to look down, he could see that even from a height Isby revealed no surprises. Already it was beginning take on the appearance of a lumpy black line. The steeply sloping slate roofs had already shed much of the snow and once past the church Straight Street bisected a straggle of farm buildings and headed beyond the open fields straight to the horizon.

Moving up a few more rungs he guessed he must be near the top and a tinny rattle just above his head confirmed it. Looking up he could see that a flexible hose connected to the end of the pipe by a jubilee clip was flapping in the wind. Taking even more care he climbed the last rungs of the ladder until he was level with the top of the chimney.

Evidence of past hooter failures littered the wooden planks sealing the chimney aperture. Most were rusty klaxon horns, but dangling from a small metal tripod was a trumpet which must have been used to replace the previous hooter. The hose had blown clear when the button was last pressed, and a length of insulating tape was all that secured the trumpet to the tripod. He leaned over the rim of the chimney to unwind the insulating tape from the bell. It was a weather-beaten object thick with verdigris and scratched in places where it had blown against the tripod. All that remained of the original finish was a small patch of gold lacquer, but the motion of the clouds reflected in that spot gave it animation, and he viewed it with a compassion normally reserved for live things. Unwinding more tape from the blowing end he removed the stub of a klaxon horn which had been forced over the mouthpiece, then looked for something to replace the trumpet. A large galvanised iron funnel lay conveniently at hand beside a drum of bitumen paint and he settled for that.

Working quickly, he used the screwdriver blade on his penknife to adjust the mounting bracket until the funnel was securely fastened to the tripod. Next, he pressed the klaxon stub into place and wound the remainder of the insulating tape onto the hose so that it would fit tightly inside the funnel. Following a quick check, he tucked the trumpet inside his bomber jacket and descended with caution.

Reaching the bottom of the ladder just as the Agriframe security guard tacked downwind past the entrance, he raced through the warehouse and upstairs to the office and waited a few seconds before pressing the button. His efforts were rewarded by a deep rasp, powerful enough to snap open eyelids the length and breadth of Isby.

Pleased with the result, he took the trumpet to a bench and examined it carefully.

Externally, it was in a sorry state, but nothing was missing and there were no serious dents. He turned it over. The cork on the drainage key needed replacing and it required three new felt discs under the finger plungers, but that was easy. The most important job was to free the valves. He went downstairs to the washroom and using a hand-basin, immersed the trumpet in a strong mixture of detergent and hot water. A greenish scum replaced the bubbles and the process had to be repeated several times before the valves were free enough to return without sticking. Drying it off with paper towels he returned to the office and unscrewed the three knurled collars holding the finger plungers and valves in place. A can of light oil lay conveniently to hand amid the electronic bits and pieces on a bench, and dabbing each plunger with just the right amount of oil he replaced them in order of removal. A slice of cork from a bottle stopper served to replace the pad on the drainage key and he completed the task by wiping the instrument over with a lightly oiled rag. The clean up had revealed a decorative pattern of roses entwined around the bell and some ornate lettering which announced: 'The Brash Superior' Elkhart Indiana.

He worked the finger plungers. The action was good, and it was only then that he thought it odd that he should know so much about trumpets. He had a toy trumpet once, but had never laid hands on a real one before. He pressed his lips together and blew lightly into the mouthpiece. The note was clear but a little shaky. He tried again and soon found the correct fingering for the scale starting on 'C'.

Strange, surely it wasn't that easy to play the trumpet?

A few nursery rhymes came to mind. He played a bad 'Humpty Dumpty' but it wasn't long before he knew the valve combinations, and correct lip pressure for each note. It was as if he had been playing for years and just needed some practice.

He tried some popular pieces; playing what he could remember and simply making up the rest as he went along. All sorts of tunes clamoured for attention; happy tunes, boring tunes, snatches from 'Sleaze Factor' and the old recording that brought him to his feet outside Rilltot's social club.

He tried to play what he could recall, but it was full of half tones and unusual melodic twists. Images of Rose flashed before him whenever he succeeded in capturing the mood of the piece. Her half smile; the frown; the mock surprise when he first asked her to go out with him, and then the harsh photos of her betrothal to Barney Rockyman.

The elderly instrument responded beautifully; dropping to a crackle in the low register and sounding high notes without shrillness. When at last he laid it on the bench he felt so much better. He now had a way to bemoan his loss. A wisp of breath curled up from the bell in the cold air of the office. Now he could say what he wanted to say without struggling for words, and winking at him like a seductive eye, the small patch of lacquer hinted at much more than that.

From behind came the sound of clapping.

'Where did you learn to play the trumpet like that lad?'

Mr Benson had arrived and seemed genuinely impressed.

'I didn't.' A lengthy explanation seemed due. '…I just found it.'

'Where?'

'On the chimney.'

'On the chimney?' Mr Benson pointed upwards. 'That chimney?'

'Yes that chimney.' He pointed upwards.

'You found this trumpet on that chimney'

'Yes, when I fixed the hooter.'

'So that was the hooter! The dog nearly made it through the cat flap. How did you fix it?'

'I used a funnel.'

'Was that on the chimney as well?'

'Yes, I used it instead of the trumpet.'

Mr Benson looked carefully at him. 'I'm swallowing it so far. You went up the chimney; fixed the hooter with a funnel and came back with that trumpet.'

'That's right.'

'Then you discovered you could play it?'

'Yes.'

'I thought it needed practice to play a trumpet?'

'So did I.'

Mr Benson sat down. 'You've never played a trumpet before?'

'No.'

'And we both agree that it needs practice to play a trumpet - correct?

'Yes.'

'So how is it you can play that one?'

'I don't know, but I was wondering if I could keep it.'

'You're not likely to go up there for any more are you?'

'No, this was the only one.'

'Good.' Mr Benson seemed relieved. 'It's yours.' He eyed him cautiously. 'But why am I so confused?'

'I'm a bit confused as well,' agreed Pimple.

Beth summarised what he had told her so far.

'So you found you could play it and you've never played one before?'

'That's right'.

They were both looking down at the trumpet which lay on the hearth between them. The lacquered patch shimmered in the glow of the gas fire.

'What did you play on it?'

'All sorts, and a recording I heard.'

'Do you know what it was called?'

'No, but it was old, and a bit different.' He didn't have the words to describe the effect it had on him.

'How was it different?'

'There weren't any guitars or singers'

'Was there a trumpet in it?'

'Yes and some drums.' He wasn't sure about the other instruments.'

She played with her broach.

'It's not my business Ducks, but were you feeling down when you heard it?'

'A bit.' He concentrated his gaze on the trumpet.

She sensed his reticence.

'I'm not just being nosey, there's a reason for asking.'

She looked at him searchingly and softened her voice.

'Was it very bad Ducks?'

He nodded and gave Beth a brief account of his unhappy courtship of Rose.

She made sympathetic noises.

'I had to ask because something like that has been happening to me since Don and Malcolm died.'

She pulled the tea trolley towards her.

'You see, I didn't know what had happened to Don and Malcolm until I was recovering in hospital. The doctors wanted to be sure I could pull through before telling me, but when they did tell me I didn't really want to pull through. What with all the tubes they'd stuck in me, and the plaster and wire keeping me from falling to bits, I was in a right state. There didn't seem any point in going through all the bother of hospital just to be housebound and alone. All I could do was stare at the ceiling and listen to the radio on my headphones, and that didn't help much either.'

She paused.

'It's all relationships and shouting on the radio these days and the news didn't encourage me to join the world again, so most of the time I plugged into the hospital music channel. It was usually light classical and old pops, but then this strange tune came on and it got to me so much I had a good cry.'

She smiled in recollection.

'I suppose it was just what I needed. It pressed all the right buttons. A tune never did anything like that to me before and I pestered them to play it again.'

She laughed.

'I must have driven them batty in the hospital because I kept on and on about it. The presenter told me that I must have heard it when they switched over to Radio Hecklington and he asked them to try and trace it. They couldn't trace it, but said they had sold some old recordings and it might have been one of them.

'Was it?'

'Yes, but I only found that out later. Anyway, I decided not to die until I heard it again.'

'Is that the same one I heard?'

She spoke guardedly.

'I can't be sure, but it sounds like it might be.'

She poured the tea and shook her head.

'It's all so daft. I've been in a right pickle since leaving hospital and I don't know if I should like what's happening or not.'

She stirred the teapot and pointed to the piano.

'The ambulance men saw me into the house, and after they left I just sat down on that stool and began to play. I couldn't work the pedals properly with my leg being like it was, but I knew what to do and soon I was getting the hang of it. Going to lessons when I was young put me off playing the piano and listening to Malcolm trying to play pops didn't teach me much either, so it's all a bit strange.'

'A bit like me then?'

'Yes,' and it's even stranger now you're here.'

'Didn't you know I was coming?'

'Yes of course I did Ducks. You've been expected for some time.' She corrected herself. '...I mean not you in particular, but someone like you.'

'Oh.' It seemed he was the only one who didn't know he was coming to Isby.

She seemed to have trouble collecting her thoughts.

'I'm not making myself clear, but I get confused just thinking about it, so let me carry on as I was or I'll lose track completely.'

She resumed her story.

'When I could walk without doing any damage I went to Bassett's antique shop. I knew Chance Bassett bought old records so I asked if he'd bought a record from Radio Hecklington. He knew about our accident and soon I was pouring everything out to him right up to when I discovered I could play the piano. It was then he told me that he hadn't bought the record but he knew who did.'

She poured the tea.

'Next day he called round to say he could introduce me to the person who bought the record, and that evening he drove me to a shed on Mr King's farm and introduced me to Philip who played it for me.'

'Was it the same one?'

'Yes,' she smiled, 'and I had another good weep.'

'Do you reckon he'd let me hear it?'

'I can't promise but I'll tell Chance you've arrived.' She passed the tea. 'We've started a band you see. Chance plays the trombone, Philip plays the clarinet, Lutz plays the banjo and I play the piano.'

She counted her fingers.

'That's only four fingers, I must have missed someone.'

'What about a drummer?'

'Oh and there's Dan of course, so all we need now is a trumpet player.'

'What about me?'

She sensed his excitement and became cautious.

'I hope it is you Ducks, but we've all got to agree that you're the one we've been waiting for.'

'So I'd have to play the trumpet for you to be sure then?'

'I think so, but I don't want to build your hopes up too soon because it isn't as simple as that. Philip thinks it's all part of a strange plan and he knows more about it than anyone else.'

'What sort of plan?'

'It's no good me trying to explain it. Chance will have to do that. I get confused just thinking about it.'

'It sounds a bit complicated.'

'It is complicated, but everything seems to be turning out the way Philip said it would.'

She frowned.

'I probably shouldn't say this, but it's getting a bit creepy for me. Maybe we'll wake up and find it's all been a dream.'

They stared at the trumpet for a while then Beth gave him the TV remote control and announced she was going to bed.

Later in the bedroom he reflected on events since his arrival in Isby. It had been a strange couple of days, but he didn't want to wake up even if it was a dream.

9. Tin Roof Blues.

The tone arm of a vintage turntable swung inwards to the centre of the record and tracked from side to side in the unrecorded groove.

No one spoke as Philip unfolded himself from one of a circle of poultry feed sacks to walk over and remove the record. He moved with a slow energy conserving lope suggesting fatigue through lack of sleep or illness, and stooping low into his own shadow placed the tone arm on its rest and carefully lifted the record from the turntable. Above him, a camping lamp threw an energetic circle of light onto a squadron of moths and the other listeners.

He straightened up.

'Was this the recording you heard Pimple?'

'Yes.' Pimple could barely speak through the constriction in his throat. It had moved him even more than he thought possible on a second hearing.

Philip placed the record in a specially constructed box. 'You have listened to 'Dead Loss Blues' which was recorded by the 'Magnolians' on the 'Revelation label'. Only a few pressings were made so this is a very rare example.'

Beth dabbed her eyes. 'It always makes me cry when I hear it.'

Chance Basset rose from his sack.

'Well, congratulations Philip. I admit to having doubts about your supposition, but the arrival of Pimple is surely all the proof you need.'

'Thank you Chance.' Philip rolled his eyes and stepped back into a cone of shadow under the base of the lamp. 'It is of course possible that Pimple has been recruited by Dead Loss Blues but we can't rule out coincidence just yet.'

'A string of coincidences Philip. First it was me, then Lutz, then Beth, and now Pimple.'

'I'm here as well!' A stocky man jumped up from his sack. It was the first time Pimple had noticed him.

'Oh, and Dan.' Chance spoke with less enthusiasm. 'But having initially harboured doubts about your idea I now find myself trying to convince you of its validity.'

Philip fluttered a hand. It was white and waxen like a plant grown in the dark.

'It is only a supposition Chance, no more than that. I could be wrong. All that matters now is our ability to faithfully perform the music of Blue Gums Foster. I don't need to remind you that our recruitment is imperfect anyway, so it is even more important that Blue Gums be accurately paired.'

'I think you are being unfair to yourself Philip.'

Philip leaned out of the shadow. The light moulded gaunt hollows in his face.

'I am simply trying to be rational in an altogether irrational situation. We have to be objective and objectivity doesn't always embrace fairness however much we may wish otherwise.'

Chance gestured helplessly.

'But perfection is rarely achieved, and I'm afraid we may stagnate while you search for it.'

Philip returned to the shadow.

'And I'm afraid that we may sink the ship for a half-penny worth of tar. This week has led me into areas of knowledge which frankly I am ill equipped to tackle. Beyond that I can say no more.'

'That's a relief!' Dan stood up, bowed, and sat down again.

Chance asked Pimple to pass him his trumpet.

'Well, I've been making some enquiries of my own Philip.' He held up the trumpet. 'This is a Brash Superior which was produced in limited numbers for marching bands. That must be significant.'

Philip crinkled his mouth - it might have been a smile. 'Significant only if you are comparing trumpets on chimneys with swords set into stone.'

'Yet another coincidence? Surely not'

'I don't know. It is quite possible that Blue Gums played a similar trumpet, or even that trumpet, but we have already ventured into the incredible. Pre-ordained trumpets would be too much to cope with.'

'You will excuse me!'

The exclamation came from a bald and noticeably angry young man who had been introduced as Lutz the banjo player. 'I am asking myself why am I listening to all these words. Why am

I not playing my banjo, or Beth the piano, or Chance the trombone or Pimple the trumpet? He is here to play is he not?'

'Please!' Philip raised his hands. 'There is something I must know.' He spoke directly to Pimple. 'Have you had any 'Deja-Vu' sensations recently?'

'I might have.'

Chance translated the question. 'Have you ever felt that you were re-living something that had happened to you in the past?'

'Well, yes.' He recalled the moment at 'Funlands' just before Madame Zelda invited him into her tent. 'Once at Southness.'

'When was that?'

'Last April.' Then he remembered gazing into Pipers Lane Millpond when he was with Rose. 'The next time was a bit like being in the future.'

Philip rolled his eyes back and took counsel from within.

'I would like to hear more about that.'

'But not now!' Lutz brandished his banjo. 'I will play, Beth will play, Chance will play, and Pimple will play or listen as he pleases! And you will play - yes?'

Philip turned to Pimple as he loped over to pick up a clarinet from the top of the piano. 'You must tell me about your experiences at the first opportunity.' He blew into the clarinet and produced a thin reedy squeak. The straight lines of the instrument complimented his angularity and using it as a pointer he explained some changes he had made to the music.

'I have pencilled in the modulation to 'E flat' for the last eight bars of 'Ringlets' and we can dispense with the drum break. It was only put in as a concession to popular taste in later commercial recordings.'

Dan pulled a face.

Suggesting 'Stomp On' as a good piece to warm up with Chance unfolded a list of tunes and spoke to Pimple.

'Most of the pieces will be new to you, but feel free to join in on any you think you can tackle.' He spread oil onto the slide of his trombone and worked it vigorously up and down. 'OK, here we go, 'Stomp On' on the count of three!'

Chance stamped on the hard earth floor and the opening bars of 'Stomp On' resonated round the shed with the subtlety of a barrel organ in a bathroom. It was simply an expression of exuberance and not much else, but Pimple reached fever pitch.

Between the misplaced notes and rhythmic contradictions he discerned an inspired trumpet part, and unable to contain himself any longer reached for the Brash well before the first ensemble passage was complete. He knew exactly how the piece should be played, and that the correct tempo lay somewhere between Chance's oscillating foot and the regular thump of the bass drum. Playing three ringing notes to provide beacons of pitch and timing, he repeated the theme at exactly the right pace, prompting the other instruments to reconcile their differences in favour of rhythm and harmony.

'Take it Pimple!' yelled Chance.

He blew a fiery extemporisation, completing each sequence with an anticipatory phrase that was only partly satisfied by the next one. For a full twenty-four bars he primed the air with expectancy then resolved it with a single chiming note that led Philip and Chance into the last chorus.

'That was magnificent!' Chance turned to Philip. 'That must have settled your doubts Philip?'

Philip barely changed expression.

'Not entirely - but.' He turned to Pimple like an approving schoolmaster. 'May I welcome you into our band, providing of course, that you wish to join us?'

'Yes...thanks I'd like to.' Pimple beamed with pleasure.

A note of caution entered Philips voice. 'I am now persuaded that Dead Loss Blues has been the recruiting agent for our band. That being so it also follows that we have come into being to perform the music of Blue Gums Foster with humility and not for profit or self aggrandisement.'

Chance frowned.

'Isn't that laying it on a bit thick Philip?'

'We are playing before a live audience tomorrow evening Chance, and applause can be a heady thing especially if it is experienced for the first time.'

'I doubt if we'll get much applause in the Puritan Arms'.

'Perhaps not, but now is the time to guard against vanity. Public acclaim can be just as corrupting as monetary reward and we mustn't be tempted into pandering to crude popular taste.'

Dan rattled a drum.

'Why not give them a 'talk in'? We're good at those!'

'And I say 'Ringlets'!' Lutz glared at Chance and Philip. 'We play 'Ringlets' and 'Julep Rag' and 'Angry Man' - angry like me. We play until - how do you say it? Until your cows are coming home. And we are not stopping to talk so Pimple will learn our tunes for tomorrow!'

Chance seemed doubtful.

'Do you think you would be able to learn our repertoire in time for tomorrow evening Pimple?'

'I reckon so.' He was certain he could.

'Let's go for it then. We'll start with 'Ringlets' then work through the book playing each sequence twice, so that Pimple can join in on the second time round.'

Chance brought 'Ringlets' to life on the fourth stamp of his foot, and holding back until some melodic consistency had been achieved, Pimple joined in to endow 'Ringlets' with a grandeur that the composer never intended. It was a pattern that he followed each time without difficulty. Some of the compositions were simple blues sequences masquerading under different titles and he became bored with their predictability. He even found himself appraising the musicianship of the others. 'Angry Man' and 'Julep Rag' were complex pieces requiring more instrumental dexterity than Chance or Philip were able to provide. Forgetting that he had only touched a trumpet the day before, he became impatient at their limitations.

By the time Beth had closed down the lid of the piano the wind was gusting hard against the shed and the camping lamp swung erratically from its length of fencing wire.

Chance grinned provocatively at Philip. 'So, do you still have doubts after hearing that?'

Philip returned his clarinet to the piano top. 'No. Quite clearly Blue Gums is matched.' But he spoke wearily, and loping across to his bed in the darkest corner of the shed added: 'Now I only have fears.'

'Fears about what? Really Philip you are being pessimistic to the point of exasperation.'

Philip pressed both hands to his temple. 'It is just too much too soon Chance.'

Chance spoke with concern.

'Possibly, but you've been doing too much for too long Philip. Come and stay with us at least until this spell of cold weather is over.'

Philip rocked his head in his hands. 'Thank you but not now. I must reach my limits to have any hope of success. You know that.'

Chance went over to the bed and laid a hand on Philips shoulder.

'I know how important it is to you, but I'm not going to sanction your apparent desire for self destruction. That may sound cruel Philip, but I think you are being foolish and would be failing my duty as a friend if I said otherwise.'

Philip lay back on the bed and stared upwards for a few moments, then turning to Chance said: 'Thank you Chance, but I must do it my way.'

10.<u>Oriental Man.</u>

Chance reversed his car away from the shed onto a narrow track flanked by farm machinery.

'Well I tried Beth.'

'You tried very hard Chance.' She spoke from the back seat. 'But if that's what he wants there's nothing we can do.'

He turned on the windscreen wipers.

'I worry about him on nights like this.'

'Is that his home?' asked Pimple.

'There's no simple answer to that, but we owe you an explanation after talking over your head for most of the evening.'

Chance glanced into the rear view mirror.

'Have you told Pimple about the band Beth?'

'Just a bit, but I didn't want to muddle him up. I'm muddled enough as it is.'

'It won't be easy for me either.'

They came to the end of the track and Chance frowned into the back-glare of the headlights.

'OK, I'll make a start.'

They turned onto the main road.

'You may find much of this hard to swallow, and frankly so do I, but our band has come together in such a remarkable way that we can't simply put it down to coincidence. Something extraordinary seems to be happening to us, and so far Philip is the only one to offer any explanation for it.'

They slowed down for a bridge.

'I met Philip soon after he had resigned his lectureship in compositional philosophy at Wrangle. He resigned because the Academic Council refused to acknowledge Blue Gums Foster as a major figure in American music despite the evidence he had placed before them. By then he had documented most of Blue Gums life, but couldn't account for some gaps, and decided on Isby to continue his work because it was a quiet town free from the usual city distractions.'

'Was he living in the shed then?'

'No, he was renting a flat in Straight Street. His move to Witherdyke came later.' Chance paused. 'I won't go into the details, but like Beth and yourself I also heard Dead Loss Blues during a very unhappy time in my life and it had a profound effect on me. Then one morning while serving in the shop I heard it again on Radio Hecklington.'

'And just to think,' cut in Beth, 'I was crying in my bandages at the same time.'

'I was in a better position to track down the record though.' continued Chance. 'Once I had served my customers I phoned Radio Hecklington, who told me that someone from Isby had already bought an old record they played on their morning show. They had no information about the record and wouldn't say who bought it, so my only option was to put a message in the local paper hoping that the purchaser would contact me.'

They slowed down for a junction.

'It was a pleasant surprise when Philip came into the shop and invited me to his flat to hear the record.'

A signpost directed them to Isby-Le-Fen or New York.

'I naturally assumed that like me, he had bought the record because he really wanted to hear it again. But there we differed. He only wanted it because it would complete his collection of Blue Gums recordings. I was even more surprised when he maintained that Dead Loss Blues was a mediocre piece compared to the brilliance of earlier work, and over several evenings he played his entire collection so I could judge for myself. Frankly I'd had quite enough of Blue Gums Foster by the time he put on Dead Loss Blues, but it moved me even more on the second hearing. So, far from agreeing with Philip, I expressed amazement that such an inspiring performance could have been lost on him.'

'Philip doesn't think 'Dead Loss' is much good then.'

'I wish it was that straightforward.' Chance spoke with feeling. 'Philip judged 'Dead Loss' to be just an ordinary blues spiced up with a few changes to make it sound distinctive. He is an expert in musical composition so I couldn't disagree with him on those grounds. I simply repeated my surprise that he could be so unmoved by it.' Chance sighed. 'Anyone else would have put it down to simple personal preference, but Philip pressed me to explain my passion for the piece, so I told how it had affected me during an unhappy period in my life.'

A flurry of sleet rapped the windscreen.

'Had I known the effect my explanation was to have on him I would have remained silent.'

Beth leaned forward from the back seat. 'You can't blame yourself for that Ducks, he would have done the same whatever you said.'

'Perhaps, but I regret being the first to start him thinking along those lines.'

He dipped the headlights and waited for an oncoming vehicle to pass.

'You see it was our meeting that led Philip towards his remarkable idea that Dead Loss Blues might come as a revelation to just a few selected people who happened to be going through a miserable period in their lives. It seemed ridiculous to suppose that just one short piece of music could single out certain individuals from the millions of unhappy people all around us, but he couldn't shake off the notion and had to follow it up.'

They turned off to Isby.

'He wrote down the full musical score by repeatedly listening to the record and analysing it bar by bar. It was then he noticed how unusual some of the harmonic changes were. The notation could have been transcribed straight from an oriental score and this led him to wonder whether anyone else had helped with the composition.'

Chance broke off. 'Are you following this?'

'Yes.'

'Very well, but if you think the next bit is crazy you're not alone.'

'It's weird' added Beth.

Chance continued.

'Quite by luck Philip gave himself the clue he had been seeking by repeating 'dumpity dum' or 'dumpity dum dum' as he counted each note and rest.' Chance demonstrated this by tapping his fingers on the steering wheel. 'Perhaps he became bored with the repetition, but he startled himself by repeating 'Dhorji Dhumdu', 'Dhorji Dhumdu' in place of 'dumpity dum dum'.'

The yellow glow of street lamps heralded the approach of Isby and he turned on the indicator.

'It seems that Dhorji Dhumdu was an unconventional Tibetan mystic who fell out of favour with the Dalai Lama and migrated to France.'

They turned into Church Street.

'I doubt if more than a handful of people have heard of Dhorji Dhumdu, but when his name sprang to mind Philip felt sure that not only had he found the reason for the oriental notation in Dead Loss Blues, but he might also have found the reason for the profound effect it had on some listeners.'

They arrived at Beth's house and went through to the kitchen where Chance continued his explanation.

'It was in his student days that Philip first heard about Dhorji Dhumdu during a lecture on musical notation. The lecturer chose Dhorji's 'Kunming Quadrille' because it was based on the seven tone scale, and unusually for such a piece, it gained popularity in Europe. It seems that Dhorji wrote it soon after arriving in Paris but was fiddled out of his royalties by an unscrupulous agent. For a while he earned enough for his needs by selling quotations, but he also excelled in the mystic arts, and was extremely proficient in astrology. Accounts of his uncanny predictions were common among his devotees, but he suffered harassment from the French authorities because of his association with radical student organisations and must have decided to leave France before being arrested.

He simply vanished, and apart from the 'Kunming Quadrille', the only evidence of his stay in France were the quotations which had been compiled and printed by an admiring student. Fortunately the student was farsighted and generous enough to send copies to most European universities and after the lecture Philip obtained one from his university library. He recalled being puzzled by one entry. Slipped between sentiments such as, 'It's love that makes the world go round.' and, 'It's not what you know but who you know.' was: 'Chattanooga here I come.'

It meant nothing as a quotation and he assumed that the student had perceived wisdom where none was intended. If, however, it was a statement of intent, then it would have been very significant because Dhorji might have travelled to Chattanooga before Blue Gums died.'

'So Philip reckoned they might have got together then?'

'Exactly, and he lost no time in trying to prove it.'

Beth placed two mugs on the kitchen table. 'It's still a mystery to me.'

'And now it gets really difficult.' Chance placed his hands flat down on either side of his mug. 'Philip reasoned that Dhorji would have been drawn to the Smoky Mountains because they had much in common with his Kunming home and offered a clear view of the night sky. Selecting the peak of Parsons Bald as a likely spot, he sought evidence of Dhorji living in the area.

Firstly he contacted the Chattanooga Office of Information, and then Mirabelle Foster who was Blue Gums only known daughter. They were both long shots, but his luck held. The Chattanooga Office of Information had recorded the finding of a prayer wheel close to Parsons Bald. It was never claimed, and to their knowledge it is now in the Mayors Office at Gatlinburg.

The reply from Mirabelle was even more encouraging. She felt certain that her father had journeyed north, but didn't know why. Then, long after his death she found a used bus ticket from New Orleans to Gatlinburg in his old wardrobe. Slidebone Walker and Clarinet player Reed Williams who both played with Blue Gums in his later years, also mentioned occasions when Blue Gums vanished for days on end.'

Chance looked at Pimple over his mug.

'Let me know if you've had enough. I can continue with this at anytime.'

'It's alright, I'm following it.'

Beth joined them.

'He might as well have it all in one lump, then he can explain it to me.'

Chance resumed.

'One difficult question remained, and it stumped Philip for weeks. Why should Blue Gums go to so much trouble to meet an elderly Tibetan on a mountain? He could barely see the day through without a quart of bourbon, and a gruelling mountain trek would have been a harrowing prospect, so why?'

'That's a hard one.'

'Yes, and Philip despaired of finding the answer until Lutz arrived.'

Chance raised his spoon for emphasis.

'Lutz was also greatly affected by 'Dead Loss' during an unhappy episode in his life and like me he couldn't understand why it failed to affect Philip.'

He grinned.

'Lutz was more direct though. He told Philip that he had 'Ears of cloth.''

'Then I arrived,' said Beth.

'It seemed odd that four musicians should have come together in Isby of all places, after hearing Dead Loss Blues.'

Chance waggled his spoon.

'Philip could see that a pattern was emerging, and this led him to the incredible notion that Dorji and Blue Gums might have pooled their talents to produce a piece of music so powerful in its effect that it would become the recruiting agent for a future band.'

'Dead Loss Blues?'

'Yes.'

'They had strong motives. If they succeeded, future generations would hear their music and they would at last receive the acclaim they so justly deserved.'

At this point Chance expressed his doubts.

'Even if I had faith in the predictive sciences I would say they had set themselves an impossible task, but your arrival is exactly in line with Philip's reasoning.'

He shook his head.

'I have no idea where all this will lead, but if Philip is correct, our destinies were determined ages ago by those two remarkable men in the Smoky Mountains.'

'So Philip reckons I'm like Blue Gums?'

'You can't be exactly like Blue Gums because this is a different age and a different country, but you may have much in common.'

Beth replenished their mugs.

'Are you still following it Ducks?'

'Yes.' Pimple nodded. 'Philip must be a bit like Reed Williams then.'

Chance shook his head.

'No, the beauty of Dead Loss Blues still eludes Philip, and that, in a round about way brings me back to your first question.'

He stirred his coffee and frowned.

'Unfortunately, Philip was born into a wealthy land owning family and enjoyed a loving and stable childhood and the means to rise well above the rough and tumble of the world we know.

He shook his head sadly.

'I doubt if you would have recognised him then. He was an energetic and even humorous person to be with. But once convinced that his comfortable circumstances prevented him from experiencing the emotional impact of Dead Loss Blues he decided to simulate in his own life, some of the hardships that Blue Gums had to endure.'

Chance sighed regretfully.

'He left his flat in Straight Street and persuaded a local farmer to rent him that dreadful shed at Witherby Top. Next, he telephoned his fiancée and said something terribly offensive to her with the predictable result that she never wanted to see him again.'

'Sounds a bit daft.'

'It is daft,' agreed Chance. 'Philip is a brilliant academic, but he has allowed an obsession to lead him onto a self destructive and stupid path. His health is clearly suffering and not surprisingly Dead Loss Blues still fails to have the desired effect on him.'

'So he's not really meant to be our clarinet player?'

'Probably not, but I doubt if Blue Gums and Dorji expected their recruitment to be perfect anyway, and Philip, more than anyone deserves a place in our band.'

Chance rose and put his empty cup on the draining board.

'You've had to take in a lot at one sitting and if you think it is all too far fetched then you're in good company. I still have misgivings after taking it in small doses.'

Beth followed him into the hallway.

'You explain it so clearly, but it's still a jumble to me.'

Chance opened the door.

'Well I may be able to explain it, but I really don't understand it.'

Pimple helped with the washing up, and later in the bedroom laid the Brash on the dressing table and mulled over what he had been told. Nothing Chance had said seemed at all far fetched, and that was the problem - it just wasn't far fetched enough.

11. The Entertainer.

He pressed the hooter button and a deep masculine rasp tore through the air. Grinning with satisfaction he returned to his letter.

Dear Mum and Dad, he had written. *'I hope this finds you as it leaves me. It's cold here, but Isby is all right and my landlady is a good cook because she runs a fish and chip shop. There isn't much to do at work because we are running out of window frames. I found a trumpet last week and started playing in a band. We had a good session in the Puritan Arms on Saturday night.*

That just about covered events since he'd waved goodbye to his parents from the train at Wenthem station, but he couldn't say much more about the band because it would worry his mum silly.

Still, it had been a good night in the Puritan Arms. Jack Benson and his wife had stayed to the end, and then there was the man in the yellow suit who bought them a round of drinks. Philip stuck to water and refused to play any popular requests, but everyone else seemed to enjoy it, especially when they marched round the bar playing 'Chinklets.'

He checked over what he had written, but it seemed to contradict his father's advice. *'You are on your own now son,'* he had said through the carriage window. *'It's no good thinking the world owes you a living. Remember you only get out of life what you put into it. Hard work never did anyone any harm. It didn't do me any harm now did it?'*

When the train pulled away he thought back to how tiny and insubstantial his parents had looked against the huge tarpaulined stack of freight towering above the station buildings. Not so long ago they had been inexhaustible fountains of strength, knowledge and affection. If there was such a thing as a circle of importance then No76 Cowgrass Estate was at the very centre of it. But now he wasn't so sure. Perhaps it was something to do with travel broadening the mind, but the blustery fenland wind seemed to hold more promise for him than Bleak Leigh ever did. Unfortunately it wasn't the sort of promise he wanted to tell his parents about, so he tore off the page and restricted his message to a bland description of Isby.

Jack Benson arrived as the phone rang, and picking it up, listened with undisguised alarm.

'How many?'...'Did you?'...'Moss? Yes that would be the man alright'

He beckoned urgently.

'Quick lad, get me our holdings of one by two Vistavacs.'

Guessing the call had come from the site manager of the Tillingham development Pimple checked the stockholdings and scribbled down the quantity he had loaded onto the morning transporter.

Jack Benson grimaced at the figures.

'Look, will five hundred tide you over until next week? In the meantime I'll shake up Crantree.'

He moved a circuit board from the writing pad.

'Tillingham want three thousand on site next week. They say they put in a preliminary request to Dave Moss last summer. You were there then, do you remember anything about it?'

'No, but they had trouble with the galvanising plant.'

'What was wrong with it?'

'The extractor wasn't working.'

'They would have fixed that soon enough.'

'Yes but...' He quickly checked himself as he pictured the extractor fan blades that Dave had shown him when he first started at Receipt and Despatch. Perhaps he had better keep quiet about them.

The phone rang again and Jack Benson winced as he listened. 'You're right, I didn't know. Could you say that again - only a bit slower so my ulcer can swell gradually?'...'Thanks. I'm supposed to be at the hub of things here so I shouldn't really ask this, but have you put in requests for anything else I should know about?'

He scribbled on the pad and again turned to Pimple.

'Tillingham again. Since the Vistavacs took us by surprise, did we know about the four thousand 'Plastikoates' they ordered in November?'

He phoned through to Crantree and Pimple listened carefully. He remembered noting down the low stocks of Vistavacs before reading the dreadful news about Rose and Barney Rockyman in the Gazette. Mr Tranmere would be hopping mad if Dave had mislaid an order that big.

Jack Benson frowned into the phone.

'Receipt and Despatch? Is Dave Moss handy? I want to talk to someone about window frames.'...'Yes, window frames, they're squarish with big holes in them and I want some please.' ...'Well, you make them don't you?'... 'America! What's he doing there?'... 'Who's handling everything then?' He put on a voice. 'Sorry for being so dreadfully tedious but can I talk to him about window frames?'

He replaced the receiver with exaggerated care.

'Dave Moss is in the States, and Tranmere is handling everything, except he's not there either.'

'Dave didn't say anything about going to America when I was with him.'

'Well he's there now, and unless we can rustle up seven thousand window frames we might as well join him.'

He did some calculations on the jotter pad.

'That's a pile bigger than this depot.'

Pimple thought hard. That many frames couldn't have passed unnoticed. He formed a picture in his mind: '…a pile bigger than the depot.' Could it possibly have been that huge stack of freight at Wenthem station?'

'Do you reckon they could have been sent by rail?' he asked.

'Hardly likely with the new transporter fleet.'

Pimple described what he had seen.

'About as big as this depot you say?'

'A bit bigger I reckon.'

'It's worth a try, anything's worth a try. I'm desperate lad. If the wife gets wind of this I'll be on her potato field before you can say 'Skylights'.'

He returned to the phone.

'Wenthem Goods? This may seem a daft question, but have you noticed about seven thousand window frames lurking in some corner of your backyard?'...'Rilltot, yes that's correct.' He gave the thumbs up sign. 'Night delivery last October'...'OK, but didn't you have any forwarding instructions?'...'Doesn't make sense to me either'... 'You've only got a small yard'... 'Well, I wish they were cluttering us up - there's coconut palms at the bottom of ours'...'It's a nuisance to me as well, if we don't get them soon we'll have to make our own. Look, can I make an executive decision and get them released?'…'Only through D H. Tranmere.'…'Yes that's clear enough!'

He spoke to the ceiling as he put the phone down, then pointed to the wall calendar. 'Surprise, surprise! Tranmere's warming up to that eclipse alright. He's had nightshifts delivering those frames to Wenthem goods until Swiftrack refused to take any more.'

'They'll be collecting storage charges won't they?'

'Yes, whopping great big ones!'

Jack Benson regarded him with a hint of admiration.

'So far you haven't done too badly lad. Now if you can tell me what Tranmere is up to I'll buy you a trumpet for each day of the week.'

He flinched as the phone rang again.

'Yes he's here alright. I haven't mentioned it yet but if he wants an agent I'll soon be looking for another job.'

He passed the phone over.

'Pimple?' It was Chance. *'Are you free this evening?'*

'Yes.'

'Good. I haven't time to go into details, but Lenny-Le-Strange plans to hold his next show here in Isby and he wants us to appear on it.'

'Oh?' The name was vaguely familiar but no more than that.

'He bought us a round of drinks on Saturday night - remember?'

'Was that the man in the yellow suit?'

'Yes. Surely you must have heard of the 'Lenny-Le-Strange Show.' Try to make it here before seven this evening. Beth knows, but I need to chase up the others.'

He put the phone down.

'What's the 'Lenny-Le-Strange Show'?'

Jack Benson snapped his fingers.

'That's who he was! I knew I'd seen that face somewhere. You must have seen the 'Lenny-Le-Strange Show' - Tuesday nights on KTV. He was in the pub while you were trumpeting.'

'We only watched BBC at home. What sort of show is it?'

'Tap dancing grandmothers; singing cats; that sort of thing.'

He smiled. 'Like a show everyone watched when I was young and beautiful. He takes it to different towns each week and gets the locals to make idiots of themselves. Don't tell me he's putting it on here?'

'Sounds like it?'

'Has he asked your lot to go on the show then?'

'He wants to talk about it tonight.'

Jack Benson gazed pointedly round the office.

'Well, unless something happens pretty sharpish it doesn't look as if there's going to be much for you here. Better give that trumpet a polish and make the most of it.'

12.Big Butter and Egg Man.

Lenny-Le-Strange swung one leg over the other and leaned back until the front legs of the armchair cleared the carpet.

'Right!' He clasped his hands behind his head.

'Thanks a million for getting these guys together Chance.' Beaming elastically he gimballed his head around to include everyone. 'Now you might not believe this people, but Yours Truly was driving back from Manchester yesterday and stopped here to grab a few lungfulls of serenity by the church - you know? Anyway, I must have taken the wrong road out because I was orbiting potato fields and stuff hours later. 'One mans métier is another mans poison.' as the saying goes, and believe me infinite potato fields are poison to Lenny when he should be halfway down the M1, and homing onto the girl he loves!'

'We say that all roads lead back to Isby,' declared Chance.

'Well, you're not kidding, and I'll tell you for why. I came across a signpost pointing to New York. My mind was starting to blow by then, you know? 'Fantastic!' I thought. Lenny's found a shortcut across the pond, and that folks would have saved me a bundle in air fares! Anyway, I found this sort of straight lane and ended up back at the church feeling gutted and in dire need of sustenance, especially of a liquid nature. Then I spied this swinging sign showing some guy in a big hat doing his thing with a pint pot, so I booked in at the tavern across the road.'

He lowered his hands and patted the armrests.

'Now I like to lay my cards on the table, you know? Dixie and Mozart, it's all the same to me, but I go for Lamborghini's with electric seat adjusters and my Kensington hideout. Showbiz is like that. You're either in or not in, and not being in is strictly non-Lenny - OK? That's why I make sure my shows are good, and that means very good!'

He screwed his hands together in simulated avarice.

'That way I make-a-plenty money you understand? No, seriously guys, these days it's all kids getting heavy on gang rap and jerk, so when I heard you giving it that great Dixie last night I decided to put Isby on the map by throwing in a spot of nostalgia for the oldies.'

Chance sounded a note of caution. 'We don't really play Dixieland music Lenny. We are trying to rekindle an interest in the early music of New Orleans, and particularly that of Blue Gums Foster before it was exploited for commercial gain.'

'Truly, truly!' Lenny waggled his fingers. ''Rabbit Warren' are making it with rural revival, so why not this Blue Gums stuff, it could take off.'

Chance turned to Philip. 'We would be playing to millions of television viewers, so what do you think?'

'I think we would be playing to millions of television viewers.'

Chance looked perplexed.

'That's what I said. I was asking for your opinion.'

'I don't have an opinion, but I do have a question.'

'Yes?'

'Why?'

'Why? Well, because millions of people would hear the music of Blue Gums Foster.'

'I doubt it.'

'How can you doubt it?'

'They would be seeing us, but I doubt if they would be listening to the music of Blue Gums Foster. Television is primarily a visual medium.'

'It also has sound.'

'If I wish to hear music I don't go to the television set.'

'You might?'

'Only if I wished to see the musicians.'

'Why should that be a problem?'

Dan stood up. 'It's a problem because he hasn't got a TV!' He bowed and sat down again.

Philip ignored the interruption. 'I didn't say it was a problem Chance.'

'Then what are you saying Philip?' Chance edged towards impatience. 'You seem reluctant to appear on Lenny's show but won't say why. All we need is a simple yes or no.'

'But you are putting supplementary questions to me first.'

'I simply don't understand.'

'Very well let's start with the most important question.' Philip spread his hands to encompass the room. 'Why are we all here this evening?'

Chance tilted his head apologetically to Lenny. 'To discuss Lenny's offer of course. Really Philip I would have thought that was obvious.'

'It is, and it should be just as obvious that our first question is to ask whether or not this show is in line with our aspirations.'

'You surely don't think that playing to a wider audience would do us harm - do you?'

'It may not do us harm Chance, but I do care if it trivialises the music of Blue Gums Foster.'

'Why should it?'

'The music of Blue Gums Foster is intensely emotional because it stems from a lifetime of poverty and oppression. To perform it faithfully requires humility. I can't imagine anything less likely to promote humility than an appearance on this show.'

'So you think that some of us would be tempted to play to the cameras.'

'Of course, how could it be otherwise? This show is tailored for popular viewing.'

'Isn't that rather patronising Philip? You are charging us with immaturity before the event.'

'No, that is exactly what happened in the Puritan Arms last night.'

'Come now. Perhaps the march round the bar was a concession to an enthusiastic crowd, but it was also an expression of our own exuberance. Surely there's no harm in that.'

'I was thinking of the 'Birdie Song.'

Chance lowered his voice to respectful dissent. 'Correct me if I am wrong Philip, but isn't it true that Blue Gums himself was obliged to play popular requests in the Licentious Ballroom?'

Philip trembled with indignation. 'How can you justify the excesses of last night with the struggle of a poor black musician desperately trying to earn a living in early New Orleans? The obligation you speak of simply meant he was free to eat or go hungry. Our plain obligation to him is to treat his music with respect.'

Chance began to assemble his defence, but Lenny spoke first.

'OK. Now that's really something! It's great to know you've got a feeling for this Blue Gums guy. No seriously I mean that. What's wrong with respect anyway? Believe me it pays off sometimes!' He produced a sincere face to go with his sincere voice. 'Straight up folks, I don't care whether it's Dixie or Mozart, but last night it was all happening in the Puritan Arms. Don't ask me why. I'm just an atmosphere monitor - you know? But that pub was full of real people who were listening with their minds, and that spells good news to Yours Truly!'

Philip nearly smiled.

'Your position is quite clear Lenny. My concern is about the ambiguity in ours.'

Chance combined exasperation with reason.

'Of course vanity and fame often go together but we haven't even played outside Isby yet. We would be more likely to have stage fright than an urge to show off. Honestly Philip are we to closet ourselves in a practice room denying opportunity after opportunity to preserve the purity of music that may never be heard again? I don't think Blue Gums and Dorji intended that either.'

'I'm sure they didn't,' agreed Philip. 'And before I'm assigned the role of party pooper - neither do I. My caution stems from a desire to spread the music of Blue Gums Foster as it should be played, but rightly or wrongly I detect in you an eagerness to step into the spotlight regardless of this.'

'My inclination to stardom disappeared along with my youth,' parried Chance. 'If I seem eager then it's simply because I don't want an opportunity to pass us by.'

Dan spoke loudly to Beth.

'Great crop of carrots this year!'

Lenny pressed the air like a conductor beseeching pianissimo.

'No, straight up, I think your outfit is great - OK? So don't get hung up for not playing Dixie. Britain loves amateurs and that's why Yours Truly gets top ratings on the box.'

Chance eyed Lenny with alarm, but it was Lutz who spoke.

'We are going on this show. Yes, or No?'

'Not without Philip Lutz. We must have a full band.' Chance shrugged his shoulders as if confirming a lost cause.

'Then we are to vote with our hands up like this!'

Lutz threw an arm into the air and eyed Philip frostily.

'Yes for up!'

Chance shifted uneasily. 'This is a difficult position Philip. I don't like resolving this with a show of hands.'

Philip spoke wearily. 'Why should you be in a difficult position? There's no need for a show of hands. Quite clearly you all wish to go on the show regardless of it's suitability for a serious performance of our music.'

Someone made a noise.

Philip continued. 'I am not refusing to go on the show. I am simply asking you to consider your reasons for wanting to appear. We would be slipped in between crooning babies, performing ferrets and anything else that Lenny can muster locally. I am simply voicing my objections as strongly as I can.'

Chance was taken aback. 'So you are not refusing to go on Philip?'

'How can I refuse Chance? I must simply try to ensure that our appearance is not a complete disaster.'

Chance spoke warily. 'I wish we could do something to make you feel happier about it.'

Philip rolled his eyes. 'There is something that can be done by way of preparation.'

Chance tensed as he waited for more details.

Philip continued. 'We lead pampered lives, yet we are trying to play music steeped in adversity and prejudice. An afternoon of hard labour on Mr King's farm immediately before the show, would, in part simulate the unforgiving lifestyles endured by those early musicians, and might encourage us to perform their music with greater empathy.'

He paused and leaned slightly forward.

'Parsnips are ready for lifting on the East field.'

Chance sensed rebellion.

'But surely Mr King would prefer experienced...' he began, but Lenny had already jumped to his feet.

'Now that's really something! When Lenny homes onto dedication he gets serious, and right now he's really serious because he's just heard solid dedication from you guys.' His lapse into the plural went unchallenged. 'Believe me, dedication comes over on the box, so when you march into the spotlight straight from that parsnip field, everyone will know you are the real business.'

Sensing that Lenny had somehow committed them to hard labour without causing open revolt Chance reacted quickly. 'Well at last we seem to have reached agreement Lenny.'

Lenny shook hands and dispensed smiles. 'Jerry my producer will be getting it together for the big day. If you need to get in touch with Yours Truly just phone KTV. They all know where I am.'

With the exception of Philip, everyone filed onto the street to see Lenny off. A gust of wind ruffled his hair revealing extensive balding, and his knees cracked as he stooped to enter the Lamborghini, but once inside, the soft interior lights restored some of his show-business credibility. Giving a perfunctory wave he moved off with just enough tyre squeal for a TV celebrity, and they watched as the Lamborghini swooped into intermittent pools of darkness between the street lights before aiming itself towards the M1 and London.

Beth said: 'I expected him to be different somehow, but he's just like that on the show.'

13.Breeze.

The blustery wind had at last calmed down to a breeze, but in lieu of fierceness, had acquired a late afternoon edge.

Pimple reached the dyke side of Mr King's field and maintaining the pace he had set for himself, reversed direction and started on the next row which would take him back to the far perimeter hedge.

Behind, a row of full baskets lay ready for collection. His arms ached and a rawness on the inside of his thumb promised a blister to come. Yet there was something satisfying about putting each full basket aside, and it was even more satisfying to know he was leading Chance by half a row and Philip by nearly a row.

Dwarfed by the field, Philip was working towards him from the perimeter hedge, and in the light of his slow progress it seemed odd that he was the one who wanted everyone else to lift parsnips without payment. The matter had of course, been heatedly discussed inside Isby Antiques long after Lenny had gone. The finer points of the debate had been lost to Pimple, but some familiar phrases came to mind such as: *'Strenuous activity being a great leveller.'* *'Shared experience enforcing a common aim.'* and: *'Less time for posturing.'* It was also quite evident that he and Lutz were of the greatest concern to Philip. Enough had been said about the 'vulnerability of youth' to make that clear. The purpose, as he understood it, was to put everyone in the right frame of mind just before the show. Even so, lifting parsnips seemed a strange way of going about it.

Mr King seemed doubtful as well. He wasn't accustomed to an unlikely team of lifters offering him a Saturday afternoon of unpaid work. Neither was he fully persuaded by the explanation given by Chance beside the tractor and trailer. The secretary of the 'Striped Marshwort' conservationists' had that way of speaking, and it usually led to trouble. On the other hand it was hardly likely that a respected local businessman would arrange for a team to vandalise his parsnip field. So, accepting their help such as it was, Mr King had grouped them in a half circle and lifted some parsnips to demonstrate the technique.

'Lifting parsnips,' he said, 'was like playing Dixie.' Some tunes were fast and some tunes were slow. The main thing was to keep going at the same speed otherwise you'd lose the rhythm. So it was with lifting parsnips 'Some lifters were fast; some lifters were slow.' Good lifters knew their best speed and stuck to it.

Warming to the theme, Mr King extended his analogy to a symphonic variation of the seasons. There was the pianissimo of winter, building up to the accelerando of early root crops and spring blossoms. Then came the grand fortissimo of late summer and autumn harvesting before nature eased off once more to the rallento of coming winter. Mid season crops added tone colour, and June strawberries he likened to a burst of the snare drum.

'I suppose you could say we were a musical family.' he concluded. 'My brother Charlie plays drums, but farming keeps me away from the cello.'

With this in mind Pimple scanned the field.

Beth was making surprisingly good progress, but no one else seemed to be heeding Mr King's advice. Philip was making very hard work of it. Swinging his body from the waist he grasped each parsnip with both hands and dumped it into the basket like a prisoner doing penance with heavy rocks. By now he had drawn level with Chance who used the opportunity to break off his spasmodic advance from the perimeter hedge to have a few words. They were too far downwind to be heard, but it wasn't hard to guess that Chance wanted to discuss the show. They would soon be onstage, and the opening tune still hadn't been decided. 'Chinklets' had been suggested as a lively piece to start with, but Philip preferred the slower 'Mississippi Moan' as a more profound opening to: 'Distance the band from the mediocrity which would be streamed into millions of homes.'

Evidently unconvinced by anything Chance had to say, Philip continued to work stubbornly onwards until distance made further conversation impossible. Arms akimbo, Chance gazed after him for some time, then, in a burst of angry energy showered handfuls of parsnips into his basket.

At least they had agreed on a name for the band, and that had been difficult enough. From now on they would be known as 'The New Magnolians' and it was already spelt it out in adhesive gold lettering on his new trumpet case.

Lutz called to him.

'I see you are also taking a rest my friend. Do you not feel ridiculous?' He tipped a thick woollen ski cap to the back of his head and at once looked older. 'I am feeling ridiculous.' There was dissent in his voice. 'This...' He picked up a parsnip and held it aloft. 'This is a parsnip - Yes? And I am asking myself why is it not a banjo or a spanner with my wages at time and a half? Do you not ask yourself such questions?'

'I suppose so.' Pimple kept his voice down.

'Quite.' Lutz released the offending vegetable and followed it scornfully into the basket. 'Tonight we will be tired like anything and my chords may be not so good, or your trumpet so excellent perhaps?' He glowered in Philips direction. 'And all because of words my friend, words, words, words!'

Lutz had clearly intended his outburst for general consumption, and Pimple quickly resumed his work. He wasn't ready to be cast into the role of a rebel, and if lifting a few parsnips was the price of playing before millions he wasn't going to make a big fuss about it. He could become famous, and if Rose knew he had appeared on television she might even wish she'd thought twice before marrying Barney Rockyman.

He stopped to savour the prospect of a regretful Rose, and conjured up a suitably remorseful image which just about encompassed his field of view. But Dan had intruded into it and was now becoming an irritant. There was little about Dan to attract attention. It didn't matter where he was or what he was doing, because his surroundings always seemed to soak up whatever personality he had. Surely Dorji and Blue Gums wouldn't have deliberately chosen anyone quite so unnoticeable to be their drummer - they must have intended someone else.

He quickly turned his attention to Beth, who was now ahead of Philip and catching up with Chance and Lutz, but he was still well ahead of them. By the time everyone had emptied their last load of parsnips into the trailer and stacked their baskets they would have to make their way to the show. He checked his watch and felt a thrill of anticipation. Soon he would be seen and heard throughout Britain, and unaware that Dan had lifted more parsnips than anyone else, he continued his work with renewed energy.

It was dusk when Mr King parked his Land Rover by the dyke. The sky had cleared and a bright half moon matched the intensity of the lamps along the New York to Isby road. He could hear singing, and watched the small column break step and climb the style leading to the Church. The words of 'Little Boll Weevil' wafted across to him above the rumble of traffic. *'...A swaying in yo' cotton home yo' watch ma baby workin'.'*

His brother Charlie was going to the show that evening and would make a fool of himself if given half a chance. Still, it might be worth turning on the television if he had nothing better to do.

He thumbed some earth from a parsnip and tossed it into the trailer. They hadn't done too badly. There was enough to make up a load for Covent Garden, and that meant another early start. He'd give the opera a miss this time though. He'd seen 'La Traviata' until he was up to the hind teeth with it.

Another snatch of 'Little Boll Weevil' drifted across to him.
'...An' thinkin' nothin' thro' the day 'cept eatin' an' a eatin'

He started the Land Rover.

'Still, it takes all types,' he murmured.

14. There's No Business like Show Business.

An amplified squeal cut through Isby Drill Hall as the continuity assistant guided them through snaking electrical cables and lighting equipment.

'Don't do that Barney!' she screeched.

The curtains rippled and a face appeared in the gap.

'Look, you're uptight! I'm uptight! We're all uptight! Feedback - OK? Just me and an antediluvian mixer console - OK?'

OK!' she screeched back. 'Don't have hysterics Deary!' She turned to Chance. 'It's always like this before a show. Who are you by the way?'

'The New Magnolians. Lenny wants us to appear just before the interval I believe.'

'Magnolians? She wrinkled her forehead and spoke to a walkie-talkie. 'The Magnolians are here Jerry, do we have props?'

'Who?...Oh yes.' Jerry seemed to remember. 'Felt hats, macs, and a reflective disc on the bass drum. Don't fit the disc until they are onstage; important that OK? 'Crabapple' know, but remind them will you? Do something if they're not scruffy enough…Should have come in straight from a parsnip field...well something like that.'

She ushered them backstage and again spoke into her walkie-talkie. 'Props needed backstage ASAP! And we have a woman'…'Yes a woman sweetie'…'No problem for me either, but felt hat and a mac? - Fix it please.'

The props arrived, and fashioning a sackcloth bonnet and shawl for Beth the continuity assistant gave everyone a length of coarse twine. 'Put on the macs,' she instructed, 'and bunch up the waists with this.' She viewed the overall effect before a wall mural of the 21st Lancers then rushed back into the hall, her voice fading amidst the clatter of tubular chairs being set into rows.

Chance eyed Philip uncertainly. 'I had hoped that props wouldn't be needed, they make us look like a troupe of Worzel Gummidges.'

'And we will be expected to behave like a troupe of Worzel Gummidges.' said Philip flatly.

Chance waited for elaboration, but none came, so he passed round his hastily scribbled prompting sheets. 'Chinklets' headed the list and still Philip said nothing. He just glanced at his sheet and laid it aside.

'There is a preference to start with 'Chinklets',' said Chance cautiously.

Philip moved to a shadowy part of the drapes. 'Very well.' His voice had an amorphous quality as if the stage props and his recent labours on Mr King's field had sapped him of all dissent. 'It really doesn't matter what we play.'

'You don't mind?'

'I'm indifferent, which isn't quite the same thing.'

'I wish you had more enthusiasm for this show Philip.'

'So do I, but I will do my best.'

Chance seemed reassured. 'I know you will, and I understand how you feel, but I'm confident it will go well.'

'I hope you're correct,' said Philip. 'I fear it could be a painful experience.'

On the other side of the drapes, lights flashed, microphones were tested, and the show group Crabapple tuned up.

Pimple felt a thrill of anticipation. Was he really going to be heard and seen by millions of viewers?

He opened the trumpet case. The Brash lay snugly in its cradle of green velvet, and exuding a special energy of its own; the lacquered patch reflected the nearby surroundings and converted them into images of a working past. Bare light bulbs were transformed into the golden globes of luxury speakeasies, and the hatted forms of Lutz and Chance became gangsters making sinister plans in darkened recesses. It was another world. A world of unconfused morality where bad was really bad, and novelty and excitement were as yet unjaded by excess. A world where to jitterbug was to court infamy and where a single sneaked kiss was the culmination of an evening romance. Girls flapped their hands in chorus lines across his imagination, and golden and distorted he ogled back from the foreground. Would he ever experience such excitement? And was this show really going to be the first stepping stone to fame and fortune?

He removed the Brash and blew lightly into the mouthpiece. The note was soft but it combined with the ambience of the hall to produce a depth of tone, which, by contrast made Crabapple sound harsh and strained.

'You will play well tonight my friend,' said Lutz with conviction. 'But are you not nervous?'

'A bit I suppose.' He felt confident of his own ability, but had doubts about Chance and Philip.

Lutz produced a leather bound hip flask from his banjo case. 'Then you will join me, for I am nervous like anything. You have tried the schnapps - yes?'

'I don't think so.'

'Then you must.' Lutz unscrewed the top of his flask and separated it into two small silver cups. He filled them both to the brim. 'It is drunk - so.' He downed the contents of his cup in a single gulp. 'You will try now. It goes down, how do you say? Without touching the sides.'

Pimple tried, and what little he did try was enough to tell him that two, possibly three, would take him to optimum trumpet playing condition.

'It is good - yes?'

'Not bad at all.'

'You will have another?'

'Thanks.'

They drank in unison and Lutz gazed dreamily at his cup.

'Helga my girlfriend, she gave me this flask for schnapps when I was leaving her to come to Isby. We were drinking many schnapps together at her home in Bad Oman. When I drink I think of her.'

'That's nice.' A suffused warmth had already ascended to chin level.

'But tonight we are the same my friend. You have no girlfriend and mine is not knowing what happened to me.' Lutz removed his hat. 'She is in Bad Omen and I am without hair.' He smoothed his head and sighed morosely. 'All gone, yet I was having hair before I came to Isby.'

'What happened?'

'I was to demonstrate a new tractor shipped from Frankfurt but oil was leaking from the gearbox. I was to drive it next day at the Isby Show and all night I worked under it with oil on my hair.' He grimaced. 'I was thinking it would do no harm and my tractor demonstrated well, but then hair was on my pillow, and soon I was having no hair at all.'

'Hair today, gone tomorrow,' quipped Dan who, unnoticed had been hovering nearby.

'I was not knowing what to do with myself,' continued Lutz. 'There would be joking at work, so I asked my manager if I could see a specialist in hair.' He frowned thoughtfully. 'He said I must visit only his hair specialist in Harley Street. Why? I was thinking did he need a specialist in hair when I was knowing him with so much hair? But he was paying the bill - so I went.'

Lutz concentrated hard on putting his thoughts into words. 'It was strange because in the waiting room I was thinking I had been there before. It was, let me say, like old times, and then I was hearing music, beautiful music.'

'Dead Loss Blues?'

'Correct my friend, and when it finished I was wanting like anything to hear it again.'

'Just like me.'

'Yes.' Lutz pushed the two small cups together and screwed them back on the flask.

'And then you started to play the Banjo?'

'Yes, but often I am wishing that I had hair without playing Banjo.'

He gestured hopelessly.

'Helga was knowing me with hair. If she saw me now she would not be thinking bald is beautiful.'

'And that's the bald truth of it.' concluded Dan.

Beyond the stage came the murmuring of an audience settling down, and beckoning with her walkie - talkie from the rear curtain, the continuity assistant whispered that the show was due to start and led them to a row of specially allocated seats.

The lights dimmed and an announcement came from several loudspeakers suspended round the hall.

'Ladies and gentlemen we will be on air in a few moments, and for the benefit of viewers throughout the country don't be afraid to make a noise. Remember, this is your own real live show, so when the red light comes on lets hear from you!... Wait

for it... Are you ready?... One, two, three... OK we are on the air... Now!'

Crabapple thundered out the theme tune; the curtains swept apart, and Lenny-Le-Strange bounded onto the stage.

'Great! Really great! No, I mean that!'

His suit blazed yellow in the spotlights.

'No seriously!' He fanned both hands to stem some applause. 'It's fabulous to be back in Isby, and did you notice I said, 'back in Isby'. That's right people because believe it or not Yours Truly has been here before!'

He paused for the significance of the event to sink in.

'You have a saying here which goes: 'All roads lead to Isby' - correct?'

There was a ripple of affirmation.

'Correct, and its true believe me, because I arrived here twice on the same day. No straight up guys, Isby was cool the first time, but infinite potato fields the second time round was too much of a good thing when I should have been homing down the A1 to my London pad.' He shrugged. 'Still, Yours Truly knows when he's beaten, so I booked in for a night in the local hostelry and woke up with the birds.'

He paused long enough to receive the echo of his own voice.

'Yes... well...no seriously, what's wrong with fields and stuff anyway? I thought. Why not put Isby on the map and freshen up the viewers at home with a dose of real country air?' He closed up to a camera and said 'Oooh - Arrr!' in a West Country accent, then moved centre-stage towards a curtained enclosure flanked by two assistants.

'So let's get down to business. Most of you will know the rules by now but I'll re-cap just in case. The Finger of Fame will choose just one person from the audience to answer four questions.'

He produced a large sealed envelope from an inside pocket.

'For each correct answer the prize money doubles. Two hundred pounds for the first correct answer, four hundred pounds for the second, eight hundred pounds for the third rounded up to two thousand pounds for four correct answers.'

He lowered his voice.

'But there's another way of winning, and with millions watching who knows where that may lead?'

He became sincere while Crabapple played softly in the background.

'You see folks, deep down Yours Truly knows that everyone has a talent for something. It might be a card trick, a dance routine, a song, or maybe just a story. Believe me, I've seen what ordinary folk can do and this show is all about giving ordinary folk the chance to entertain ordinary folk. Remember, you only have to step into the spotlight and the cash and a fabulous prize could be all yours.'

A sense of occasion edged into his voice.

'So now it's your chance to show Britain what you can do because...' He swept his arms outwards and upwards. 'Because tonight, Isby-Le-Fen, the Finger of Fame points at you!' Crabapple exploded into a chordal summary of the introductory theme and the stage assistants drew the curtain aside to reveal a huge pedestal mounted hand pointing its index finger at the audience.

Lenny stood beside the finger.

'If you're too shy to come onstage you can propose someone else, but Isby gets the raspberry after two refusals. Let them hear it Daphne!'

An assistant pressed the raspberry button while Lenny pulled a face.

'So don't get the raspberry Isby! Now remember, this is a real live show, and Yours Truly has no idea who the finger is going to choose. Daphne will set the finger in motion while Moira and Myrtle will walk among you to see which lucky person gets the chance to win one of the really fabulous prizes we have tonight.' He pointed dramatically to the finger. 'Set the finger in motion Daphne!'

Crabapple played while the hand swung ponderously on its pedestal. A narrow beam of light from the fingertip settled on a lady who Pimple recognised as the Postmistress. The hand flashed on and off to indicate that the choice had been made.

'And who has been chosen Moira?' asked Lenny.

Moira tossed her hair back. Her voice came back strained and unamplified. 'The finger has chosen Mrs Fossitt Lenny, and Mrs Fossitt is taking the chance!'

'Then lead the goodly lady forward!' enthused Lenny. He spoke into a camera. 'It's is all happening here tonight folks.'

Mrs Fossitt walked onto the stage as he waved a handful of notes at the audience. 'That's one hundred pounds you've earned just for taking the chance Mrs Fossit, and believe me there's more where it comes from.'

Spectacled, with her hair drawn back tightly into a bun, Mrs Fossit curtsied first to the audience and then to Lenny.

'Thank you. I hope I will be able to fulfil your expectations.'

Lenny raised his eyebrows. 'Indubitably, and indubitably again. What a genteel contestant we have to start the show.' He closed up to her, 'But can I address you like what your friends call you?'

'You can call me Cecily or Isabel, either will do.'

'So it's Cecily Isabel Fossit.'

'Yes. Even my husband couldn't rescue me from sibilance.'

Lenny stood back in mock horror.

'Goodness! - it's not catching is it?' He threw a sideways glance at a nearby assistant. 'Write that down Daphne, I'll need it for the next show. But seriously Cecily, you were once a Miss Fossit and now you are a Mrs Fossit, have I got it right?'

'Yes, I married another Fossit you see.'

'Once a Fossit always a Fossit, are there any small Fossits?'

She smiled demurely. 'I have seven children.'

'Seven Fossits!' exclaimed Lenny. 'How about that people, and they say the great British family is dying out!'

'Well six are adopted,' she added hastily. 'It's surely very selfish to have a large family of one's own these days don't you think?'

A buzz of approval came from the audience.

'Now isn't that something?' Lenny rested a hand on her shoulder. 'I mean we're always hearing about the nasty side of human nature, you know; road rage, muggings, city fiddling - all that sort of thing. Then I come to Isby-Le-Fen and somehow I know everything is going to be just fine.' He held the microphone to one side and spoke to the camera. 'Everything's going to be just fine viewers, don't worry, the human race isn't doomed yet!'

He returned to her.

'That's really something Cecily, and I mean that, but would I be correct in guessing that hubby earns the daily bread while you attend to your brood?'

'Not quite, we both have full time jobs. I run the post office.'

'We've got Superwoman with us tonight. Is Superman with you?'

'No, it was my turn to go out, but we always...'

'Well,' broke in Lenny, 'with seven Fossits to look after I don't have to ask what he's doing.'

He led her to the front of the stage.

'But now we come to the exciting part of the show Cecily.' He again turned to his assistant. 'What prizes do we have tonight Daphne?'

Daphne tossed her hair back. 'There are eight really fabulous prizes tonight Lenny. We have two home karaoke's from 'Lonepose'. Three family holidays in Ibiza from 'Bingotours'. Five years subscription for 'CrushLove' donated by 'Banal Arts', and a complete limited edition of Naples Street Urchins donated by 'Humility Ceramics'.

'So that's the selection on offer Cecily,'

The stage darkened except for a patch of coloured light swirling before the Finger of Fame.

He held the envelope before Mrs Fossit.

'It's your choice Cecily. You can answer the questions in this envelope, or you can step into the spotlight and that dream holiday with hubby and the kids plus two thousand pounds could be yours.'

He closed up to her.

'Have you ever imagined that you were once a superstar entertaining thousands in front of the television cameras?'

'I did once, but that was a long time ago.' She toyed with her broach. 'It was just a girlhood fantasy of course.'

'Well now is the moment to make that girlhood fantasy come true. You aren't nervous are you?'

She inclined her head thoughtfully.

'I was, but now I feel strangely uninhibited. It must be those coloured lights, or a menopausal trauma perhaps?'

He used the envelope to fan alarm from his features. 'Yes, well...Great! So what are you going to do for us Cecily? Remember Britain is watching you.' It sounded like a warning.

'I would like to recite.'

Lenny signalled Crabapple for a drum roll and ushered her into the spotlight.

'Great!' He pointed dramatically at Mrs Fossit as he withdrew backwards from the centre of the stage. 'Cecily Fossit this is your moment of Fame!'

'Thank you.' She curtsied to the audience. 'A poem about death ladies and gentlemen.' Lenny stiffened in the shadows.

'Death,' repeated Mrs Fossit, by Hubert King. She folded her hands across the front of her skirt and began.

Thinking killed my golden urge,
The imagery is black and grey.
A sceptic acme subtly changed
Into this morbid lethargy.

There's death for you, there's death for me
and creatures great or small.
Lolling tongues in pens of blood.
Death's bounty for us all.

That kindness to the soldier.
The act of gallantry.
Courageous deeds in battle,
for death's efficiency.

She invited everyone to join in with the chorus.

There's death for you, there's death for me
and creatures great or small.
Lolling tongues in pens of blood.
Death's bounty for us all.

I heard the oceans sighing.
I saw the skylark die.
And mother earth was greying.
So many sucked her dry.

The audience joined in with enthusiasm.

There's death for you and death for me
and creatures great or small.
Lolling tongues in pens of blood.

Death's bounty for us all.

And in this gloom joy hurts.
A light through dungeon walls.
Ecclesiastic rites are stilled
in misanthropy's halls.

She raised her hands 'Altogether now!'

There's death for you and death for me
and creatures great or small.
Lolling tongues in pens of blood.
Death's bounty for us all.

The audience responded with gusto and raising her voice above the applause Mrs Fossit concluded: 'Hubert King is of course our very own poet and his recitals in Dyke Lane are well worth going to.'

Lenny jumped into the spotlight and appealed to a wider audience. 'Well how about that viewers? As I said, it's all happening in Isby tonight.'

He quickly led Mrs Fossit to the prizes.

'And what has Cecily scored on the Applause Monitor Daphne?'

Daphne tossed her hair back. 'Cecily has scored nine points, so she wins two thousand pounds plus five hundred pounds bonus and a prize of her choice.'

Mrs Fossit chose the family holiday. 'Someone may welcome a break in the sunshine.' she added.

Lenny presented her with the cheque. 'But there must be some words of advice you can give to all those hardworking mums watching us tonight.

She smiled. 'Early to bed, no TV, fizzy pops or mobile phones, and if necessary an occasional hard slap round the back of the legs.'

He whispered urgently into the microphone. 'Quick young Fossits, turn off the TV, Mum's on her way!'

A chorus of young voices welled up from the audience.

'We don't watch TV!'

He rummaged through his gallery of faces. 'Help, we've got a posse of Fossits! Set the finger in motion Daphne before they chase me out of town!'

Once again the Finger of Fame swung into motion. This time the light fell upon someone who stood up and refused to take his chance.

'It's not that I'm a bad sport like, but there's someone who'd be a better turn than me and he's in the house.'

Moira hurried towards him.

'Careful Isby that's one refusal,' cautioned Lenny. 'Who is the nominee Moira?'

Moira tossed her hair back. 'The first nomination tonight Lenny is for the Reverend Michael Flint, and I understand he is the Vicar of Isby.'

'And is the Reverend Flint prepared to take the chance?' asked Lenny.

'I am well prepared Mr Le-Strange!'

The reply required no amplification, and well ahead of Moira, the Reverend Flint strode confidently onto the stage.

Beth joggled Pimples arm and whispered.

'He's a wonderful man Ducks. I don't go to church very often, but he visited me lots of times after the accident and gave Bob and Malcolm a lovely funeral.'

The Reverend Flint shook hands firmly with Lenny.

'An opportunity indeed Mr Le-Strange. I have never stood before so many in this town and I intend to make the most of it.'

'And there's one hundred pounds in the collection box already Reverend'.

Lenny acquired a serious face. 'But joking aside, and it's the first time we've had a real live Vicar on the show, the Church is having trouble finding enough customers these days isn't it?'

'It is, and when one considers the bargain we have on offer, the trend is as remarkable as it is sad.'

'Agreed,' Lenny infused concern into his voice. 'But what went wrong? I mean why is the Church losing its popularity?'

'If I received one pound each time that question was asked, St Luke's would have a leak-proof roof by now.' The Reverend Flint glared into the lights. 'But you are all on the button when it comes to rushed marriages and character testimonials aren't you!'

'Rhubarb!' yelled someone from the audience.

'And that to you sir!' The Reverend Flint leapt over to the raspberry button. 'My, what a grotty self centred lot you are!'

Alone for a moment Lenny smiled badly into a camera.

'The fact is Mr Le-Strange,' continued the Reverend Flint. 'We have created a wonderful selection of recruiting agencies for the Devil and many amongst our number display an eagerness to enlist.'

'But isn't the Devil a bit old fashioned these days? You know; fire and brimstone - all that sort of stuff?'

'I am not one of those trendy idiots who wish to re-fashion the church by watering down Hell!' The Reverend Flint took a central position on the stage. 'Hell, my foolish friends, is just as hot as it ever was!'

'But you don't want to frighten folks away from the church do you?' Lenny stepped forward to include himself in the dialogue.

'I don't know where you come from Mr-Le-Strange. But the 'Horsemen of the Apocalypse' wouldn't frighten this ungodly shower!'

The Reverend Flint thrust his chin forward.

'But you have plenty to be frightened about. Oh yes! And so do you!' he glowered into the nearest camera. 'Yes I mean you out there sitting idly in front of your television. Who have you cheered up today? What about the neighbours or that lonely gent? Do you really have nothing better to do than watch silly shows like this?'

Lenny angled his head between the Reverend Flint and the camera.

'It's alright viewers, don't change channel, Sunday half hour is tomorrow!' He quickly pulled an envelope from his inside pocket and made signalling motions with the other hand. 'But leaving aside controversy, now it's time...'

'A last word to this lot before we continue Mr Le-Strange!' thundered the Reverend Flint. 'One way and another you have all found time to come here this evening, so let me remind you that tomorrow is Sunday and the doors to St Luke's will be open at nine sharp. Nigel Fitzpatrick will be starring on the organ. Bishop Collier will be master of ceremonies, and by popular demand the choir of St Botolphs will make their second appearance. I promise it will be a brilliant show and for some, it could be a belated, but profound awakening!'

He shielded his eyes and looked into the audience.

'As for you Cecily Fossit, I intend to take issue with you later. 'Misanthropy's Halls' indeed!'

Beth sighed with admiration. 'He's just like that in church. You'll have to come with me one day Ducks.'

Pimple wasn't so sure that he would enjoy a service conducted by the Reverend Flint, but further thoughts were cut short by the continuity assistant whispering urgently for them to go backstage.

'Lenny wants you to go on next. He feels that the show could do with some light relief... er ... music I mean. The present guest will finish soon, so get ready and wait for Lenny to announce you...best of luck.'

Going backstage they collected their instruments and lined up in a corridor formed between the curtains.

'Watch my foot when Lenny announces us,' instructed Chance, 'and don't forget the four bar break leading to the chorus.'

Through a gap in the curtains the Reverend Flint could be seen throwing endless coloured balls into the air. It was a dazzling performance and when he caught the last ball between his teeth, the cheers and catcalls raised the applause monitor to eight on the scale.

'Fantastic! What more can I say?' declared Lenny through involuntary facial twitchings. 'Believe me when Lenny's lost for words it means he's really knocked out!'

Bowing to the applause, the Reverend Flint straightened to his full height and amid loud cries of encore raised up his arms. 'Thank you ladies and gentlemen! But let me remind you that only one person ever completed a trick like this and you would be wise to think about it when the bells of St Luke's are ringing out tomorrow!' So saying, he deftly flicked his wrists and produced two items which he dangled before the audience. One was a small bread loaf and the other was clearly a fish.

'Nine sharp at St Luke's!' he roared. 'Be there!'

Lenny sprang to the microphone. 'How about that folks? Your very own juggling vicar, and it's show time at St Luke's tomorrow - so don't you forget it!'

The Reverend Flint chose the Naples Street Urchins and the main curtains closed behind Lenny.

'Sensational and believe me there's more to come! But now for something different.'

The spotlight moved to the curtain.

'Right behind me is a hot little package straight from the parsnip fields of your very own town. Yours Truly heard them over a pint in the local, and take it from me these guys are really dedicated to the music they play. When you hear Chance Basset and the Mangol Worzels you'll be hearing sincerity with a big 'S'. So pin back your ears and prepare for some of the hottest 'Dixie' you'll hear this side of the Pond!'

Chance pawed the air with his foot and brought it hard down on the count of four just as the curtains parted. The boards of the stage trembled, and Pimple tightened his embouchure for the ascending run of demi-semi quavers into the introductory bars of 'Chinklets'. But Philip broke ranks, and ignoring Lenny, strode directly to the front of the stage.

'One moment Chance!' This nonsense has gone quite far enough!'

The audience rustled uneasily.

'Ladies and gentlemen, we have been grossly misrepresented, and to continue under these circumstances would be humiliating for us and misleading for you. We are not a troupe of performing bumpkins calling ourselves the 'Mangol Worzels'. We play the music which evolved in the Southern United States early last century. It is an intensely emotional music because it is an expression of the hardships endured by so many black Americans in those times. Our labour on Mr King's farm was intended in part to simulate those hardships. It was certainly not intended to convey the impression of jolly rustics doing silly things with musical instruments.'

He placed his hat over the lens turret of a camera and turned to Lenny as he untied the binder twine and shed his mac.

'Sincerity, Lenny, usually comes with a small 's' and we will not be tricked into compromising our values for the purposes of popular television.'

Lenny, his bald patch glistening in the lights, moved towards Philip as if he had something vital to say, but he was beaten to it by Lutz who was already uttering something in German as his fist made hard contact with Philips nose.

15. Strike Up The Band.

Pimple raised his head a few inches above the pillow then slumped back and stared vacantly at the ceiling.

Polished by a fitful sleep, the awful events of Saturday evening came back with renewed clarity, and for the umpteenth time that weekend he re-lived the appalling finale to their brief appearance on the show.

It was all so vivid. The enraged glint in Lutz's eyes as his fist sped to its mark. Lenny's rush forward and the delayed gasp of shock when the audience realized they had witnessed a genuine moment of unleashed fury on national television.

Even the slightest sounds rang inside his head with perfect clarity. The squishy sound of Lutz's fist on Philips nose; the metallic tinkle of the clarinet mouthpiece cap bouncing into the footlight gully, and the dull thud of Philip dropping backwards onto the stage.

Yet the episode lacked consistency. It was like being cast in a badly scripted play where the performers were obliged to act out of character after the moment of high drama. It was Dan, not Chance, who had rushed to attend Philip, and it had been Dan, who, in the ensuing confusion had arranged for Philip's speedy removal from the stage.

But Philip's response was most surprising of all. After gaining consciousness he actually thanked Lutz for not punching him before he had finished speaking. He even claimed that the band could now perform in public with its integrity intact. It was hard to understand what he meant by that. Surely no one would want to hire a band with a reputation for self-destruction?

The sounds of a waking Isby filtered into the room, but he continued to stare miserably at the ceiling. So, far from becoming a celebrity he had been embarrassed before millions of viewers and might never have the chance to perform in public again.

A heavy lorry rumbled past setting up a sympathetic buzz in the house, and someone, surely not Lutz, was whistling below in the 'Isby Tractors' yard. He rolled over to look at the alarm clock and groaned again, but louder this time. The alarm setter was down, and with the hands at five past eight he was already late for work. Consternation followed despondency. Beth must have overslept as well. He really would be for the high jump if a transporter was delayed.

Jumping out of bed he scuffled round for clothes he had left in untidy heaps the night before, and rushed to the bathroom. Minutes later he had sealed the door against Beth's snores, and keeping his head down to preserve a degree of anonymity, rushed from the house.

It was a bright cheery morning.

High above the church a squadron of seagulls enjoyed a rare opportunity for some still air soaring, and running to the junction he crossed over to the Puritan Arms in time to come face to face with the mayor rounding the corner with his dog. Further along, Mrs Fossitt was cleaning the post office windows, and out for his morning jog, the Reverend Flint swept past in his tracksuit. Everyone seemed eager to get to grips with the new day and he tried to cast aside his forebodings. But the attempt was short lived. On reaching the line of advertisement hoardings he heard a disturbingly familiar sound, and watched horrified as three empty transporters nosed out of the yard and turned away in convoy towards Freeze Enderby.

Now he was in big trouble. The drivers must have lost patience waiting for him to open up, and it wouldn't be long before the Tillingham site manager was on the phone ranting about his window frames. A fourth, then a fifth transporter roared up to the gates panicking him into a last desperate spurt, but it was too late, and he arrived gasping into a cloud of diesel fumes.

Resting for a moment, he caught his breath while the depot cat brushed against his leg and made false sorties to urge him onward. He followed the cat to the entrance and groaned for the third time that morning. He had left the entrance keys on the bedside table. What Mr Benson would say to him didn't bear thinking about.

Meowing noisily while he worried what to do next, the cat strutted to and fro, then, in a gesture of feline impatience pressed the flat of its head against the entrance door and opened it a few inches. Had Mr Benson beaten him to it? He went through the door then stopped in bewilderment. This wasn't the depot, it couldn't be. It was more like the entrance foyer of a plush hotel.

A thick red carpet continued under a pair of swing doors through which he could see easy chairs and low coffee tables. Where was the clocking machine?

Like someone who had accidentally strayed into the wrong house he went outside again to check the surroundings.

A glance was enough to assure him that externally, at least, it was the depot, yet the clear sunlight revealed architectural features he hadn't noticed before. He hadn't, for instance, been aware of the white vertical lettering on the chimney when he first climbed it. It spelt 'Chimney' which conveyed the obvious, and if intended to be read with 'Rilltot Fabrications' which he knew was on the other side, then 'Rilltot Fabrications Chimney' seemed unduly possessive for such a large company.

He pinched himself hard. Perhaps he was running away from the recent traumatic events by creating his own world of virtual reality. But this was a solid sensation, and nothing like the one he had experienced when he was with Rose at Pipers Lane Millpond.

He entered the building again. The cat was waiting by the swing doors and it darted through the gap as he pushed them open. Hanging his bomber jacket on the pegs provided, he continued along a carpeted corridor to a second pair of swing doors, then to another pair of swing doors. But by now he had become so accustomed to the improbable that the profusion of swing doors flitted by as a minor oddity.

'Well here goes,' he muttered, and again led by the cat, entered a spacious room strewn with crates and folding partitions. It looked too extensive to have been the warehouse because the low ceiling and panelled inner walls exaggerated the dimensions. But the air compressor was still in place by the far wall, and the window to Mr Benson's office was visible through an unfinished section of the ceiling.

The cat made itself comfortable on some discarded packaging, and the swing doors closed shutting out all external noise. Nearby came the sound of rustling paper behind some folding partitions which had been arranged into an open cubicle, and walking to the open end he arrived before Mr Tranmere. A full moustache sprouted from his top lip and eyes gleaming he looked up from a formidable pile of paperwork.

'Ah! Just the person I wish to see.' In one flowing movement he shook hands and pointed to a nearby chair. 'Make yourself comfortable.'

He surveyed Pimple with evident approval, and pulling a folder from the pile of paperwork said: 'You must be wondering what all this is about?'

'Well, yes.'

'Can you guess?' Mr Tranmere opened the folder.

'No, it's a bit of a surprise.'

'I'm sure it is.'

Mr Tranmere smiled; his moustache tilted unevenly as if it were held in place by a ball of wax. 'Not what you expected first thing Monday morning?'

'No.' He sensed that Mr Tranmere was about to place his elbows flat on the folder.

'Well, firstly let me allay any worries you may have about your future with us.' He placed his elbows flat on the folder until his head was just above the desktop. 'Your talents are essential if this new venture is to succeed, so have no doubts about your continued employment.'

'Thanks.' This was reassuring in view of his late arrival.

'There will of course be some contractual changes, but we can get down to that later.' Mr Tranmere raised himself from the desktop. 'What you see here is the launch of a cherished ambition. It is something I have planned over many years and something that I now dare to hope may lead to a new beginning.'

'Oh good.'

'For too long the wishes of ordinary people have been distorted and manipulated into base desires by ruthless entrepreneurs who profit by encouraging a climate of suspicion and selfishness. I have met them in boardrooms and at leisure and know how they work. We live in a beautiful world Pimple, but they present it to us in malevolent packages, wrapped up to corrupt every age and circumstance.'

The divers watch hovered threateningly above the desktop.

'They are gross individuals who rob the young of innocence; the elderly of security, and everyone else of trust, yet they have the effrontery to wrap themselves in virtue!'

The watch descended hard onto the desktop.

'Seems wrong,' said Pimple.

'It is wrong and has to be challenged.' Mr Tranmere rose slightly from the desk. 'But how do we provide enlightenment in an age when slogans trim reason from prose, and egoism is encouraged to triumph over altruism?' He looked expectantly at Pimple.

'That's a difficult one.'

'Extremely difficult, but the answer may soon be provided in this very building.'

'That'll be good.'

Mr Tranmere leaned forward over his desk. 'That is why this project must succeed, and you will play a vital part in achieving it.' He eyed Pimple intently. 'But I must impress on you the need for absolute secrecy. Can I have your assurance that nothing I might say will go beyond these walls?'

'You can count on me Mr Tranmere.' He hoped that a forthright expression of loyalty might lead to something more specific.

Mr Tranmere subsided in his chair.

'I know I can count on you. You have already proved trustworthy in that respect and I must apologise for keeping you and Benson in the dark for so long. The depleted holdings of Plastikoates and Vistavacs must have been a constant worry, but to have divulged the project in advance could have placed both of you in the position of accomplices should it have come to the attention of any hostile members of the Board. Beside which, I had an excellent confidant in Dave Moss who was able to regularly update me on the supply situation.'

'Tillingham's nearly run out.'

Mr Tranmere spoke reassuringly. 'The critical items have already been despatched direct from Crantree, and Swiftrack will deliver the remainder of the order over the next few days.'

'It's a big pile.'

Mr Tranmere smiled wryly. 'Historically modest for Rilltot I can assure you. Wentham was chosen for the consignment because it was unlikely to be visited by our directors. There is no golfing nearby, and nothing to attract the shooting fraternity. Isby stockholdings were kept to a minimum to facilitate a speedy move. A cluttered yard and full warehouse would have delayed rapid conversion of the premises.

'Does Mr Benson know?'

'I called Benson before leaving Crantree. It was a hurried departure, but I had a loyal team standing by and the move had been planned in meticulous detail beforehand.' A far off look came into Mr Tranmere's eyes.

'As a young officer I was once required to lead a night supply convoy through enemy territory, and was strongly reminded of that occasion as each transporter slipped its handbrake and rolled silently into the darkness down Spring Hill. Such moments are to be treasured. The thrill of sailing close to the wind knowing that any second all could be lost, then the elation of success against the odds. All of us should have just one such experience in a lifetime.' He shook his head regretfully. 'Sadly my wife fails to appreciate my sense of adventure. She took a dim view of my rush from the fireside chair to make the necessary arrangements.' He smiled. 'Your appearance on the 'Lenny-Le-Strange Show' took me completely by surprise, so I had to act immediately.'

Pimple squirmed with embarrassment. What had that to do with the changes to the depot?

'Much remains to be done of course,' continued Mr Tranmere, 'but the equipment will be installed within a few days, and Benson assures me that Chimney Studios will be in business early next week.'

'Chimney Studios'? will we be recording then?'

'Of course.'

'But we didn't play.'

'Quite, and for that reason it was a magnificent performance. A spirited rejection of the tawdry offerings currently ladled out as popular entertainment. I am confident that the first New Magnolians album will sell in millions.'

He opened a magazine with a garish cover, and passing it across the desk indicated an article ringed round with a blue marker. Headed 'Trendz' and written by Mick it said:

'And what about the Lenny-Le-Strange 'botch-up'? Did 'Yours Truly' take a bashing? Zowee! Pow! Zap! Smash! - right between the eye wrinkles. And I'm not kidding either folks ... you know? Straight up Lenny you were superfluous (Careful 'Mick' that comprehensive education is showing) to requirements. It didn't need a vicar to administer the last rites after that postmistress shoved you into the nether-regions did it? Believe

me Lenny you were six feet under and that was before the lanky guy put the lid on it, or should I say the lens cap on it. Well I mean - you know? Blacking out Lenny - seriously folks it isn't done is it 'old' chap.

So what's cool? 'Whatever' garrotted their keyboard player at Wembley last month so maybe it's back to trumpets and blowy things, - different maybe? The web doesn't give much on the 'Blue Gums' guy except he was some ancient cat who didn't give a monkey's for anyone... interested? - So, 'Hey Grandpa it's Déjà Vu!'

He was baffled by much of the text, but it was a relief to know that Philip's hat must blacked out the TV camera which would have captured the moment of violence.

'Very encouraging don't you think?'

'Well, yes.' He couldn't understand why though.

'But we are at a fragile stage, and must act quickly. Fortunately our directors know little or nothing about the affairs of the company, so I have taken it upon myself to assume a role that they have long neglected. In short it is my intention to present the Board with a 'fait accompli' which is why speed and secrecy is essential at this stage. Moss is currently making arrangements for your appearance in the USA.

'America?'

'Immediately after the release of your first album.'

There were so many questions. How could Mr Tranmere know the band was worth recording if he hadn't even heard them?

He asked the last question first.

'Do you reckon we're good enough?'

'Of course, you need have no doubts about that.' Mr Tranmere lowered his voice. 'But by now you must have gathered that the New Magnolians are more than just a band.'

'Philip reckons that Blue Gums and Dorji Dhumdu worked it out years ago.'

Mr Tranmere formed his hands into an arch and spoke cautiously. 'We mustn't assume too much. They may not have been infallible, so we have to be prepared for that, but I have good reason to believe that you may discover a treasure infinitely more valuable than anything yet extracted from the ground.' He tugged at his moustache as if even he doubted its authenticity. 'I can't be precise at the moment. This is a risky undertaking and you will of course understand that I must retain the trust of others who are also dedicated to its success.'

He rose from the desk and gave Pimple a bulky envelope.

'This contains draft contracts for the New Magnolians. Please deliver them personally and convey my desire for speed and confidentiality. The terms and conditions will be acceptable, and I have provisionally booked the functions room at the Puritan Arms so that we can discuss details over dinner on Thursday evening.'

They went through to the first set of swing doors where Mr Tranmere extended his hand.

'Thank you for another enlightening meeting Pimple.'

'That's alright'

'And remember; confidentiality is of the utmost importance.'

Outside in the yard it was quite dark, and a car sped past the entrance gates with dipped lights. Strange, there were even stars twinkling overhead. Surely he hadn't been in there all day? He checked his watch. It was just ten thirty. He looked back at the building. It had taken on a purple hue as if it were part of a skilfully fabricated stage set. Then he noticed a brilliant yellow crescent high above the church.

No doubt about it, Mr Benson was correct. Tranmere had grown a moustache; he had gone 'Bananas' - and here was the eclipse.

16.Till We Meet Again.

A burst of spring sunshine cut through the sitting room window as 'Chinklets' erupted from the speakers of Beth's new music system.

He never tired of listening to the band's first album, and returning to the carpet zipped up his case and prepared for another bout of self admiration. Titled 'Back to Earth', the gritty monochrome sleeve pictured the band standing solemnly in Mr King's field one grey February afternoon. The sleeve notes were wholly a tribute to Blue Gums Foster, and only after a great deal of persuasion did Philip agree to list the musicians. Arguing against any commercial promotion of 'Back to Earth', he also ruled out contact with disc jockeys, and refused to have anything to do with the formation of a New Magnolians fan club because it would encourage vanity and focus attention on them and not the music.

With so little publicity 'Back to Earth' sold very few copies, but Mr Tranmere seemed strangely unperturbed. After ensuring that the recording was satisfactory in every respect he had instructed Jack Benson to keep the studios producing at maximum capacity before returning to Crantree. Within a few weeks the premises were stacked high with copies of 'Back to Earth' and additional storage had to be arranged at Agriframe. Then suddenly they were struggling to produce and distribute enough.

The demand came from an unlikely source.

Just before the parliamentary recess a senior cabinet minister resigned unexpectedly. His resignation shocked the government and the media soon busied themselves trying to find out why.

The minister insisted that Dead Loss Blues had such a profound effect on him that he could no longer bear the duplicity of political life. Disbelief and ridicule followed his explanation, but efforts to unearth additional and more entertaining reasons came to nothing. It was unclear if the minister had heard the original recording of Dead Loss Blues or the New Magnolians version, but nation-wide intrigue had sent sales into the millions and many more had claimed that Dead Loss had also changed their lives for the better.

Pimple moved his luggage to the hallway and gazed approvingly at his reflection in the mirror. Strings of blue notes from golden trumpets patterned his shirt, and his choice of blue jeans and trainers followed some earlier posing before the bedroom dressing table.

Above him, the irregular bumps and thuds which had been criss-crossing the ceiling now moved over to the landing and soon Beth arrived at the bottom of the stairs. She smoothed the front of a beige suit. 'That's the best I can do with myself these days, so it will just have to be good enough for America.' She sighed. 'Now, have we remembered everything?'

They went through a checklist of essentials; left a note for the milkman, then locked the door and waited outside for the taxi.

He looked back at the house and tried to quell a nagging despondency that had been with him since waking. He had been happy in Isby, much happier than at any time in Bleak Leigh, yet he couldn't shake off the feeling that he might not be making the return journey.

They arrived at the station for a brief departure ceremony arranged for them by the mayor and town council. A small crowd had already assembled on the car park, and he was quickly besieged by some boisterous teenagers. A girl thrust a pen and her copy of 'Back to Earth' towards him. 'Your four bar stop chorus in 'Baton Rouge Shake' really grabs me!' she declared. 'It's wicked!'

He thanked her with the casual modesty he had cultivated during similar encounters and signed the other CD's presented to him.

'I suppose I'll have to get used to more of this in America,' he mused, and pleased that none of the others had received quite so much attention, walked over to join them with the mayor and councillors.

The mayor winked knowingly at him. 'You were doing well for yourself there wack - more than your fair share I'd say.' He turned to the Reverend Flint. 'Agreed Michael?'

'Too much, too soon I fear.' The Reverend Flint allowed his glower to rest on Pimple. 'And does your absence from my church stem from sincere doubts about the Christian message or general apathy towards all things spiritual?'

'I don't know.'

The Reverend was unimpressed.

'Perhaps Saturday evenings in the Puritan Arms dampens your enthusiasm for Sunday mornings?' He extended his glower to the others but continued along less severe lines. 'Indeed, I expect to see all of you at St Luke's on your return. I'm sure I don't need to remind you that the music of New Orleans owes as much to it's gospel traditions, as to the downright profane. A concert of hymnals by the New Magnolians would be a welcome boost to the roofing fund.'

Philip and Chance agreed with enthusiasm.

'Excellent, then we will arrange a suitable date on your return.'

Filtering his gaze through two lowered eyebrows the Reverend again turned to Pimple. 'And remember young man: 'If the trumpet gives an uncertain sound, who then shall prepare himself for the battle?'… Corinthians chapter fourteen, verse eight.' His gaze scoured the blue notes and golden trumpets then slowly rose to eye level. 'I suggest you read it and inwardly digest.'

'Right lads!' The mayor called for order and rapped a pewter tankard sharply on the table which had been placed before the station entrance steps. 'This lot have a train to catch, so be sharp about it!'

The councillors and dignitaries assembled behind the table and the mayor began his speech.

'Now you all know I'm a man of few words, so I won't rabbit on about this and that, except to say that I'm pleased you've turned up to see these troopers off to the States. We're going to miss them at the Puritan Arms. They've helped the pints slip down a deal easier on Saturday nights and in a 'Priddles' house that's real achievement. And that leads me to this.' He brandished the tankard. 'Half pint tankards are a bit of a rarity in these parts I'd say, but the Yanks were never happy with pint pots - couldn't cope with them you know. This one belonged to one of my dad's old wartime buddies and it's been littering our mantle-piece for years.' The mayor spoke directly to Chance. 'Now you might not know it yet gaffer, but you'll be going north soon after you arrive, and when you get there search out Mayor Garbor and give him this. It's his grandad's old drinking mug and he knows its coming.'

Chance shared a puzzled glance with Philip before stepping up to receive the tankard and thanking the mayor and councillors.

'Mr Mayor, on behalf of the New Magnolians let me thank you and everyone here for this unexpected send off. I know I speak for all of us in expressing our appreciation of the support and encouragement you have shown to us in these early days.'

Chance passed the tankard down to Lutz.

'Good Ho,' concluded the mayor. 'Have a grand time lads and don't do anything I wouldn't…Right Jim?' He nudged the councillor at his side and winked at the crowd.

After more autograph signing they collected their cases and started up the steps to the platform, but some laboured wheezing behind caused Pimple to hesitate and look back. An elderly lady was waving an autograph book towards him, and he went down to her. She shakily opened the book.

'Don't let me hold you up Ducks but I'm not as young as I used to be.'

The book was crammed with autographs, and he had to flick through several pages to find a space big enough for his signature.

'There are plenty of trumpet players in there,' she added, 'but you're the best so far.'

None of the autographs meant anything to him.

'The trouble is,' she grumbled 'they've done it all before.'

He squeezed his signature below a confident scrawl dated February 2012 and waited for her to say who had done it all before.

'Blue Gums and Dorji I mean.' She gripped him by the arm as he returned the book. 'They keep trying you see, so don't be too upset if it doesn't work out. Playing the trumpet isn't everything. Remember Ducks, you've got plenty of life ahead of you.' She looked searchingly at him then released his arm. 'But I mustn't hold you up.'

Disconcerted by what she said, he hurried to join the others. How could she have known about Dorji and Blue Gums? And if those autographs really did come from trumpet players what had happened to them?

Jack Benson and his wife were chatting to Beth as he arrived on the platform.

'Blimey it's 'Hooter Lips'!' Jack Benson shielded his eyes against the shirt. 'Someone call the fire brigade, the lad's burst into trumpets!'

'Take no notice of him,' said his wife. 'It's just jealousy. He never had the shape for clothes like that. The last time he dressed up was during a chemical scare at Agriframe.' She smiled in recollection. 'Plastic overalls and a gas mask… did a deal for his appearance I remember.'

An announcement was made and the train to London appeared as a darkening spot in the distance.

'Well this is it lad,' said Jack Benson. 'The Express to fame and fortune, so keep your trumpet well oiled, we depend on it. Oh yes, and stay away from chimneys.'

The train slid into the station and discharged just one passenger onto the far end of the platform.

'And mind those Americans,' added Jack Bensons wife. 'They're not like us you know.'

There was plenty of room in the carriage and they were able to sit together. He squeezed his luggage into the stowage space between the seats and sat next to Beth by the window. The train moved off and drew level with the passenger who had just disembarked. He was about the same age but overweight, and glanced about uncertainly as he walked splayfooted to the exit.

'Could be his first time in Isby,' thought Pimple. 'Probably feels a bit like me when I arrived.'

The rows of greenhouses mirrored light back into the carriage, and by now the flat fenland had transformed itself into a patchwork of colour. Acres of tulips and bright green shoots sprang from the black soil, and all was vigorous and new. Even the traffic sparkled as it sped along the Tillingham road and the whole scene was floodlit against a purple backdrop of recent rainstorms.

He sighed.

So, just when Isby had shaken off the drabness of winter they were leaving it for America. It was like spurning a plain girl who had striven to look her very best in the face of exotic competition from afar.

He almost envied the chubby passenger who would now be plodding along Straight Street and wondered why he had come to Isby - but wait a minute! Wasn't he carrying a small black case? Yes, he was carrying a small black case. It was too small for a trombone but about right for a clarinet - or even a trumpet. He thought back to the autograph book presented to him by the old lady. Plenty of trumpet players had signed in that over the years, so could there just be a chance that he was about to be replaced by that chubby bloke? It was a worrying possibility and he considered it until they were only a few stations away from London. At last he concluded that there was nothing to worry about. After all, the old lady did say he was the best, and his performance on 'Back to Earth' was clear proof of it anyway. Feeling easier, he leaned back against the head rest and smugly recalled his contributions to each track. Let's face it: even if that chubby bloke was a trumpet player he would have to be pretty good to beat the competition wouldn't he?'

They arrived at the airport by late afternoon and queued at the airline desk. He had never seen so many nationalities in one place before, and from their appearance and choice of airline it was quite easy to guess where they were going. Some were harder to pick out though, like the fierce looking individual with the black eye-patch and bandoleer who was standing to one side of their queue.

Chance was the last to check in, and as he walked towards them Beth whispered urgently. 'Look Ducks, that nasty man is going after Chance!' She gripped his arm, and following her gaze he saw with alarm that the man with the eye-patch had pulled something from his bandoleer and was pointing it at Chance.

'Chance Basset?'

'Yes?' Chance froze.

'I'm Captain Kidd and I'm here to get some answers from you!'

He waved a microphone at Chance.

'Really!' Chance stared at the microphone and recovered sufficiently to be annoyed. 'Is that approach necessary for outside interviews?'

'Not for performers who care about their fans.' Captain Kidd closed in. 'So don't expect the sober suited and deferential treatment from me.'

'I'm not getting it, that's plain enough. Anyway why should I talk to you?'

'No particular reason, but your fans might like to know why you are giving them the brush-off?'

'Are we?'

'Come off it, you know you are. They're crazy about you. So what's the angle? Are you working hard at being inscrutable, or is it just natural disdain?'

'It's neither, apart from the fact that it's our business and we have a plane to catch.'

Chance started to move away.

'Don't give me that Mr Hoity Toity. You've made it everybody's business.'

'What do you mean?'

'I mean getting that Cabinet Minister to throw a wobbly. How's that for a start?'

'We had nothing to do with that?'

'Nice timing though wasn't it?'

'You certainly know how to be offensive.'

'You make it a pleasure. So, why are you giving your fans the brush off?'

'We're not giving anyone the 'brush off' as you put it.'

'No? With 'Back to Earth' grabbing the whole nation and you lot sneaking off to the States to cash in on the publicity. I'd call that giving your fans the brush off, or have you got a fancier way of putting it?'

'That may be your way of putting it Mr Kidd. But our fans enjoy the music we play because it is strictly non-commercial and we have no desire to trivialise it by pandering to the worst excesses of the popular music industry.'

'Well well, aren't we virtuous? Is that why you pulled the plug on the 'Lenny-Le-Strange Show'?

'That's outrageous. We were set up.'

'You were set up?' Emphasising the 'You', Captain Kidd spoke slowly - speeding up as his incredulity mounted. 'You dress up as yokels knowing that a few million viewers are watching. Then you throw a tantrum and black out the show.'

Chance reddened. 'That's a gross misrepresentation of events.'

'Is it? Captain Kidd brought his eye forward.

'You do funny things to a cabinet minister: hi-jack a top rated show: create enough intrigue to alert MI5 then swamp us all with 'Back to Earth'. What makes you think I'm that stupid?'

'Well you look stupid, and I don't care if you believe it or not. We are simply trying to play the music of Blue Gums Foster as honestly as we can.'

'And making a packet out of it as well,' cut in Captain Kidd. 'Banging a bongo or blowing a bugle isn't good enough for you buzz heads these days is it? If you're not prancing naked in a video clip or screaming expletives at nuns it's got to be some ancient soothsayer - or in your case - an ancient trumpet player. Anything will do just as long as it's too obscure for the rest of us to understand. That's the truth isn't it?

Chance shook with indignation.

'This is outrageous! We didn't hi-jack the Lenny-Le-Strange Show. We didn't do 'funny things' to that cabinet minister and we would never exploit the music of 'Blue Gums Foster'!'

'So, you've sold our kids mega-pounds of integrity have you?' The microphone trembled in Captain Kidd's hand. 'And now it's 'Hullo America!' This business makes me cynical but you really are the pits, and I'm up to here with it!'

He levelled the microphone under his chin to show how far up he was with it.

'Is that so?'

Chance lowered his voice and dared to push his chin slightly forward.

'Then tell me. How cynical is it for our integrity to be questioned by someone pretending to be a Pirate?'

Captain Kidd ripped off his eye-patch and Chance stepped smartly sideways in case this was a prelude to violence.

'This!' announced Captain Kidd 'was given to me by the drummer of 'Sludge' because he doesn't like suits - OK? Pirates are uncontroversial right now - OK? So I'm staying this way until the situation changes - OK?'

Everyone closed in to peer at what was, by any standards, a monster black eye. By way of a shared glance Lutz and Philip acknowledged that the force applied in this instance had been considerably greater than in their previous roles of giver and receiver.

'Anyway, what about the rest of you?' Captain Kidd clenched the microphone between his teeth and replaced the eye patch. 'Do all of you get a kick from giving your fans the brush off as well?'

'Don't answer him.' Chance raised his hand dismissively and walked away, 'He's just trying to stir up trouble.'

It may have been the abrupt way Chance terminated the interview that sparked a flicker of rebellion in Pimple. After all why shouldn't he say something? He didn't quite know what he was going to say, but the urge was there. A few words floated into his head and sorted themselves into order as he stepped forward. Aware of the eyes upon him he said: 'I don't know about the fans Mr Kidd, but Blue Gums was great, and I reckon if more people played trumpets there wouldn't be half so much trouble about.'

Captain Kidd considered this for a moment then placing a hand on Pimple's shoulder said: 'Does that go for flutes as well?'

'Yes.'

'And Harps?'

'Harps are alright.'

Captain Kidd closed his eye in thought…'It's coming to me…I think I've got it… Yes, I've got it now… In fact I like it.' He replaced the microphone in his bandoleer. 'Pimple has just spoken hasn't he?'

'That's right,' agreed Pimple

They boarded the aircraft and Beth asked him to take the window seat so she could straighten her leg in the aisle. Starry pinpricks of light shone through a decorative panel which ran the full length of the cabin, and settling down music warbled from consoles above the passenger seats. No doubt about it, for the first time in his life he was inside an aeroplane, and this one was about to take him to America.

Pressing his face to the window he watched preparations for the flight. An engineer in white overalls shone a torch into the jet-pipe of the inboard engine and coming towards them against the lights of the terminal buildings was a small tug towing a train of baggage trolleys. Close by, but not visible from where he sat, a ground power unit started and jets of cool air squirted down from nozzles mounted in the consoles. Within a few minutes the loading operation had been completed, and the cabin shook slightly as the freight hold door was secured.

'It won't be long now,' he thought.

In the centre row, Philip and Chance were concentrating on some foolscap sheets, and working her way down the aisle with a tray of boiled sweets a cabin attendant reached over to him and said: 'First time flying Honey?'

He nodded and she smiled. 'They won't stop yo' knees from knockin' but they might stop yo' ears from poppin'!'

A puff of smoke emerged from the outboard engine, and soon they were moving backwards in a slow circle onto the taxiway. A tow tug raced past the wingtip and they surged forward past lines of floodlit airliners. The music faded and two of the attendants choreographed emergency procedures at the head of each aisle. He read the safety instructions and reached under the seat to feel for his life jacket, but Philip and Chance continued to work on the sheets right through the demonstration, seemingly unconcerned about being blasted thousands of miles across the Atlantic.

They turned onto the slipway to the main runway, and he could see other planes queuing behind. Ahead, a Jumbo Jet rumbled down the runway until it became indistinguishable from the lights of West London - later to emerge as a ponderous silhouette in the night sky.

Swinging onto the runway threshold they hesitated for a moment, then the engines crackled and he was pressed firmly into his seat. Giving the safety belt an extra tug, he sucked hard on the boiled sweet and watched the runway markers merge into a luminous strip. Beyond them, moving more slowly, but fast enough all the same, were the terminal buildings, and in the nick of time, or so it seemed, the tyres stopped rumbling and the runway dropped away. Various mechanical whirrings beneath the cabin floor were followed by the solid double clunk of the retracting undercarriage, and at once the ride became smoother. Now, on easier terms with the elements, the plane commenced a steep climbing turn and below them, flat and glowing, night time London stretched to the horizon. Sliding the papers into a large envelope, Chance glanced around as if confirming that they were in the air, then moved his seat back and closed his eyes.

Beth spoke.

'I wonder what comes next Ducks.'

'We'll soon find out.'

'I don't want too many surprises.'

'I reckon we'll get a few.'

But he really wanted to concentrate on the moment, and turned again to the window.

The thick clouds were now below them, and the cosmos glittered grainily beyond the wingtip navigation light. This was the first time he had seen it with such clarity and just one wispy cloud sped past to emphasise its stability.

'I reckon there's some answers out there,' he thought.

But it had been a long day, and he was well into sleep before the first wave of sadness washed over him.

17.<u>Way Down Yonder In New Orleans.</u>

The 'Pontomatic' nosed along Airline Drive towards a temporary flyover, and tilting upwards, the bonnet headed towards a sky full of lively cloud formations before dropping down again to a boring succession of gas stations, motels, and overhead power lines.

So far New Orleans was nothing like he had expected, and if it was to live up to the rapturous description given by Chance then it would have to change pretty quickly. Still, he should have known better than to arrive in America full of preconceived ideas, and he certainly should have known better than to drink all those 'Best Buddy' beers because of the diversion and technical delay at Atlanta Airport. Related to this, he hadn't expected to arrive at New Orleans Airport hoping there would be no fans to jostle him. As it happened there were no fans to jostle him, but Dave Moss was there with the 'Pontomatic' and plainly at ease in his new role of liaison manager.

Following a salvo of questions from Chance and Philip, Dave turned his attention to Pimple. 'Long time no see.'

'It's a bit different from Receipt and Despatch.'

Dave smiled faintly. 'It's a small world.'

'Tranmere didn't stay long at Isby. I suppose he's organising things from Crantree is he?'

'Aye.'

I bet he's given you plenty to do?'

'Aye,' Dave gazed steadfastly at the road ahead, 'but it's all in a days work.'

'I suppose there will be a few changes at Crantree now?'

'A change is as good as a rest.'

'How's darts going?'

Here Dave was more forthcoming. The Machine Shop Supervisor had led Rilltots to victory in the Industrial League and Red Ears had won a place on the 'Belchards Trophy' team.

But it was becoming difficult to talk without shouting because the conversation in the seat behind was growing louder by the second. Seated between Philip and Chance was Dr Isiah Ross who had once played banjo with 'Chalmette's Sycophants'. As Chairman of the New Orleans Heritage Foundation he had welcomed them at the airport and hadn't stopped talking ever since. By now he could be heard well above the road noise and hiss of the air-conditioner.

He was a wizened little man with a falsetto voice, who appeared to have been shrunken by time and sunshine until he was several sizes too small for his suit. His jacket lapels were enormous, and a black bowler sat so low on his head that only a square of his face could be seen. Yet he held strong views about the niceties of dress, and it was this that had brought him to the boil.

'An' don't no man talk to me about Paris. Paris's far as I'm concerned ain't nothin!' Twenty-five ten dollar shirts, that's Paris to me. Yip, twenty five ten dollar shirts an' an' empty sinkin' feelin', but Paris.' He shook loosely inside his suit. 'Paris ain't worth a dime.'

The recollection of shirts stolen in a Paris hotel had been sparked off by Chance who had asked Dr Isaiah if he, like many New Orleans residents, had family connections in France. Now eager to steer his thoughts away from the episode, Chance asked if he had been to Britain.

'Yip indeedy,' enthused Dr Isaiah. ''Strand Palace Non-Iron'…best shirts I ever had.' He extended his neck for Chance to check the brand label. The shirt stayed roughly where it was, and a quick glance was enough to confirm that it was indeed a 'Strand Palace Non-Iron.' 'Best shirts I ever had.' repeated Dr Isiah.

Philip tried to guide him away from shirts.

'We understand that Blue Gums Foster occasionally played with 'Chalmette's Sycophants' Doctor. Is there anything you can tell us about those times?'

Dr Isaiah tortoised his visible features into disdainful wrinkles. 'Man, that cat was no dresser. Put his clothes on with a bailin' fork. I never knew a man who didn't know how to dress more than him. Wore sneakers everywhere; sneakers in Antoine's, sneakers in Crazy Sarah's. I never knew that cat without he was wearin' sneakers. You'd think he was intendin' runnin' everywhere, 'cept he couldn't run. Yip, he even died in sneakers. Naw'lins was dressy then. Even the Americans took to the habit o' wearin' polite dress, an' the children walkin' two's and three's to chapel Sundays, lace an' all. Naw'lins was real dressy then. Yip, it sure was.'

His skin smoothed out like stretched Crimpolene, and yipping back to the well groomed New Orleans of his youth, Dr Isaiah closed his eyes and retracted fully into his suit. The transition was sudden, and with questions still unanswered, Philip and Chance stared blankly at the bowler.

At last Philip said: 'I think we should pay our respects to Blue Gums as soon as possible. He never had a decent burial, and Mirabelle did say how much she would like to give him a traditional New Orleans funeral.'

He spoke to Dave Moss.

'Do you know if Mirabelle has made any arrangements for putting her father to rest Mr Moss?'

'Aye, on parade at ten sharp tomorrow with instruments at the ready.'

'Excellent.'

Gradually the scene beyond the windscreen became more like the New Orleans that Chance had described, and soon they were on a wide street gleaming with hotels, movie theatres, and department stores.

'Canal Street', chirped Dr Isiah emerging from his snooze. 'Never did build the canal.'

They continued into narrower streets lined with older buildings fronted by elaborate wrought iron balconies, then slowed down and turned sharply into an alleyway. Facing them was an entrance gate leading into a garden courtyard canopied by the branches of a huge magnolia. There was just enough room for the car, and Dave held the doors open against some flowering shrubs for everyone to get out.

Beyond the intervening foliage a shaky voice gasped 'A... one! A... two! A... three!' then came some tentative pats on a drum, and a brassy burst from something that sent a cloud of coloured birds streaking towards alternative roosting spots. Unsure whether this might be a prelude to the American National Anthem they stood respectfully for a few moments until the knotted threads of sound unravelled into the familiar theme of 'Stomp On'.

'Stomp On' ended as uncertainly as it began, and led by Dr Isiah they picked their way through the greenery towards a patio where a few elderly musicians were seated.

Philip gazed in awe.

'Goodness!' he whispered. 'It's Slidebone Walker and Reed Williams.'

Slidebone refreshed himself from a bottle of bourbon as Philip loped reverentially over to him, and grinning from ear to ear wiped a shirtsleeve over the neck of the bottle and held it out.

'Care for a short snort Squire?'

Philip hesitated uncertainly.

'Simply whopping just lazing here under the old magnolia don't you think?'

Slidebone rocked to and fro' in his wheelchair opening his mouth wide enough to show his tonsils. At first nothing could be heard, but soon a low wheezing cackle blended with the rustling leaves and rumble of an overhead jet. Slidebone refreshed himself again and after another bout of wheezing and rocking said: 'I been practisin' see. Knowin' all these weeks you was comin' I been practisin' an' practisin'. Then Mirabelle, she told me. These English cats, they don't want no long speeches. Not after travellin' from London to Na'wlins they don't. But after all that practisin' man, I had to say sumpthin!'

Philip entered into the spirit of the moment.

'Slidebone with a brogue like that you would be welcome at any exclusive London club.'

'How about that?' Slidebone spoke wistfully. 'I alus wanted to play dominoes.'

At this point a shadowy figure emerged from the main building and without a trace of unnecessary movement descended the short flight of steps to the patio. Without doubt she was the most beautiful woman Pimple had ever seen. Dressed in a black gown, her hair glistened black and the texture of her skin made it hard to discern where the gown ended and she began. Two plain gold earrings provided just enough colour to emphasise the monochrome nature of her beauty.

Placing a hand lightly on the back of Slidebone's wheelchair she gently eased the bottle from his grasp and offered it to Reed Williams who moved faster than his age should have allowed.

'You've done well today Slidebone,' she smiled. 'Only half a bottle since breakfast and there should still be enough for a nightcap.'

Slidebone turned two watery eyes up to her. 'Ma'am If I'd had a good woman like you alus by me I'd never needed none anyhow.'

She stooped to kiss him lightly on the forehead and turned her attention to Philip.

'Philip, it's so good to see you again, and we've so much to talk about, but now I guess you'd appreciate a rest more than anything else - right?' She gripped Reed Williams by the wrist and levered the bottle from his fingers.

'Well,' Philip seemed doubtful. 'I understand we will be paying our respects to your father tomorrow. Perhaps we should complete the arrangements for that first.'

She smiled knowingly. 'You old martyr. Gee Philip, you haven't changed one bit - you've still got that masochistic streak.' She took him by the arm. 'Now, introduce me to everyone, then we can go inside for coffee and cookies and Isiah will show you to your rooms.'

Pimple couldn't take his eyes from her. She possessed that star quality he had attributed in varying degrees to others, and more recently to himself, but she had it in bucket loads.

Repeating each name as she was introduced, Mirabelle gave everyone her undivided attention; somehow conveying a personal interest that went far beyond casual conversation. Even Lutz remained wistful long after she had spoken to him.

'And this is Pimple.'

He warmed up as if he was under two sun lamps.

'Pimple, yes, Pimple.'

Taking both hands she repeated his name and leaned back as if to see him better. It could have been Auntie Joan checking his annual growth rate, except Mirabelle's touch affected him like an infusion of Pointers Special.

'Now, we've met before.' It was a statement and the implication of it barely filtered through in time for him to answer.

'We might have.' He couldn't have met Mirabelle before, but didn't want to disagree.

'You don't seem very sure.'

'It's my first time in America.'

'Strange?' A breeze of doubt ruffled the texture of her forehead. 'Are you well travelled?'

'I get about a bit.' He instantly regretted the casual swankyness of his reply.

Philip tried to solve the puzzle.

'Perhaps you recognised him from the photograph on the sleeve of our CD?'

'It wasn't a photograph.' She released his hands but continued to study him. 'I just know I've seen you someplace.' She tilted her head. 'Think about it, we'll come up with the answer sometime.'

They turned to walk back to the patio, but she hesitated.

'Philip you haven't done your duty, we've missed someone.'

'I don't think so.' He cast his eyes about.

'I know we've missed someone.' She used her fingers to count off the names: 'First it was Chance, then Beth, then Lutz from Bad Omen, then Pimple who I've met before. With you that makes five, and there should be six, right?'

'Oh there's Dan of course.' He spoke offhandedly. 'He's over there.'

'Then lead me to him,' she demanded.

Set against the bushes Dan might have been the gardener, but as Mirabelle approached he took on the air of a lonely traveller, who, having just emerged from a forest wasn't quite sure how to react to his first human contact in months.

'Dan,' she mixed concern with welcome. 'You were almost forgotten, but it sure won't happen again while you are here.' She threw a reproving glance at Philip. 'And I guess you're going to tell me that you haven't been here either?'

Grinning awkwardly he said that it was his first time in America as well.

She turned again to Pimple, then back to him. 'Strange, yet I feel I know both of you so well.'

The question hung in mid-air while she took time to diagnose in Dan something she had previously missed.

'Dan?' Her voice had a therapeutic quality. 'You need to know you are really welcome. It's great to have you here.' Then she came in close to squeeze his arm. 'I mean that Dan, I really do.'

He swallowed as he watched her return to the patio with the others, then everything went blurry, and alone again, but now acknowledged, he searched for a tissue.

18. Oh! Didn't He Ramble?

The sky threw down a flat colourless light and their clothes hung limply in the humid air as Philip knelt to lay a wreath at the base of the tomb. The sentiment, composed by Dave Moss in anticipation of the event read: 'Better late than never'.

Raised on a substantial marble plinth, the tomb was fashioned in the style of a classical Greek temple complete with fluted columns. It was an imposing structure and confirmed that in death at least, Blue Gums had at last received just acclaim.

Mirabelle added her own small posy of fresh flowers and spoke quietly to Philip.

'I figured he'd appreciate a roof over his head. He was never too sure of getting one in the past.'

'Is that why you moved him from his first place of rest?'

'Yes but...' She hesitated as if uncertain whether this was the right moment to reveal her thoughts. '...Well.' She made up her mind. 'You may not know this Philip, but only recently I discovered who my true mother was and I wanted him to be with her.'

'So you know who she was.' He spoke with caution. 'Are you pleased now that you do know?'

She smiled uncertainly. 'Maybe, maybe not. The last time you came we thought it might have been one of three women - right?'

He nodded.

'I've never mentioned it to anyone before but I've always known there was one more possibility.'

'A fourth woman?'

'Yes, a fourth woman. I suppose I didn't want to admit it to myself, but I did some checking and straight away knew she was my mother. I just knew it. I couldn't be the way I am if it was someone else.' She hesitated again. 'I guess I'm a bit reluctant to tell you this, but it was Maria Hoodoo.'

'You mean Hoodoo the Voodoo?' Philip hushed his voice to an intrigued whisper.'

'Yes, the flowers are for her, and if you look closely you can see small crosses scratched on the tomb by folks who believe she still has magical powers.'

'Incredible, I know very little about her, but I understand she was a benign voodoo.'

'That's what they say, but she had her mean moments too. She couldn't stand fathers drinking habits and they had some awful rows, which is why they never settled down. But just as I knew she was my mom I knew she loved him.'

'Fascinating,' murmured Philip.

'I did just wonder if you'd figured all this out.'

'I had absolutely no idea, but it's significant because it could help to explain how your father knew about the existence of Dorji Dhumdu so far north in the Smoky Mountains. Maria Hoodoo would have been sure to know about the arrival of such an eminent mystic. She may have even arranged their first meeting.'

'I guess so.' A tinge of reproach entered Mirabelle's voice. 'But your letters have been sketchy these days Philip. How was I to know about this Dorji guy?'

'I'm sorry Mirabelle, I should have kept you better informed, but it was only recently that I placed so much importance on your father's association with Dorji. Their partnership seems so remarkable that I have been reluctant to say anything I couldn't confirm. That's why I hope to find some solid evidence during our stay here.'

'Do you still aim to go to the Smokies?'

'Yes.'

'When?'

'As soon as Dave Moss can confirm the arrangements.'

She furrowed her brow at the tomb. 'I'm not sure why I'm saying this; could be it's womanly intuition, but promise me one thing?' She laid a hand on his wrist and he waited for the promise he had to make. 'Don't get too upset up if it doesn't work out.'

'Don't you think we will find anything?'

'It's not that. It's just that you've cut yourself off from so much because of father, and I don't want you to get hurt.'

She moved closer to Philip. It wasn't a deliberate move because Pimple was watching and listening intently. It was just that the gap between them narrowed, or to put it another way - it wasn't quite so wide as before.

At last Philip said: 'Thank you Mirabelle.'

They gazed at the tomb for a few more moments then Mirabelle said: 'I guess it's time to lay you down properly Papa.' She signalled Dr Isiah. 'Be ready to march Isiah. Traffic will be building up downtown.'

'Yip Ma'am,' chirped Dr Isaiah, and wielding a folded umbrella he marched stiffly over to Pimple. As Acting Parade Grand Marshal he wore full mourning attire with a diagonal sash over his topcoat emblazoned 'Musicians'. Because of his past acquaintance with Blue Gums, the honorary position together with the sash and umbrella had been bestowed to him by Parade Grand Marshall Baldy Garner during a brief ceremony the evening before.

Crossing his chest with the umbrella, Dr Isiah lifted the other arm, and Pimple prepared to play 'Flee as a bird'.

'Cut him loose!' squealed Dr Isiah.

Pimple launched his notes at a leaden sky while everyone bowed their heads. A short respectful silence followed then Dr Isiah raised both arms and yelled through the lapels of his jacket.

'Oh didn't he ramble! Didn't Blue Gums ramble, Yip! He rambled all around. Yes sir he sure did ramble!'

Dan rapped the side drum, and forming into pairs, they turned into line behind Mirabelle who was ready with Slidebone in his wheelchair. Marching stiffly to the head of the small column Dr Isiah unfurled his umbrella and waved them forward. Slidebone sounded a mighty blast to lead the band into the first bars of 'Didn't he ramble' and playing furiously they marched through the cemetery gates onto the street.

'Yip Yip!' yelled Dr Isiah. 'That cat sure did ramble… Man, didn't he ramble!'

Tourists took photos from the sidewalk and they were soon joined by some local boys who whooped and skipped alongside. One of them kept level with Chance until 'Didn't He Ramble' clattered to a halt.

'Hey where you from?' asked the boy.

'From England.' replied Chance.

'You all English?'

'Some of us are'

The boy skipped back to his friends. 'They're limeys' he announced.

'Yeah so what?' chorused the others.

'So?' The boy fixed a commercial eye on the thickening crowd of onlookers then raised a leg high above his head and pirouetted round like a ballet dancer. 'So?' he replied. 'The rain in Spain falls mainly on the plain.'

'What was that?' chorused the reply.

'I said.' The boy laboured each vowel. 'That the reen in Speen falls meenly on the pleen.' 'The reen in Speen falls meenly on the pleen.' mimicked the others.

Still keeping level with the marching column they performed their own version of a familiar show sequence augmented by high kicks; hand clapping, and more than a spattering of cruel parody. The choreography was impressive, and the entire performance lasted just long enough for a cap to be passed through the tourists.

'Thanks limeys!' yelled the boy. 'Yeah thanks limeys!' repeated the others, and together with the hat, they ran back the way they had come.

Having been given time to catch his breath, Slidebone then launched into 'Stomp On' at a furious tempo. It was only just possible to march at such speed, and Beth bobbed up and down like a cork on rough water. They were making better progress than the traffic, and the crowd they had collected soon fell behind to pursue less exhausting activities. A row of gloss painted wooden houses served as a sounding board as they veered round the corner into St Peters Street and past the faded facade of the Licentious Ballroom.

'Yip Yip!' screeched Dr Isiah above the flurry of squeaks and growls saturating the air about him. 'That cat sure did stomp at the 'Licentious'!'

Slidebone was enjoying himself enormously. Unencumbered by the need to keep step, he advanced like some ancient artillery piece taking random blasts at anything or anyone that took his fancy. It didn't seem possible that elderly lips pursed against brass tubing could make so much noise. Grinning horribly he loosed off a whole tone scale at the door of Antoinett's Restaurant and a rasping glissando at a horse drawn buggy which stopped sharply enough for the occupant to slide from her seat.

It was like taking part in an old time Hollywood movie where the action had been speeded up for effect. But it was all getting out of control. Chance and Philip had long ceased to contribute anything worthwhile, and Beth had oscillated free from the column, so it came as a relief when the multi coloured birds erupted above the rooftops like a salvo of artillery rockets.

Just in time they wheeled into the entrance of the Heritage Foundation and away from further public scrutiny. Slidebone sent a last withering blast into the courtyard, and like battle weary soldiers the column broke up and headed for anything which could be slumped onto.

For a while nothing was said; the comparative silence being broken only by loud breathing and some mischievous cackling from Slidebone.

'Man was that the craziest 'Stomp On' I ever played!' he wheezed.

'An' praise be, we ain't never heard 'Stomp On' played like that before!' came a voice from above. 'You sure collected some hot cats today Bone!' The murmur of other voices filtered down to them through the magnolia canopy.

'We've disturbed their afternoon nap,' explained Mirabelle. She smiled maternally at Slidebone. 'You blew a hurricane for Papa today Bone.'

'Sure wanted to Ma'am.'

She dabbed the top of his head with her handkerchief, and spoke reflectively - almost to herself. 'Yes we really laid Papa down today.'

Thanking everyone for giving her father such a fine send off, she wheeled Slidebone to the entrance and turned briefly to announce that the reception would be in the main hall that evening. She then gave a little wave, but something other than a smile tugged at the corners of her mouth.

19. There'll be A Hot Time in Old Town Tonight.

Pimple leaned over the bedroom balcony. Behind on the bed, a lightweight suit was laid out ready for the formal reception that evening, and hanging out to dry on one of the steel cables supporting the magnolia canopy was his father's anorak. His mother had insisted he took it when he first went to Isby, but only the most extreme weather would have persuaded him to wear it. A wet afternoon stroll with Lutz persuaded him of it's unsuitability for New Orleans as well, but Mr Tranmere had told them to take waterproofs and it had been written into the contracts.

He sighed.

So Philip must have persuaded Mr Tranmere to include the Smoky Mountains in their tour even before they left Isby. That meant getting up early next morning for the trip to Gatlinburg, and another early start for the mountains after their stay with the mayor. But what was the point of all of them, especially Beth, trudging up mountains anyway? Weren't they supposed to be making themselves famous in America? If Philip thought it was such a good idea why didn't he go on his own and tell them about it afterwards. After all, Blue Gums was dead and Dorji Dhumdu wasn't likely to be up there was he? So what was Philip expecting to find apart from a few bones? No one else knew, and from his conversation with Mirabelle by the tomb he didn't seem to know either.

The outspread branches of the magnolia blocked the view down to the courtyard as effectively as they blocked the view upward from it, and sideways there was even less to see. The sun shutters hinged outwards from the French windows and boxed in the balcony, restricting forward vision to the wall of the Heritage Hall on the other side. Whoever commissioned the building must have had an obsession for privacy. Even the corridors were obstructed by half partitions making it necessary to zigzag from room to room, and the heavy drapes and carpeting let through the wrong sounds. A creaky floorboard, soft tremors from the ceiling above, and voices muffled to low conspiratorial murmurs created a climate of innuendo and sinister goings on.

He looked at his watch just as the chimes of St Louis Cathedral jangled discordantly with the wail of an outbound freighter.

The reception in the Heritage Hall was just one hour away; not long enough to go anywhere, but too long to wait with nothing special to do. He was looking forward to playing, but the formal reception wouldn't be much fun. There would be speeches, and it was quite clear who would be doing most of the speaking. Philip and Chance had been working on their notes since leaving Isby and it wasn't difficult to guess what they would say. A string of familiar utterances came to mind: 'Approach with humility.' 'Due deference.' 'Avoidance of crude commercialism.' 'We will never misrepresent.' It was all so predictable.

He looked back into the room. Then there was Dan. Given a choice he wouldn't have shared a room with Dan, but like the mountain trip, he hadn't been given a choice. Dan wasn't too bad really, but he would be a lot better if he wasn't always telling jokes and trying to draw attention to himself. Admittedly he had been quite subdued since coming to New Orleans, but that was no reason to take any chances.

The roof of the hall stood out in sharp silhouette against the afterglow of dusk, and thrown into shadow, the magnolia canopy rippled like surface water on a deep pool. It was an eerie effect, and his attention was drawn to the changing patterns as the canopy rose and fell in the low light. Soon he was totally engrossed. He had seen something like it when Godfrey Smith had his first computer, but this was bigger and more compelling. At the same time, a rising anxiety warned him against repeating the creepy experience at Pipers Lane Millpond, and with difficulty he averted his gaze. But the sensation lingered, and the low mutterings and the scraping of walking sticks drifting up from the patio did little to relieve his disquiet.

It wasn't possible to see what was happening until a door opened at the top of a shallow ramp built onto the side of the Heritage Hall. Framed clearly in the doorway was Dr Isiah, and trooping up to him were the stooped forms of the residents.

Dan joined him on the balcony and they watched in silence as the door closed on the last resident to enter the hall.

'It's a rum place lad' he said.

Pimple agreed. Dan had mirrored his thoughts exactly.

The interior of Heritage Hall was long and narrow.

Illuminated portraits and photographs of well known musicians lined the walls, and several tables had been placed end to end to make a central banqueting area. Everything needed for the public performance was ready at the head of the hall. There was no stage, but a few chairs; a piano minus the front; a drum kit, and a microphone. A large tin marked 'Donations' was bolted to the entrance table, and an even larger notice announced:

'Special Tonite!' the 'Winjy Mooney Five,' and 'The New Magnolians.' 'Requests 5 Dollars / No Pops or Classics.'

Philip, who had been talking solidly for ten minutes, at last placed his sheets of foolscap on the table and spoke directly to the President of the Heritage Foundation.

'So, we will do our utmost to achieve for your music the recognition and acclaim it so justly deserves. Be assured Mr President, we are fully aware of the honour bestowed upon us and the responsibility it entails. We will perform your music with humility, and promise not to misrepresent it as so many have done in the past.'

He sat down to a spattering of applause.

The President motioned the waiters to distribute juleps then rose in reply.

'Thanks Philip, I guess that about sums it up.' He reached for his glass: 'Ladies and Gen'lemen. On behalf of us and our departed cats let's rise in a toast of appreciation to these fine English visitors.' He raised his glass to a chorus of snapping kneecaps: 'The 'New Magnolians!'

Most of the juleps were downed in a single draught prompting the waiters to rush round with refills. Throughout the speeches Pimple had looked for any notable diners, but age had masked the faces that once featured in music magazines and on the sleeves of old records. Baby Todd of 'Guy Werchants Fast Eight' was just about recognizable as the President, and Lord John; banjo player and oldest surviving member of the original 'Magnolians' dozed beside Slidebone Walker.

There were more ladies than he had expected, and while many were advanced in years, their dress seemed over frivolous for the occasion. The plump woman seated opposite Beth could have been Sister Henrietta Hennessey, but the rate she was downing juleps would have barred her from most sisterhoods. He guessed that the person seated next to him was 'Spattered Brown' who was once house pianist at 'Crazy Sarah's' and so named because of his blotchy complexion. There were no other faces of interest so he allowed his gaze to stray to the top of table where it rested just long enough on Mirabelle to confirm that she was indeed the most beautiful woman he had ever seen.

A waiter came towards them balancing a julep provocatively on his tray, but Lord John snapped awake in time to down it and order another.

'Goddam it!' complained Spattered Brown. 'I ain't had more than one julep 'cept the one I had on comin' in!' He grimaced at Lord John until his blotches touched. 'Bum!' he declared.' I seen that string picker booze so hard his eyes filled up like bourbon optics. Booze! Booze! Booze! I ain't seen no one booze like it, and man if you have, let me know, it'd sure be sumthin' worth watchin'.'

'You play the piano don't you?'

'Stride piano.' corrected Spattered Brown. 'I play stride piano. You one of those English dudes ain't you?'

'Yes.' He answered to English - not knowing what dude meant.

'Then you ain't heard stride piano on account you ain't heard no pianists.' Spattered Brown paused to reflect. 'Ain't no pianists in England any good…been there once. No pianists and nothin' to eat 'cept cheese. Cheese rolls, cheese sandwiches, cheese on toast…just cheese.'

A tray of juleps came between them.

'You want to hear stride piano?' Spattered Brown pulled a mint leaf from his glass and chewed it open mouthed. 'Then you just came to the guy who invented it. No one plays better than me. 'Back 'O' Town Bump', 'Left Hand Strollin', 'Bayou Strut'… all composed by me.'

'You used to play at 'Crazy Sarah's' didn't you?'

'I was 'Crazy Sarah's'. 'Crazy Sarah's' weren't nothin' without me!'

He narrowed his eyes at Slidebone and Lord John.

'An' those bums proved it 'cos it went to nothin' after they got there.'

'What about 'Blue Gums?' Pimple spoke with deference. 'He played at 'Crazy Sarah's' didn't he?'

'Yeah, that bum went there too.' Spattered Brown curled his top lip over a yellowish set of dentures. 'Couldn't tell what position he was aiming for, like whether he was intendin' standing up or lying down. Never did know which way up he was goin' to play.'

Pimple jumped to the defence of Blue Gums. 'Well I reckon he was a great player.'

'You jokin'?' Spattered Brown sneered contemptuously. 'That bum had the smallest lungs in the business.'

'How do you know?' - It was becoming difficult to stick to his mother's advice about respecting the elderly.

'I know 'cos he played sort of blubbery, like he was having trouble gettin' enough air. With that belly there weren't room for much else.'

'He sounded clear enough to me.'

'He was a bum.' Spattered Brown spelt it out. 'B.U.M, bum, an' he had a bum band.' He twirled a finger inside his glass to extricate the last mint leaf. 'An' you comin' from England, how'd you know, bein' there ain't no trumpet players in England?'

'Well you're wrong there for a start.'

Spattered Brown added a leer to his sneer.

'I'm listenin''

Pimple thought quickly.

'There's Godfrey Littlejohn, and Harry Witmore and…well…I play trumpet.' He instantly regretted his last words.

Spattered Brown grinned horribly.

'Now ain't that nice for you.'

He leaned back and twirled the mint leaf over the tip of his tongue.

'Yeah, caught me while I was dozin' this mornin'. Kind'a pretty it was…reminded me of old ladies sittin' an' knittin' in gardens, an' honey and tea, an' bicycles, an' cheese. Yeah, lots o' cheese. Sort'a like you'd expect from an English dude.' His lips curled upwards stretching his blotches into tiny mocking half-moons. 'Yeah, sure was pretty. Put me in mind o' my niece practisin'… Nice high school trumpet.' Spattered Brown put a

thumb to the tip of his tongue and waggled his fingers at Pimple.
'Peepity, peepity, peep!'

A julep arrived between them, and hoping it might cool his ears, Pimple grabbed it and gulped it down. He was conscious only of a burning dislike for Spattered Brown and something less definable lying battered and curled up inside. He tried to concentrate on the inanimate objects before him. There was the tablecloth; the remains of his oyster fritters and French fries; the crinkled napkin and napkin ring made by Napkin Ring Inc of Charleston…anything but Spattered Brown. He sought refuge by gazing into the empty glass, but it didn't help much. Even the frosted ice which circled the rim of the glass began to break up into Spattered Brown shaped blotches. Spattered Brown permeated everything. Worse still, it was quite clear that the torment was far from over. He had grabbed the only julep between them and Spattered Brown wouldn't like that. He'd be thinking up something really dreadful. Another 'Nice high school trumpet.' would be bad enough and 'Peepity peepity peep!' would be unbearable, yet something much worse was bound to come.

A waft of damp elderly breath evaporated on his cheek and the click of loose dentures close to his ear told him that Spattered Brown was closing in for the kill. He closed his eyes and braced himself.

'Wha! Wha!....Geeeeee!'

He opened his eyes in surprise. That was nothing like the sound of a badly played trumpet, or a badly played anything, but he kept looking away from Spattered Brown in case this was a weird prelude to some really awful humiliation. Along the table Beth was chatting with Sister Henrietta Hennessey, and next to her immersed in thought, Mirabelle was turning her tumbler round and round - except! His scalp prickled with fright. Mirabelle wasn't looking at her tumbler at all but straight past him, and the pupils of her eyes had become malevolent black pinpricks. He froze in his seat, not daring to move anywhere near her line of sight. Beside him, the scraping of a chair being moved hurriedly aside and a wheezy sound like air escaping from a punctured tyre, suggested that Spattered Brown was the recipient of this terrible attention and he didn't want anymore of it.

Waiting until Mirabelle's eyes flickered and went out, he inched round until he could see that Spattered Brown had gone, leaving in his wake a faint musty odour.

Another julep arrived and it quickly joined the others. Feeling a little better, he allowed a few moments to pass before plucking up enough courage to look at Mirabelle again. She was pouring some water for Beth and must have sensed his gaze because she turned and placed a finger across her lips by way of a signal to keep the episode a secret between them.

At the front of the hall preparations were already being made for the evening session, and hoping to shake off the horrors of the last few minutes, he left the table and wandered over to the photographs and paintings displayed on the walls. The street and river scenes of early New Orleans pictured marching bands and smartly dressed musicians on paddle steamers, or outside restaurants and dance halls. Many of the paintings were formal portraits. King Lawrence posed in a leather studded chair, his cornet lying casually across his lap, and in the next frame, a youthful Reed Williams stared out from the portico of a fine house. The colours were rich and the postures proud, as if the subjects had achieved high office in day jobs and just happened to have their instruments with them when the artist put brush to canvass.

Hoping to find a picture of Blue Gums, he stopped before a photograph of the original Magnolians. A young Slidebone Walker and Reed Williams were pretending to joust with their instruments over the head of Gemma Singleton, who, as the subject of the contest was trying to hold them apart. Lord John was leaning against the piano with his banjo the wrong way round, but Blue Gums was nowhere to be seen. Working his way along the wall, he arrived at a far corner of the room and joined the others who were grouped around a glass display cabinet with Baby Todd and Dr Isiah. The case contained a banjo riddled with bullet holes and Baby Todd was providing an explanation.

'It was mighty rough in Chicago those days.'

'Sure was, sure was.' confirmed Dr Isiah.

'What did you do after it happened?' asked Chance.

'No choice. We looked straight ahead and carried right on playin''

'But surely Baby?' began Chance.

'Call me Todd. Maybe Baby is my real name, but I spent a lotta bruised knuckles in Austin trying to live that down.'

'Call him Todd, call him Todd!' repeated Dr Isiah.

Chance obeyed. 'But surely someone rushed to help him Todd?'

'Uh! Uh! The question was re-directed to the banjo by a slow shake of the head. 'No one rushed in Chicago those days, you moved smooth and slow…no jerks.'

'S'right, S'right,' agreed Dr Isiah. 'No jerks in Chicago, just smooth and slow.'

'It must have been a harrowing experience,' said Chance. 'I understand he was held in some esteem by his fellow musicians?'

'You said it - I didn't like him much either.'

Philip spoke. 'He had a successful band here in New Orleans of course. Chicago must have made a considerable impact on him for him to remain there?'

'Yeah, - about thirty five calibre.'

The largest portrait in the hall was of a guitarist, and Chance pointed to a length of cable leading to a speaker cabinet. 'This looks like an amplified guitar?' He spoke as if someone were to blame.

'Sure is,' affirmed Baby Todd.

Philip frowned. 'I wasn't aware of any outstanding New Orleans musicians who used amplified guitars.'

'Ahead of his time,' declared Baby Todd. 'Big John Stannard - came from Austin like me and settled here. Greatest guitar picker ever lived. Alus found his notes fair and square without havin' to move his hands overmuch.'

Philip sought reassurance from Dr Isiah. 'Well it's pleasing to know that New Orleans remains a bastion of acoustic instrumental playing.'

'Sure is.' Dr Isiah bent his head in thought. 'Greatest guitar picker ever lived -snazzy dresser too.'

Baby Todd beckoned a waiter. 'We go dry when the doors open. No liquor allowed during public sessions.'

'Why is that?' asked Chance.

'We don't want anyone buying drinks for the duty band. They gotta last the night.'

'I suppose the frailties of age must be a problem.'

'Yeah, mainly booze and death.'

'No doubt some of your top players have to drop out because of illness?'

'No problem, we just pull out the second best ahead of their place on the roster.'

'So they all have a fair share of the playing?'

'Or their fair share of time off dependin' how you look at it.'

'You mean they don't always enjoy playing?' Chance seemed surprised.

'Most don't enjoy playin' - period. And then we've got to be careful who plays with who. They might have been in rival bands sometime. That's when they can cut up real rough.'

'So you have to be diplomatic.'

'Yeah, and if that don't work we drag 'em out kickin' and hollerin'. You wouldn't believe how cussed they can get. Without Mirabelle we wouldn't have a band some nights.'

'She must be respected.'

'You can bet on it.' Baby Todd relieved a waiter of his tray of juleps and placed it within general reach. 'Mirabelle's got a way of persuading. I've had them cussin' at me for hours then seen them come out meek as kittens for her.'

Pimple reached for a Julep. Mirabelle had a way of persuading - no doubt about that.

As they talked the Hall began to fill up. No seats were provided, so customers sat directly on the floor reading information sheets provided by the Society. They spoke in whispers and gazed about in reverence like pilgrims who had arrived at some hallowed sanctuary. The chairs at the head of the hall were labelled 'Band Only'.

'Some of the band can stand,' explained Baby Todd. 'But we made a rule that everyone sits - not good for their dignity havin' one higher than the other.'

A trombonist arrived followed by a clarinet player who pointedly his moved his chair some distance away before sitting down.

'Uh Uh!' observed Baby Todd. 'Trouble already. Semprece Bailey and Shakes Rice …both sweet on Henrietta. She was makin' eyes at Semprece over dinner.'

The trumpet player arrived some moments later and stared sourly at a tin helmet mounted on a stand. A row of concertina-like wrinkles spanned the bridge of his nose and he glared at Baby Todd.

'Hey where's the Canadian helmet? I ain't playin' into no Yankee helmet!'

Baby Todd ignored the outburst.

'That's Winjy Mooney. We call him 'Winjy' on account he's alus winjin' and complainin'. Nothings ever right for Winjy.'

Winjy tried again. 'Gee Baby! Ya oughta know better than givin' me the Yankee helmet. Can't get no tone outa Yankee helmets.' His nose hinged upwards as he spoke.

'Call him Todd! Call him Todd!' warned Dr Isiah.

'Yeah call me Todd!' demanded Baby Todd. He slowly finished his julep. 'Could be a tough set guys. Help yourselves to juleps, you're on after the break.'

Baby Todd pulled a box full of helmets from beneath the entrance desk and selected a Canadian helmet which he handed to Winjy before taking his seat behind the drums.

Winjy allowed the American helmet to clatter noisily onto the floor while he placed the Canadian helmet on the stand, and without acknowledging his fellow musicians or the audience, tapped his foot twice and started to play. Pimple hadn't heard the tune before, but the juleps had taken much of the sting from Spattered Brown's merciless summary of his playing, and he assumed the role of critic. Dismissing the trombonist as no better than Chance, and the clarinettist even worse than Philip, he went on to place himself on a sliding scale of talent far above Winjy.

The piece came to a natural finish but Winjy caught out the audience by playing a full chorus on his own and concertining his nose at those who had the audacity to applaud beforehand. Outwardly smiling, Baby Todd left his drums to say something into Winjy's ear, and then to the clarinet player, who quickly moved his chair beside the trombonist.

'Flat Foot Blues' was better, but just when the theme became discernable Winjy dived behind the helmet to muffle it beyond recognition. He also had a knack for lifting compositions straight from the New Magnolians repertoire, but his nagging tone made them sound alike, and Pimple reasoned that the audience probably wouldn't know if the New Magnolians repeated the tune.

Alone with the tray of juleps he exchanged his glass for another full one and glanced around to spot the others. Chance was with Lord John, and Dan was telling Sister Henrietta the joke about the piano and the kangaroo. Only Philip and Mirabelle were listening to the band, and catching his glance, Mirabelle excused herself from Philip and walked over.

She pulled a chair across and sat down.

'I'm sorry Pimple. I must have given you a shock back there, but that Spattered Brown he got me so mad buggin' you and talkin' about Poppa the way he did. What with it being such a special day with you all comin' over to pay your respects and him carryin' on like that, well, I just snapped.' She shrugged her shoulders.

He replied as if Spattered Brown had merely stretched his tolerance.

'Thanks Mirabelle he was getting up my nose a bit.'

She smiled. 'Well I don't think anyone else noticed, so let's make it our secret shall we?'

He readily agreed, and savouring the exclusiveness she had bestowed on him finished the julep and waited impatiently for the first set to end.

The Winjy Mooney Five seemed to go on forever, but at last the interval came and the New Magnolians assembled on the spot previously occupied by so many famous and infamous musicians. He was supremely confident, and now that the moment had come was determined to surpass any of his previous performances. One thing was certain - he wouldn't be playing *'Pretty High School Trumpet'.*

Baby Todd introduced them to the audience.

'Ladies and Gen'lemen! Tonight we've got something special for you 'cos these cats have come over all the way from little ol' England. Well, maybe that ain't so unusual, but they're standin' here and that's mighty unusual.' He pointed to where he was standing. 'Now I don't hold with breakin' tradition, and we have a tradition that only New Orlin's musicians play here. But the kids over there never heard New Orlin's music until this sent them crazy.' He held up a copy of 'Back to Earth'. 'Now they're lookin' back here to where it all started, and it's spreadin' 'cos now our kids are looking' back to their roots and catching on fast. So let's have a New Orlin's welcome for the New Magnolians!'

Amid the welcoming applause Philip made a move towards the microphone but was effectively forestalled by Lutz who had already started the banjo introduction to 'Snake in the Grass.'

Pimple sped crisply through the melodic twists and turns of the verse, ably supported by Chance and Philip who were roughly in tune and more or less in harmony. Perhaps the flatness of the veteran's piano came closer to their natural pitch than the Weistein Grand at Chimney Studios. Whatever the reason, the New Magnolians were playing at their very best. 'Snake in the Grass' received rapturous applause as did the more genteel 'Muffin Man' and 'Bo Diddley Bo'. Even Philip, in an improbable moment of high exultation, sang the vocal refrain: 'Bo-Bo-Diddley-Bo-Bo!' into the microphone.

Amid shouts and whistles for an encore Chance raised his voice jubilantly. 'We've never played better, but I think we should end with just one more chorus of 'Stomp On' and leave them wanting more.'

The applause continued long after the final notes of 'Stomp On' had resonated round the hall, and only a few copies of 'Back to Earth' remained unsold and unsigned by the time the audience had left. Even Winjy Mooney came up to compliment Pimple. 'Man you sure nailed that G diminished run in the twenty third bar of 'Gorilla Strut.' His nose smoothed out. 'I heard plenty good horn players goof on that.'

Mirabelle hugged everyone in turn until she came to Pimple who she held at arms length just as she had done when they were first introduced. Her eyes shone with admiration. 'You played beautifully Pimple, really beautifully. I just wanted you to go on and on. Gee if only Poppa could have been here tonight.' She at once became more thoughtful, almost perplexed. 'But I can't shake off the feeling we've met before. I know it's crazy. It's got to be crazy because I'm sure Poppa was with me, and you couldn't have been around then.' She shook her head in puzzlement. 'But watching you play trumpet, I just know we've met someplace.'

'Maybe there's someone who looks a bit like me?' He daren't risk a straight denial.

'I guess that's possible but it wasn't just you.' She half turned as she left. '…Dan was there as well.'

He thought over what Mirabelle had said, but further consideration was overtaken by the need to focus all of his attention on stowing the 'Brash' into its case. He managed to complete the task by kneeling down, but some ominous simmerings below the waist warned of open hostilities between the oyster fritters, French fries and juleps. He would have to leave, and leave quickly.

The main door was the nearest exit and he mustered all his flagging resources to reach it. The floor tilted at each step, and grabbing the donation box, he feigned a posture that might have implied a casual need for fresh air, then stumbled to the bottom of the entrance ramp and erupted into a mass of foliage.

The courtyard was deserted, and crossing it a more shamelessly erratic manner, he reached the entrance and continued up the stairs to the gloomy corridor leading to his room. Zig-zagging between the partitions he succeeded in unlocking the door, and flopped onto the bed hoping that the room would remain steady enough for him to go to sleep. Sleep came, but it came as sequence of grotesque images and frightening encounters, one of which required him to make a perilous ascent to the top of the Crantree chimney for an interview with Mr Tranmere. A vengeful Spattered Brown was in wait, and sneering 'Peepity peep peep!' threw something slippery and odorous over him from a large bucket. He lost his footing and was still falling when he woke up.

Outside, a stiff breeze ruffled the magnolia canopy and carried light conversation over from the Veterans Hall. It would have been reassuring but for a persistent knock on the balcony doors. He broke into a cold sweat. Was it just possible that Spattered Brown had managed to climb the fire escape up to the balcony in hope of retribution? The knocking became insistent. There was even something moving behind the slight gap in the curtains. Spattered Brown might have planned something dreadful - murder perhaps? And what about that banjo riddled with bullet holes? Anyone could own a gun in America. Spattered Brown was about eighty, so what did he have to lose?

He shouted at the balcony.

'Mirabelle said she would sort you out if you bothered me again!' He immediately rebuked himself. Now Spattered Brown knew just where to aim. Panicked into action, he scrambled from the bed and flattened himself against the wall.

The knocking continued.

He had to do something. Anything was better than just waiting to be shot. He might even surprise Spattered Brown if he moved really quickly. He made his decision and rushed at the balcony doors, but fell flat onto the low coffee table which conveyed him headfirst onto the door handles. The pain jolted him into a fury and scrambling to his feet he snatched the doors open and growled: 'I'm really brassed off with you Sunshine. Buzz off if you don't want the Mirabelle treatment again!'

Something moved back as if fearful of confrontation, then it came swiftly forward and arms outstretched, his fathers' anorak enfolded him in an empty embrace. He detached it from the steel cable and clasping it tightly returned to the bed.

It had been a peculiar evening, no doubt about that, and it wouldn't be long before they would be searching for a mystery something or other on the Smoky Mountains. So the next few days were likely to be peculiar as well. And of course they had to make an extra early start to reach Gatlinburg in time for their stay with the Mayor.

He sighed, and still clasping the anorak rolled over so he would be facing away from the door and hopefully asleep before Dan came in.

20. Blue Mountain Blues.

The estate wagon veered away from the narrowing gravel track then slewed round in a half circle and nosed back towards Gatlinburg.

Mayor Garbor waited for the dust to clear then slid open the doors and assisted Beth from her seat.

'Well folks, this is as far as I can take you. It's your show from now on.' He opened Philip's map and laid it on the bonnet. 'We're here now and by noon you should be well into Cherokee country - that's here at Raging Fork.' A burly finger moved to a circled location on the map. 'Follow this gully until you come to the old logger's cabin I mentioned earlier, but watch out for copperheads and rattlers. Snaky Jake lived there until Washington put a stop to logging operations and he reared snakes to discourage the marshal's men busting his moonshine racket. There's a path leading from the cabin to Moonshine Falls and that's the only place where you can cross Raging Fork to the east ridge of Parsons Bald.'

He looked at them intently. 'OK, you got that?'

Everyone nodded.

His finger moved to another location on the map.

'This time of year the falls should be strong enough to clear the back-rock and that's the only way to cross, but when you reach Cherokee Gap wait for a sun break and look for the rainbow. If you can't see the rainbow there's no way you can cross the falls, OK?

Everyone nodded.

His finger moved a considerable distance across the map.

'No rainbow means you'll have to take this trail round to Blakes Elbow and make it to the East Ridge from there…Got that?'

They nodded.

'One last thing...You all got cell phones?

Everyone nodded.

'Forget them, this is a dead area folks - no signals. So take care, OK?'

Everyone nodded.

The mayor pressed a button somewhere on the dashboard and the tailgate swung open for them to offload the rucksacks and climbing rope. Chance again thanked the mayor for his help and hospitality and they all shook hands.

'It's been a real pleasure having you folks and I sure hope you find what you're looking for.' He leaned out of the driver's window and grinned as he moved off. 'And when you get back, tell Mayor Bingham that he'd better make our centenary dinner in Chattanooga next Fall or I'll be over there to kick his butt!'

The estate wagon accelerated down the track leaving a trail of dust which extended into the forest and out onto the plain towards the main highway.

They turned to face the mountains.

The hill on which they were standing dipped sharply to a stream. Beyond the stream the landscape reared upwards in a series of huge misty corrugations. The furthest was topped by a bank of cloud, which, even as they watched, fell away to reveal a darker and even more formidable corrugation topped by an even higher bank of cloud. Everyone, with the exception of Beth, hitched on their rucksacks and strode briskly down to the planked footbridge fording the stream.

Once again Pimple had Dan as a companion, but this time he didn't mind so much. Dan had changed since their arrival in New Orleans, and the change had become so marked that it was like being with a different person. He no longer tried to draw attention to himself, and during their stay with Mayor Garbor had been quite content to listen to the mayor's endless stream of anecdotes without contributing any of his own. No one had remarked on the change, but he now attracted greater respect.

Crossing the planked footbridge they started on the first hill. The footpath skirted a clump of rhododendrons then re-appeared as a thin wispy thread high above them. For the first time Pimple felt that the onus of starting a conversation was up to him.

'It's going to be a long walk.'

'Bound to be lad.'

'How far did Mayor Garbor say it was to Cherokee Gap?'

'About ten miles.'

'Do you reckon we'll make Moonshine falls today?'

'We should.'

'I hope so. I don't want this to last long.'

Dan's grin contained experience. 'It's not so bad once you get your second wind.'

A shakiness about the knees, and a constriction in the throat suggested his first wind was fast running out, and they hadn't even cleared the rhododendron bushes. It had never occurred to him that he might be the only one who would have difficulty in keeping up the pace.

Beth was making much better progress, and Philip and Chance were close to the hilltop forest. He felt sure that Dan was holding back for his benefit, and chastised himself for taking full advantage of Mayor Garbor's hospitality on top of his previous excesses at the Heritage Foundation dinner.

'Have you climbed any mountains?' he asked

'A few times with the army.'

'Were they as high as this?'

'No, but they had ways round that. A string of dummy grenades and a bazooka made it a fair walk.'

The hillside steepened, and they had to step over boulders and small shrubs intruding onto the path. The constriction in his throat had grown to the size of a tennis ball and the rucksack booked out from the park ranger station flopped uncomfortably on his back. They walked in silence until it was possible to pick out the individual trees in the forest, then Dan returned to the subject of their conversation.

'Our climbing instructor said he knew us better than our mums did.'

'Why was that?'

'He claimed that no mother had seen us so knackered as he had.'

Pimple listened through a cocoon of pain. With each step the sharp headache, which was now centred between the eyes, sent shock waves to his toes and fingertips.

'What was the army like?' he rasped.

'Rough, but it's supposed to make a man of you.

'Did you go anywhere?'

'Iraq.' He pushed Pimple's rucksack upwards as they walked. 'You seem to be struggling lad, is that better?'

It was much better, so they stopped and Dan adjusted the straps to make the rucksack ride higher. At once climbing became easier; soon to be further improved by a 'Best Buddy' flavoured burp which heralded his second wind and relieved the headache. They reached the top of the slope, and passing a notice warning visitors not to feed the bears, entered the forest. Mist condensing in the upper foliage of the taller trees came as cooling droplets, and step by step walking became almost enjoyable as he settled down to his best rhythm and balance.

They drew level with Lutz and Beth.

Lutz smiled grimly. 'And how are your lungs my friend. Are they well exercised for harder trumpet blowing?'

'I've got my second wind now.'

'Ah! So you have two winds? I have only one wind, but is it not enough? I am not having to blow the banjo.' He glared in the direction of Chance and Philip. 'And what are we looking for my friend?'

'Philip reckons Dorji lived here.'

'Then we will find only bones.'

'There might be a few more things lying around.'

'Hmm.' Lutz seemed doubtful, 'I am thinking we are searching for a tall story.'

Dan placed a hand on Lutz's shoulder. 'No need to search for a tall story chum. We're we're in one.'

They joined Chance and Philip at the other side of the forest. Facing them was a much larger version of the hill they had just climbed, and behind it, blue with distance and filling most of the horizon was an imposing formation capped by a domed summit rising above an encircling band of forest.

Chance consulted the map and came to a decision.

'Lutz and Beth will set the pace for this leg then Dan will take over from Lutz when we reach Cherokee Gap. After that we can all take turns to assist Beth over the steep stretch from Moonshine Falls to the eastern ridge of Parsons Bald.' He slid the map into a waterproof cover and used it to point out the next stop. Cherokee Gap is over the top of that hill. We'll have to move quickly to reach Moonshine Falls in time, but if the rainbow is visible we might even be on the eastern ridge before dusk.'

Bowed under the weight of his rucksack, Philip looked into the distance. 'What a perfect environment for Dorji to continue his work. I'm certain we are following in his footsteps.'

Cherokee Gap was a long green valley rising towards Parsons Bald like an enormous railway cutting. It had been a hard struggle getting there, and they rested on a ring of boulders circling a weathered board mounted above a wagon wheel. The board listed all the battles that had been fought in the area, and Philip, while clearly fatigued, took the opportunity to give an impromptu lecture about the shameful treatment meted out to the Cherokees by the settlers who had encroached onto their land.

'Even now,' he declared, 'many cling to the outrageous versions of history put out by early Hollywood film makers who portrayed the Cherokees as primitive savages who rejected the hands of friendship offered to them by the white settlers. Nothing could be further from the truth. The Cherokees tried to accommodate the demands made on them by the white establishment, but were swindled out of their lands by government legislation, which in effect, denied them any legal status. When Dorji arrived, it would be safe to assume he was among kindred spirits who shared his mystical beliefs and revolutionary fervour.'

As Philip spoke, his hair and clothing were whisked forward by a steady wind which sent clouds streaking along the valley towards them. It was as if they, complete with the valley, were being swept towards some heavenly destination. 'I am now confident,' he concluded, 'that this was the route used by Dorji all those years ago.'

He remained where he was for just long enough to be framed by a magnificent rainbow which curved over the lower end of the valley and coloured the slopes of Parsons Bald with a larger and paler imitation of itself. Turning into the sun Philip raised his arm towards the rainbow and acquired the mien of an Old Testament prophet.

'It seems,' he said, 'that the way is clear for us to continue our mission.'

The descent from Cherokee Gap to Raging Fork Gully took longer than expected, and by the time the old logger's cabin came into view the late afternoon shadow of Parsons Bald had extinguished the rainbow. Above them, and apparently devoid of solid support, high patches of rock could be glimpsed though clouds scurrying away from the eastern ridge. Closer to hand a brace of ruffed grouse broke cover and struggled for aerodynamic control in the growing wind.

'Snaky Jakes' cabin nestled beneath a rocky outcrop overlooking a dense hemlock forest, and mindful of Mayor Garbor's warning about copperheads and rattlers they gingerly picked their way through empty bottles and twisted copper pipes to the footpath which led to Moonshine Falls. Pimple peered through the cobwebs of a window and his curiosity was unblinkingly returned by a large copperhead coiled protectively beside a wooden ladle. The air became cold and damp as the footpath took them downwards, and hanging limply from bushes, festoons of moss brushed over them like wet flannels as they clambered over a tangle of roots into an energetic mist at the base of the falls.

Only hand signs were possible above the roar of water, but as Mayor Garbor had predicted, the falls cleared the back-rock leaving a narrow ledge just wide enough to walk across.

Dan immediately drew on his army training and doubling a rope around one of the more substantial roots ventured beneath the cascading wall of water. Shortly afterwards the rope tightened to make a double handrail, and within a few moments he returned to collect Beth. Making it clear that everyone would have to cross separately, he indicated with hand signals that the rope would shake three times before the next person could cross. Beth clung to his waist and they moved together into the watery tunnel. The rope shook three times for Chance to take his turn, and the procedure was repeated for Lutz, Philip, and finally Pimple.

Leaving the rope in place for the return trip, they struggled over a pile of rocks, then up through more bushes and a steep bank to a scree slope.

Philip screwed his eyes upwards at the glinting rock strata. 'There should be several natural caverns in this part of the face but it is impossible to tell from here. We will have to look for evidence of a route along the base of the ridge.'

They picked their way over the scree, and Pimple joined Dan to help Beth over some of the really difficult patches. Chance scanned the rock through his binoculars.

'There doesn't seem to be anything likely in this section.'

Dan made a suggestion.

'If I was Dorji, I'd make for the other side of that buttress.' He pointed to part of the face that extended forward like a giant nose. 'It sticks out from the main face and wouldn't catch so many falling rocks.'

Chance considered the suggestion.

'I can't think of anything better, what do you think Philip?'

Philip turned the binoculars to the buttress.

'It would be worth trying. Being proud of the main face it would provide a panoramic view of the night sky and there's a pine copse and some vegetation. A ready supply of wood and a small arable patch would be quite sufficient for Dorji's needs.'

The occasional clattering of rocks stressed the need to maintain a safe distance from the base of the main face, but it was an exhausting trudge. By the time they had reached the buttress, patches of mist prevented them from seeing more than a few yards ahead and the light was fading.

Chance called for a rest.

'If you feel up to it I suggest we try to find some ways up this buttress before looking for a suitable place to camp.'

As Chance spoke, Dan was angling his head towards the sound of running water.

'Dorji would need water for his cabbages, so let's head for it.'

They crossed a patch of finer scree and came across a cairn of rocks shaped like a large traffic cone. It had been put together so precisely that the sides were smooth.

Philip studied it with admiration.

'Only someone well versed in mountain craft would be capable of such expert stonework in these conditions.' He inched himself round the cairn. 'But I suspect that there will be a flaw somewhere in the construction. Dorji held the belief that no man is capable of perfection and that this applies to all human endeavours.' He knelt down to examine the cairn in greater detail. 'Ah yes! Can you see it?' he pointed to the base. 'An ordinary house brick has been used here, which is of course totally at odds with these natural grey rocks.'

Chance seemed doubtful. 'Surely he wouldn't have carried it here specially for the purpose.'

'That is exactly what he would have done Chance.' Philip replied with conviction. 'Dorji would have left no stone unturned to demonstrate human fallibility.'

Meanwhile, Dan had been walking behind the cairn in a semi-circle; stooping at intervals to take a line of sight. Satisfied at what he had seen he snapped his fingers.

'This way troops!'

Soon they were standing before a similar cairn only a few feet from the base of the buttress. Directly ahead, a torrent of water splashed down the face, and beside it a ribbon of clean rock hewn into rough footholds rose into the mist like a giant staircase.

He advised caution.

'Looks like this was the original watercourse. It must be blocked higher up to make a pathway. It could be slippery so we'd better rope up, but if the going gets tough we'll have go right back to the falls and camp out for the night.'

Making sure that everyone had roped up properly, he ascended into the mist followed by Pimple and Beth. The footholds varied in width and height but were well formed. Pimple helped Beth to maintain an even keel by pressing hard on her short side as she raised herself over the higher steps. Looking down, he watched a bank of mist transform the others into ghostly figures as it dropped over them to the warmer air of Cherokee Gap, but above, the stereophonic boomings foretold a far from serene night ahead.

The steps ended in a row of square stone blocks which had been arranged to divert the flow of a stream to the alternative watercourse. Dan drew their attention to a notch cut into the base of the first block.

'A bit of smart thinking here. This block can be levered sideways to turn the steps back into a waterfall.'

'Ingenious,' agreed Philip.

Chance was puzzled.

'Then why are the steps open now?'

Philip weighed up the possibilities.

'Someone may have been here before us. There's no reason why the route should have remained secret after Dorji's death.'

'Maybe,' Dan pointed to softer ground around the stone block, 'but they're not my footprints, that block has been moved recently.'

A clap of thunder made everyone jump.

Chance spoke warily.

'When did Dorji die Philip?'

'I don't know, and neither do the authorities.' Philip rolled his eyes. 'It is of course possible that we are expected.'

'You surely don't think...?' Chance stared at Philip in disbelief. '...I mean, well, you are not suggesting that Dorji might be waiting for us are you. He would be about one hundred and twenty years old!'

Lutz interjected. 'I am wanting to play banjo.' He strummed the climbing rope. 'I am also wanting hair.' He removed his wool cap and angrily patted his head. 'I am not wanting to go further.'

Philip spoke wearily.

'Even if Dorji had the power to extend his life it would have been contrary to his beliefs to do so. I am simply saying that our arrival here may have been predicted.'

'Then who moved the block?'

'I have no idea, although it is just possible that Dorji anticipated our arrival, and his devotees, or possibly their children have complied with his wishes by diverting the stream for us today.'

Chance was unconvinced.

'I don't see how Dorji could have possibly predicted our arrival to within hours. After all, Mayor Garbor nearly persuaded us to spend another day with him. There must have been hundreds of occasions in our lives when we have changed plans on the strength of a mere whim.'

Another peal of thunder shook the air - it was closer this time.

'And we'll have to change plans right now if we hang around here any longer.' warned Dan.

Hurriedly coiling up the ropes they continued alongside the stream into a fir grove. The ground squelched underfoot, and a blustery wind shook the trees deluging them with spray and pine needles. Roving thunderstorms rumbled in all directions and the trees moved jerkily against the stroboscopic illumination of lighting flashes.

A gust of wind ballooned Philip's oilskin pulling him sharply sideways against the trunk of a pine. He quickly returned to the path but it was evident that he was in no fit state to cope with such conditions for much longer.

More lightning streaked down to the head of the copse and the stunted boundary trees stood out against a grey wall of rock.

'I saw something up there Ducks,' said Beth, but Dan was already pointing upwards. 'There it is!'

They assembled before another steep gully cut into the rock face. There was urgency in Dan's voice. 'We'll have to move fast. We're going to get chilled unless we reach shelter soon.' He drew Pimple aside. 'Philip needs a rest and I'll have to help Beth over this stretch. How do you feel about going on ahead?'

'I don't mind.'

'Right, try to get some wood ready for a fire.' Dan gave him a torch. 'Wave this when you get there, but don't do anything daft, OK?'

He entered the gully. It was high sided and narrow but there were more steps and convenient indentations had been cut into the rock for use as handholds. Thunder crashed resoundingly between the gully walls and overhead a darkening strip of sky flashed brightly enough to illuminate the way ahead. Soon he emerged from the gully onto a stony path where he could see the top half of an impressive cave.

He hadn't expected it to be so easy, but neither had he expected to see a plume of smoke rising from the cave. He continued with caution. Could Philip have been wrong, and was it just possible Dorji was still in residence?

As he came closer he could see someone blowing energetically into a fire, and it certainly wasn't a centenarian. The smoke made it difficult to tell if it was a man or woman, but when the billowing clouds suddenly ignited, the spluttering and cursing plainly came from a 'him' and not a 'her'.

Wearing a shabby US army greatcoat, his straggly hair was topped by a head-dress of bent and broken feathers, and his face was crudely decorated with paint and fire-smoke. He was obviously a Cherokee.

Pimple cleared his throat and stepped forward into the cave-mouth.

'Hullo, not very good weather is it?'

The man showed no surprise.

'Um...' he began, and pointed to a stack of cut logs by the wall of the cave. 'Got any gum chum?' he added.

'No, but I'll ask the others when they arrive. We're here to look at Dorji's Cave.'

'Seeing is believing.'

Further into the cave he was shown a row of tin mugs resting on a ledge, and a blackened kettle suspended by a chain from the cave roof. The cave wall was scratched over with calculations, astrological symbols and writing. Most of the writing was in French but an English phrase appeared every so often. 'You scratch my back and I'll scratch yours.' 'It's love that makes the world go round.' and 'Marples must go!' were a few examples that caught his attention. They usually appeared after algebraic symbols and formulae as if someone of considerable learning had used maths to derive statements of wisdom. Further proof that Dorji had lived there was provided by a brass telescope on a tripod.

He was led outside to a stone cubicle smelling strongly of 'Lavysan', and from there to a bucket of water beside a brass urn with a pumistone chained to the rim. It was like being shown around lodgings by a landlord who was eager to be elsewhere, and it felt like a well rehearsed routine.

They went back to the fire and cramming the head-dress into the pocket of his greatcoat, the Cherokee hoisted his collar against the wind and waved his arms about to encompass all he had shown.

'Okay Dokay?'

'Yes, and thanks for lighting the fire.'

They shook hands, and moving to the entrance the Cherokee said:

'Two's company, three's a crowd.' He hesitated. 'Um, five's big crowd.'

For an instant he looked uncannily like Dave Moss, then whooping unconvincingly, bounded into the darkness leaving Pimple to wave the torch and call up the others.

21.Higgledy Piggledy.

Thunderstorms had continued to rage throughout the night, and smoke from the fire had been blown back into the cave. Warm but uncomfortable, Pimple lay curled up by the cave wall. The spare jumper and socks beneath his sleeping bag did little to soften the floor, and the knobbles and ridges grew harder as the night wore on. He would have been more comfortable had he remained beside Philip, but that would have been much too disconcerting.

The last steep foot-slog to the cave had brought Philip to a state of near collapse, but on arrival, and against all advice, he immediately began to note down the writings on the cave wall. Eventually Dan led him firmly to his sleeping bag where he sank into a shivery slumber. Without doubt he was in a bad way, and when not croaking and moaning at his fevered imaginings, the lighting flashes caught him staring wild eyed at the cave roof. It was clear that unless his condition dramatically improved, they would have to abandon the trip and get him off the mountain to seek medical care. Whatever remained in the black depths of the cave would just have to remain a mystery.

Anything could be lurking in there of course. Admittedly, the cave was above the forest and the Cherokee didn't seem concerned, but there were plenty of notices warning of black bears. Being zipped up in a sleeping bag wouldn't give much time to escape from a determined bear.

So it was fortunate that he hadn't been looking rearwards when an exceptionally bright streak of lightning crackled across the cave-mouth and probed the darkness beyond the firelight. Had he done so, further sleep would have been out of the question. But it was some hours later, just as the first rays of sunshine had begun to soak up the night deluge, that he was staring open mouthed in the direction of Lutz's shaking finger.

'It is you I am seeing is it not my friend?'

'Stroll on!' He snapped awake in an instant. 'That's me alright!'

From the back of the cave another Pimple gazed back at them over the bell of a 'Brash Superior'. Eyes twinkling in the rosy light of dawn, he was poised in a moment of high exultation, possibly during the stop chorus of 'Bo Diddley Bo' or the moving modulation from B Flat to A flat minor in Dead Loss Blues. It was undoubtedly a Pimple, and an incredibly realistic one at that.

They looked in amazement as the rising sun picked out more details.

Headed: 'Joueur de trompette ide'al' he was shown in the playing position from different viewpoints including side, plan, front and rear views. Nothing was missed. Precise dimensions were given, and even the palm tree of hair sprouting from the crown of his head was given room and measurement.

Philip sat up in his sleeping bag and stared shakily in the direction of interest.

'Goodness!' He rose stiffly. 'I expected confirmation, but nothing quite like this!'

Shunning all common-sense precautions, he pulled on his boots, picked up a torch, and clad in nothing more than pyjamas stumbled towards the back of the cave. His departure was barely noticed by Pimple who continued to stare at his own likeness with mounting wonderment, but Lutz broke into his thoughts.

'I am worried about Philip. We must wake Dan and get quickly in there after him.'

Dan grunted affably following a hefty shake. 'What's up? Cocoa time is it?'

'Just about, but look at that!'

Pimple pointed to his image.

'Well, well, Dorji's right on the button with you lad, it's a dead ringer.'

He rubbed the stubble on his chin. 'I wonder what he's done with the rest of us.'

'Philips gone inside to find out.'

Dan glanced at the empty sleeping bag and pile of clothes.

'He's in no state to go anywhere.'

They dressed hurriedly and soon everyone was standing before the cave wall where Pimple had been so meticulously reproduced. For the first time, he gathered that his head was exactly twenty-one centimetres at the widest point, and his right ear jutted out four millimetres further than the left. His eyes commanded instant attention. Crafted from clear blue quartz and gazing slightly ahead they encouraged the observer to move back into an admiring audience. It really was an incredible likeness and even more incredible at close range because the fine details consisted of astrological symbols. Hundreds of crabs linked pincers, their jumbled outlines blending to create a tangled mop of hair, and tiny fish swarmed in the complicated wrinkles on his forehead mingling downstream with larger fish to fashion his eyebrows. It was a brilliant combination of sculpture, astrology and draughtsmanship, and it was only with reluctance that he dragged himself away from it. This was exactly how he hoped he looked when playing the trumpet.

As they ventured deeper into the cave, the torchlight picked out an astounding likeness of Dan. Seated confidently behind the drums, he was depicted with one hand damping the tom-tom and the other lightly holding a drumstick which was about to make contact with the high hat. Like Pimple he was shown from different viewpoints with relevant dimensions. The detail was nearly as breathtaking and the pose nearly as flattering. Even the make of his drum-kit, 'The Earwig' was correctly styled in earwigs across the front of the bass drum.

'And very nice too.' observed Dan. 'It's not often I look like that, but when I do it's worth it.'

An equally convincing image of Beth, and a slightly less convincing image of Lutz, was displayed on the opposite wall together with a trombonist who bore only a vague resemblance to Chance.

Hushed expressions of awe echoed inside the cave as it became clear who Dorji and Blue Gums had chosen for their future band. It was also clear who had not been chosen, and it was with considerable dignity and against heartfelt appeals for him to continue that Chance announced his resignation. Expressing disappointment, but not surprise, he promised his continued support for the New Magnolians and wished them every success in the future.

It was like being in a strange art gallery where the artist had taken on the role of a judge and his subjects had no right of appeal if they failed to resemble their own portraits.

No one vaguely resembling Philip was featured on the cave wall and the chubby youth blowing into a clarinet wouldn't have passed off even as a distant relative. But Pimple knew exactly who he was. Without doubt it was the passenger with the small case who had had stepped from the very train that had started them on the journey to New Orleans.

'I hoped that wouldn't happen.' Dan lowered his torch. 'We'd better get to Philip fast.'

A prolonged moan of anguish echoed up to them from the blackness beyond, and filled with foreboding they hastened towards it. But even as they hurried, lifelike images revealed by the shaking torchlight jumped out from the cave walls. Dave Moss, Mr Tranmere, and even the Machine Shop Supervisor gazed down from their stony environs, and Pimple went weak kneed at Rose half-smiling at him between Godfrey Smith and Madame Zelda. Dorji had created a 'Who's Who' of those who had been important in his life and the startled exclamations from those around him suggested that Dorji had done the same for the others as well. Beth sighed adoringly at a homely lady holding babies, and Lutz came to a dead stop before a severe character framed by mountains. It was hard to believe that just one man could have accomplished so much. The slogans and maxims scrawled willy-nilly on the remaining wall space hinted at Dorji's state of mind as he worked feverishly against his advancing years. 'Many a good tune is played on an old fiddle.' 'If I knew I was going to live this long I would have taken better care of myself.' were just two among hundreds meticulously chiselled in English and French.

The cave roof dipped sharply downwards over some boulders and into a black pool of water. Slumped over one of the boulders, Philip might have been mistaken for a discarded pile of rags, but everyone knew that they were gazing anxiously at a frail bundle of hope worn down by overwork and finally disappointment.

Dan closed a hand gently over his shoulder.

'It's time to go old fellow.'

'I'm not here.' croaked Philip. 'I'm just not here.'

Chance offered some words of sympathy.

'No one deserves to be here more than you Philip. It must be a terrible disappointment, but please understand you are among friends who above all want you back to good health.' But Philip was inconsolable. He merely stared into the water and shivered.

'Right!' Dan went into action, and giving his torch to Lutz lifted Philip from the boulder. 'Lead us out of here and no looking at the walls. He needs something hot inside him and we need something hot inside us!'

They worked as a team. Chance helped Dan to get Philip into warm clothes, Beth filled the kettle and Pimple and Lutz re-kindled the fire. As they worked, Lutz said: 'Pimple my friend is this not all too much?' Is it perhaps that like the sparks from this fire we are burning so brightly that we will go out quickly afterwards?'

Lutz had given voice to something unsettling in his own mind. And Philip's deathly pallor served to underline it. He glumly recalled the words of the old lady who had asked for his autograph at Isby Station: *'They've done it all before Ducks. Blue Gums and Dorji I mean. Don't be too upset if it doesn't work out. Remember you've plenty of life ahead of you.'*

The 'New Magnolians' would never be complete until they were joined by the trombonist and clarinet player pictured on the cave wall, and there didn't seem much chance of that. He began to think about his own future with the band, but was distracted by a fuzzy glow circling Lutz's head. Making doubly sure he wasn't mistaken he said: 'I reckon you're getting your hair back Lutz.'

22.That Long Lonesome Road.

Dan checked the thermometer. His diagnosis was grim.

'One way or another we've got to get him off this mountain. I don't give much for his chances otherwise.'

Everyone agreed. Further exploration of the cave would have to wait for another day and probably another party.

Not surprisingly Philip had other ideas. He awoke yellow eyed and trembling, but still protested at the decision to leave when there was so much left to discover.

Chance knelt beside him.

'You are ill Philip, you must go back.'

'But I must continue my research.' Philip forced himself into a sitting position. 'This is too valuable an opportunity to miss.'

Dan left no room for argument.

'Tough! You can either walk back or be carried.'

Philip scanned the other faces for any weakening resolve.

'You seem determined.'

'We are.' Dan and Chance spoke in unison.

'You've got to get better Ducks.' added Beth.

He slumped back to the wall as if their combined resolve had robbed him of all purpose. 'It seems I have no choice.' He leaned over to reach his sleeping bag and shakily stowed it onto his rucksack.

'At least let me take your rucksack,' said Chance.

Philip rolled his eyes upwards until they became defiant yellow balls. 'Thank you Chance, but I can manage.' Using the cave wall for support, he rose, and walked unsteadily to the stone cubicle outside the cave.

Dan drew everyone together.

'It's going to be difficult. Something tells me he doesn't care whether he makes it or not. Watch him like the proverbials, and keep him within grabbing distance over the difficult bits.'

Chance took the lead down the steep gully while Dan and Lutz kept Philip between them at the rear of the column. They tackled the stone steps to the scree slope in similar fashion, and during a short break Dan handed over to Pimple the responsibility of looking after Philip.

'He's all yours down to Moonshine Falls lad, and don't give him an inch.'

Keeping close to Philip was difficult. Tackling obstacles with ashen faced doggedness, he allowed gravity rather than caution to take him downhill, so his progress was careless but brisk and they arrived at the bank above Moonshine Falls well ahead of the others.

The rainbow arced over the falls with even greater intensity than before, and from the bank he followed the direction indicated by Philips shaking finger. The heavy rainfall had powered up the falls overnight and they curved over the back rock clearing it by several meters before crashing into the rock-pool and dissipating downstream in foam and swirling eddy currents.

He followed the erratic progress of a branch as it twirled and jumped over rocks until it became trapped in a whirlpool. Every so often the whirlpool would swirl onto a nearby rock and lose energy so that it nearly, but never quite, released the branch. It had become a contest, and he became so engrossed in the watery tussle that he began to take sides with the branch. Concentrating on that small spot to the exclusion of everything else, he eventually lost track of time while something half remembered strived again and again for his attention. As the branch twirled round and round his anxiety mounted until at last it brought him up with a jolt.

Wait! This was a repeat of the experience at Pipers Lane Millpond when he was with Rose.

Sensing that something was badly wrong, he turned to Philip, but Philip was no longer at his side. Shaking with worry he looked left and right then down the slope towards the falls and the swirling branch. Philip was nowhere to be seen unless? He ran along the bank to line himself up with the falls and instantly chilled with horror. Half way along the narrow ledge in the watery tunnel beneath the falls a lanky figure stood facing the back rock. Obscured at times by the cascading water it was unmistakably Philip. At first he seemed hesitant, then glancing over his shoulder shuffled sideways a few inches to adjust his position, and placing both hands flat against the rock leaned backwards and pushed.

Shouting frantically, Pimple rushed downwards blundering through bushes and jumping over rocks to the river bank. But Philip had gone.

Icy disbelief gripped him. It was so quick that his mood hadn't time to absorb the ghastliness of the moment. Yet in its wake came the even more appalling realization that he had been trusted with Philip, and from that moment on he, and he alone would be held responsible and therefore to blame for Philips demise.

This was beyond dreadfulness. 'How could Philip have done such a thing, especially to him?'

He scanned the falls, then downstream as far as could be seen. Something like Philip would soon have to bob up unless he was jammed between some boulders at the base of the falls. He raced up the bank to look onto the water, then down again into the spray mist and sank to his knees with a groan.

The spray mist sought out large absorbent patches in his father's anorak, but his torment left no room for physical discomfort. Even the apologies - barely audible against the roar of the falls - took time to get through, and he dare not accept their authenticity for fear that they might be a cruel fiction of his own making.

Yet Philip had already emerged from the falls and was loping along the bank still gasping his apologies.

'I sincerely apologise Pimple, but I had to complete my task otherwise our mission would have been utterly pointless.'

He breathed hoarsely for a few moments while relief tussled with anguish.

'I thought you'd pushed yourself off the ledge.'

'Deliberately?'

'It looked like it.'

Philip thought back. 'Some force was needed, but with great caution. My death would have placed you in a terrible position.'

'It did.'

'Again I must apologize. My intention was to complete the task while you were distracted.'

'I don't want that to happen again either.'

'I'm afraid you are sensitized, so it may happen again. It should however be a more positive experience in the future.'

He flopped onto the grass and rolled his eyeballs. They were a deeper yellow, but he managed a weak smile and added mysteriously: 'But now of course we are at rainbows end and the treasure has been claimed.' Without further explanation he lay flat on his back and lapsed into noisy sleep, giving time for more relief to flood in.

But Philip wouldn't be able to go much further, and where were the others? Beth might have slowed them down a bit but they should have arrived a long time ago.

Below, the branch was still spinning in the whirlpool. It had been trapped for ages as well. Perhaps he should avoid looking at it, but he wanted to see it released, and his hopes mounted when the whirlpool surged onto a rock. Swinging wildly, the branch again rose upwards, but this time it snagged on the rock and taking the opportunity, skipped downstream like something live and free.

At once something went click. Colours brightened; the air vibrated; his wooziness vanished, and the others arrived.

By the time they had begun the long haul to 'Cherokee Gap' it was clear to everyone that Philip had taxed himself to the limit, yet he still stubbornly refused assistance.

And Philip wasn't the only one to cause concern.

The blond fuzz that meant so much to Lutz, yet so little to everyone else, had reduced him to an excitable chatterbox. The change had been instant, and much for the worse. Anyone within hearing distance was subjected to incessant banter about Helga of Bad Oman who would agree to his proposal of marriage within seconds of his arrived on German soil. He was a new Lutz; a bouncy and ebullient Lutz, but an unimproved Lutz.

Searching for reflective surfaces to check his hair, he would dash over to pools of calm water, and in one foolhardy moment even ventured inside Snaky Jakes cabin to obtain a shaving mirror. Only Pimple's headlong dash through the open door saved him from being nabbed by the resident copperhead.

His preparations for a life of bliss with Helga were outlined in scrupulous detail. Nothing would be left to chance. Helga, so it seemed, was a perfectionist, especially where her own desires were concerned and Lutz planned to cater for her tiniest whim. Her virtues had been catalogued as they waited to cross under

Moonshine Falls and were later extolled in breathless spasms as they plodded up the steep incline to Cherokee Gap. It seemed remarkable that Bad Oman could retain such a girl for so long, but Lutz had no doubts. With love and hair he would be would be embraced by Helga and all would be wonderful from thereon.

At last Dan called for everyone to take a breather.

Pimple selected a boulder and uncorked his water bottle. There was barely room, but Lutz squeezed beside him and he waited uneasily for the question which was bound to come. With affairs of the heart burning fiercely and only a few years between them it was simply a matter of time before Lutz would enquire after his romantic intentions.

'And you my friend.' Lutz eyed him intently. 'Have you no one waiting for you?'

'Not really.' He tried to convey some uncertainty but it was lost on Lutz.

'But you would like someone Eh?'

'I wouldn't mind.' He spoke defensively. 'But I haven't found anyone I fancy yet.' He didn't want to talk about Rose.

Lutz tut-tutted with disapproval. 'Then you will search high and low for one my friend. A man without a woman is like a fish without a tail.'

Pimple lapsed into glum silence. He didn't need to be told that something was missing in his life. It had been bad enough seeing Rose on the cave wall without being quizzed about his solitary condition. Chance was married, Lutz would soon have Helga, and Dan had been keeping pretty close to Beth since they left the cave - so something was going on there as well. He had no one, and it didn't seem likely that he was going to get anyone either. Rose was the only girl for him but he was about as close to her as he was ever likely to get. Playing trumpet with the New Magnolians had helped, but even that was threatened now. What was the point of being chosen to play in a future band if there wasn't a band to play in? Chance had resigned; Lutz was going back to Germany to be with Helga, and Philip? He gazed over his water bottle at Philip.

Every angle of Philips sparse frame conveyed wretchedness. His arms hung limply through the lower spokes of the memorial wagon wheel, his head lolled disjointedly in the hollow of his shoulder and his lower jaw drooped open. He could have been a white rancher left for dead by a rampaging band of Cherokees and Pimple put aside his own troubles to walk over and offer him water.

Philip removed an arm from the spokes of the wagon wheel. He could barely speak, and taking a few sips motioned Pimple to come closer. 'You are the first of the chosen few,' he croaked. 'Blue Gums has entrusted you to...' Pimple quickly pressed the water bottle to his lips. '...to spread his legacy...Mirabelle must…' he took some short crackly breaths '...must know I would have dedicated…' His head clunked against a spoke of the wagon wheel, but he came to just long enough to wheeze: 'My pocket...in my pocket!' His eyes glazed over, but a fading flicker of urgency prompted Pimple do as he was bidden. Unzipping the large front pocket of Philips anorak he closed his hand round a damp stone slab. Meticulously chiselled on the smoothest side was a musical score entitled 'Le Rag Galactique'. He pocketed it and looked round for help just as Dan hurried over.

'Fading out is he lad?'

'He's already faded out.'

They supported Philips head and laid him flat on the ground. 'See if you can rustle up a branch strong enough to take his weight. We'll have to make a hammock and get him to the nearest rangers post.'

Dan opened his army penknife.

'Use the saw on this if you need to do any cutting.'

Pimple scrambled up the side of the valley to a small clump of trees, and lopping a fairly straight section from a low branch trimmed off the smaller shoots as he hurried back. By the time he returned, Dan had cocooned Philip in his sleeping bag leaving three loops of climbing rope for the branch to slide through.

Dan gave his instructions.

'I'll take the first stretch with Lutz. Then it's your turn with Chance.'

An hour later they were standing dejectedly before an emergency phone dangling from a bashed enclosure and clawed post.

'Bad bearanting.' quipped Dan flatly. 'I bet that doesn't happen very often…Just our luck!' He checked Philips pulse. 'We'll just have to get help as soon as we can.'

Pimple joined Chance to shoulder the hammock for a second stretch, and they started down the slope to the bottom of the valley before the long trudge to the hilltop forest on the opposite side.

The branch hardly bowed beneath Philips weight. It was difficult to prevent the hammock swinging in the wind, but once in the calm of the valley all was still both outside and inside the hammock. Philip hadn't mentioned relatives, but if there were any he would probably have cut himself off from them just as he had with his fiancée. So the band was probably all he had, and already they could be his mourners and pall bearers.

Once inside the forest Dan and Lutz shouldered the hammock, and again Dan turned to Pimple. 'We can manage now, so dash ahead and try to get some help. You might come across some campers with transport.'

Pimple raced through the forest and down the long narrow track to the footbridge fording the stream. Then, dizzy with exertion he walked backwards up the first part of the rise to catch his breath and relieve the ache in his legs.

The scale of the landscape was huge, and he could just discern the others as small dots emerging from the forest. Turning back to face the rise he could see another small dot, and even at that distance lacking feature or form, it radiated authority and magnetism. Without a shadow of doubt it was Mirabelle, and they came together with uncanny speed.

Just one searching look told her all she needed to know.

'So it's that bad?'

He nodded.

Her eyes went watery but she spoke with determination.

'I won't let him fade out just like that.'

She gripped his shoulders. 'Did he find anything?'

'Yes.' He showed her the stone slab 'He gave me this.'

She closed her eyes in relief.

'You may be the only one who can save him. Get to the top of that rise. Dave Moss will tell you what to do.'

She hugged him hard and he was immediately charged with enough energy to reach top of the rise with breath to spare.

Dave seemed totally unaffected by the urgency of the situation and leaning casually against the bonnet of the Pontomatic, raised an arm in lazy greeting.

'Time to blow your own trumpet lad.' He angled his head at the Brash which was ready to play beside an erected music stand and a can of Best Buddy Malt Liquor. 'A spot of the old 'Galactic Rag' would go down nicely after the drive we've had.'

'It's a good job you found us?'

'A stitch in time saves nine.'

He placed the stone slab on the music stand and studied the chiselled score of 'Le Rag Galactique'. This, he could see, was much more than just a tune. The crotchets, quavers, semibreves and rests leapt from the stone with the power of dynamite and the freshness of first love.

Fired with purpose he picked up the Brash and played.

The inspired assembly of notes burst from the Bell and flew like Cupids arrows across the vast undulating panorama. 'Le Rag Galactique' embodied the melancholy of 'Dead Loss Blues' but on a far grander scale. It was a universal melancholy, a sort of colossal moan on behalf of all downtrodden creatures large and small. Yet throughout, there was an ascending mood of hope that would have lifted the spirits of anyone in dark despair.

Blue Gums and Dorji had surpassed themselves this time. Here was an antidote to all things horrible. Rhino's might keep their horns in Africa. The selfish might settle for less, and even Crantree might not be quite so nasty on Saturday nights.

A hare rose from a tussock of grass, its ears finely tuned to the incoming sound, and as further testimony to the inclusiveness of the piece, a flock of tiny birds fluttered down and tilted their heads in unison. Tears streamed down Pimple's cheeks as he played. Even Dave had his eyes closed, and on the narrow path leading down to the footbridge Philip stirred in his hammock.

The clear skies of the Southern Appalachians were now well behind them, and a dim haloed moon swung across the windscreen as they rounded a slow bend.

Behind him, and just being passed by the moon, Chance had an ear pressed uncharacteristically forward by the edge of the seat. It was surprising that this small deformation should have such a pronounced effect on his appearance. It even gave him a passable resemblance to the trombonist pictured on the cave wall, and somehow, that made his resignation seem even more regrettable. After all, the other trombonist was hardly likely to turn up, and even Dorji hadn't thought to chisel in his name and telephone number.

In the back seat Dan was leaning heavily against Beth. Beside them facing a lowered courtesy mirror, Lutz sat bolt upright but asleep, and still cocooned in his sleeping bag, Philip slept with his head resting on Mirabelle's lap. Framed for a few moments in a moving square of moonlight, Mirabelle could have been cradling a skull on a cushion.

Pimple's cheeks tingled as he recalled the barrage of kisses she had pressed upon him after Philip had been carried to the top of the rise. He had never been kissed like that before, and all the questions he wanted to ask had vanished in the heat of the moment. The most beautiful woman he had ever known had actually kissed him and had promised she would never forget him.

'All quiet in the stalls?' asked Dave.

'They're asleep.'

Dave leaned across to turn the air-conditioner up a notch.

'Fancy a bevvy?'

'I wouldn't mind.'

The dashboard cooler flap opened, and taking out two cans of Best Buddy Pimple considered how little Dave had changed since they had been at 'Receipt and Despatch'. He pulled the ring tops slowly to reduce the hiss.

'Has Tranmere made any plans for us when we get back?'

'There'll always be plans.'

'When are we going back?'

'Thursday.'

'What's today?'

'Wednesday.'

'So we're flying back tomorrow?'

'Aye.'

He felt let down. Just one session in the Veterans Hall and a mountain climb was hardly an American tour. Still, with the band breaking up what was the point of staying any longer?

He shared his despondency with Dave.

'There won't be many of us left, so I reckon that's the end of the band.'

Dave replied after a lengthy pause.

'Aye, but there's a beginning to every end.'

23.Going Home.

Pimple was the last to add his cabin bag to the assortment of luggage in the entrance lobby. It was mid afternoon, and the others were seated around a large wooden table in the shade of the magnolia canopy. Philip was wrapped up in a wheelchair and Dr Isiah flitted between them with coffee. Looking up, Mirabelle broke off her conversation with Chance and left her seat.

'My hero!' she announced, and greeting Pimple halfway with a big cuddle walked him back to the table. 'Gee am I going to miss you.' She patted the place next to her. 'Sit right here I want you beside me.'

Chance repeated his question. 'But what made you decide to drive through the night to get us?'

'I got uneasy at what might happen in those mountains.' She squeezed Philips hand as if they were answering the question together. 'Right Honey?'

Philip seemed to agree.

'Trouble was I couldn't put my finger on what was bothering me until I got to thinkin' about you wanderin' up there among those rocks. It sounds crazy, but I started thinking about particular rocks - rocks I'd seen before.'

'Are you saying you had been there in the past?' asked Chance.

'I wasn't sure. I figured I might get the answer by going back to my childhood, but it took a lot of hard thinking. Whenever I got close to remembering something I felt I was hurting Momma.' She looked ill at ease. 'You see until recently I didn't know who Momma was because she split with Poppa when I was very young. Sometimes I must have been with Poppa and other times with Momma, and I always knew that Momma never wanted to hear about my times with Poppa.' She sighed. 'I guess she couldn't bear anyone, even me, sharing him without her.'

'It must have been very difficult for you.'

'It made me kind'a closed up as a child and it's only now I feel easy thinking about Poppa. But you all being up in the mountains really got me worried so I made myself think about those rocks.' She sighed. 'It was like I was fighting with Momma to get the key to my memory. As soon as I thought about the rocks I started to get sleepy, and if I didn't get sleepy I was fancying something to eat. Gee! You wouldn't believe what she did to stop me thinking about those days.' She laughed. 'She got me hunting in the freezer for the craziest things. But then I got really mad because it was so important to me and I started crying and cussin' her for all her trickery.'

'You make it sound as if your mother was beside you?'

She nodded emphatically. 'She was there alright.'

'But wasn't all this happening in your imagination?'

'That's right, but Momma was making it happen.'

Chance was puzzled.

'But how, I mean ... is your mother still alive?'

She shared a glance with Philip.

'Shall I tell them about Momma Honey?'

'I think you should' he murmured.

She looked doubtful but continued.

'Once I knew who Momma was I got permission to move Poppa into her tomb. Deep down I always knew she loved him but I worried over it in case I'd done the wrong thing. Poppa's bones would have been scattered all over the cemetery if Momma didn't want him there.'

She paused while Chance tried not to register disbelief.

'You see,' she explained. 'Momma was Maria Hoodoo.'

'You mean 'Hoodoo the Voodoo'!' exclaimed Chance. 'She was often referenced during my Comparative Beliefs studies at Wissell.'

'Could be, folks with all kinds of troubles came miles to see her and she had a reputation for curing them. That was all kept from me, but it got mighty noisy some nights with all the chantings and dancing going on.'

'She must have had a powerful influence on you?'

'You can bet on it!' Mirabelle spoke with feeling. 'But I'm closer to her now, what with Poppa being with her and Philip and everything.'

'But you were saying how you found us?' continued Chance.

'It was strange.' Mirabelle slowly shook her head. 'I got so mad with her, considering all the money and work I'd spent re-uniting her with Poppa, and her still keeping a lock on my childhood memories.'

She became thoughtful.

Maybe she's matured. After all the crying and the bad names I was calling her I got the feeling she was changing her mind because this beautiful rainbow came into my head and I was in the mountains. Everything was so clear like she was giving me a movie show. Soon I was looking down on the rocks from high up. Then she turned on the sound 'cos I could hear wind and some wheezing underneath me. It was then I knew that Poppa must have taken me on those mountains when I was very young and I was looking down on everything because he was carryin' me on his shoulders. I must have been asleep at times, because the walk came to me in snatches. There was a log cabin and steps cut into rock. But most of all I remember being in a big cave with an old guy who was always chiselling. I don't know how long we stayed with him, maybe days, maybe weeks, but I know I was happy. He was a lovely old guy and I think he liked me being there, but some of the faces he had chiselled were so real they frightened me. He must have noticed because he led me to Poppa who sat me on his knee and played such a beautiful tune that I wanted it to go on forever.'

'Astonishing!' declared Chance. 'But you must have been very worried to drive so far to reach us. I mean… well, it must have been more than just a vague concern for Philips safety?'

She shook her head. 'Not vague Chance. Philip came here two years back remember? He knew more about Poppa than I ever did, but most of all he wanted to play Poppa's kind of music. Even then I had a feeling that he wasn't right for it, but I never saw such determination in a man. Nothing I could say was going to stop him.'

'Was that really such a surprise Mirabelle?'

She smiled thoughtfully. 'I guess not. But he's mine now.' She turned to Philip with a glance that contained enough castigation to erase further obstinacy for a long time. She continued. 'When he came back here with you guys I couldn't figure how he had gotten into such bad shape, and then he told me he was going to the Smoky Mountains and that started me fretting. I just knew he was headed for a big let down and it might be too much for him. That's why I had to remember what was in those mountains.' She half turned to Philip. 'Once Momma had given me my memory back I knew why I was so worried. The old guy had chiselled a clarinet player on the cave wall and it sure wasn't Philip.'

She caressed Philip's forehead. 'I'm sorry Honey. I didn't want you to find it out like that.'

'You did try to warn me my dearest.' he whispered.

Chance wasn't entirely satisfied.

'I'm still puzzled about the beautiful tune your father played to you. Was it 'Le Rag Galactique'?'

'Yes.' She fiddled uncomfortably with her coffee spoon.

'But how, after all these years, could you have known it had been written down. Blue Gums was a genius at improvisation, he could have made up any number of beautiful tunes on the spot.'

'I didn't know what it was called, but I knew Poppa could never have made it up.' She became visibly ill at ease.

'Why not?'

'I was hoping you wouldn't ask that Chance.'

'I'm sorry, it's just that...'

She raised a hand to stop him. 'No, you should know. It'll have to come out sooner or later.' She glanced warily at Philip. 'You see I knew Poppa couldn't have made it up because... well... I liked it too much.'

Astonishment lapped over Philips face. 'You liked it too much?'

'I'm sorry Honey,' she looked straight at him. 'But truthfully I never did care overmuch for Poppa's playing. He always sounded kind'a ragged to me.'

'Kind'a ragged. Yip Yip! Blue Gums sure was ragged!' chirruped Dr Isiah.

She became apologetic.

'I was hoping to break it to you gently but I can't help it, it's just the way I feel.'

Dr Isiah danced around with the coffee pot.

'Can't help it! Can't help it! Just way she feels!'

'I hope it won't make any difference to us?'

Philip stared at something distant. 'Well, my dearest,' he whispered at last. 'It hurts of course, but with time I may learn to live with it.'

She squashed his face in her hands and searched for any doubt.

'Are you sure?'

He managed to kiss her fingertips. 'Perhaps you will allow me to play your father's recordings in the privacy of my room?'

'Hmm…' her reply contained a trace of flirtatiousness. 'Maybe, but you won't be private for long.'

'Oh how lovely!' Beth clapped her hands together. 'I just know you'll be really happy together.'

Dan nudged her. 'Don't jump to conclusions woman.'

Mirabelle dipped her eyes coyly. 'I guess you're entitled to jump to conclusions. If we don't tell you now, you'll soon be wondering why Philip's not on the plane out.' Her eyes shone as she gazed down at Philip. 'You tell them Honey.'

He risked a smile and announced their engagement.

'I suppose I've taken him from you.' she added. 'But one way or another we'll be in touch.'

Chance was the first to offer his congratulations, followed by Dan and Beth who also revealed their intention to marry.

'It will be my second time round Ducks,' confided Beth. 'But I'll give him a good run for his money.'

Dan whispered something in Mirabelle's ear and her laughter tinkled round the courtyard. 'Gee Dan that's really funny. I never thought it would end like that.'

He grinned. 'I'll save the one about the Hippopotamus and the chest of drawers until we see you in Isby.'

Lutz stepped forward.

'And I am wishing you happiness forever and a day. I also am to marry the girl I was loving before losing my hair.' He patted the thickening fuzz on his head.

With no matrimonial plans of his own, Pimple compared his future with those around and concluded that he didn't have a great deal to look forward to. Feeling very much the odd man out, he went to Philip.

'All the best Philip, I hope it works out alright.'

'I'm sure it will.' Philip croaked his gratitude. 'Your rendition of 'Le Rag Galactique' gave me something to live for, so thank you.'

Mirabelle drew him to one side.

'I will never forget you Pimple, so be sure to let me know what's happening to you back home.'

'I'm not much good at writing.'

'Then phone or mail me.' It was a command.

Then she was holding him at arms length once again.

'I need to know how life is treating you. Promise you'll let me know if anything goes wrong.' She searched for signs of reluctance. 'Do you promise?'

He nodded.

'I want to hear you say it.' He detected a trace of impatience in her voice.

'I promise,' he said quickly.

'Just one more thing.' She came in closer. 'In the end everything is going to turn out just fine. You need to believe that OK?' She gave him one last hug and led him over to the other side of the courtyard to the Pontomatic where Dave was handing out airline tickets to everyone as they took their seats. Pimple joined him in the front, and after saying her final goodbye's Mirabelle spoke to him through the open window: 'Now remember it's all going to turn out just fine.'

Dave backed the Pontomatic along the narrow alleyway towards Dr Isiah who waved them on with the authority of a traffic policeman. They moved away quickly, and Mirabelle's waved kisses were soon blocked by the intervening traffic. Gradually the decorative wrought iron balconies and historic buildings of old New Orleans gave way to glassy towers and office blocks and they were on the road back to New Orleans Airport.

He waited for Dave to overtake a line of trucks and spoke flatly to the windscreen.

'Well, that's that I reckon.'

'Aye.'

'Have you got any plans?'

'Plans are tricky things right now.'

They arrived at the airport and Dave helped Beth with her luggage.

'I might as well go home,' continued Pimple. He spoke without relish.

'Home is where the heart is.' observed Dave unhelpfully.

'Will you be catching the next plane back then?'

'You never know.'

Dave placed Beth's suitcase onto the baggage weighing platform then added:

'Industrial Cup League semi-finals at the club this Friday. Fancy a few arrers with the production shop?'

The proposition dropped heavily onto his sagging spirits. Darts at the social club. Had it all come back to that?

'I'm not good enough for the league,' he said.

'Well now.' Dave produced his fixtures book from the inside pocket of his suit 'How about the beer leg? Sunday lunchtime, at the Green Queen, Southness.'

He couldn't work up much enthusiasm, but the alternative was listening to Gardeners Forum with his mum and dad.

'Alright.'

Dave added his name to the list.

'The coach leaves the club at ten thirty.'

'Will you be there?'

Dave walked backwards a few steps.

'Maybe…but tomorrow's another day.'

He checked in at the airline desk and joined the others at security control where he removed his trainers and placed them and his cabin bag onto the conveyer. His bag was moved to another table overseen by a large official.

'Open your hand baggage please sir.'

He unzipped his cabin bag and pulled the top apart to reveal the trumpet case inside.

'What's in the case sir?'

'A trumpet.'

A U.S customs official narrowed his eyes and stepped forward. 'OK it's a trumpet. So let's see the trumpet can we?' Pimple removed the case from his cabin bag and opened the lid. The customs official carefully examined the Brash then consulted a visual display screen on the counter.

'You got a permit for this?'

'No?' Trouble seemed to be brewing.

'No permit Huh?'

'Didn't think I needed one.'

'You need a permit for antiques. Where did you get it - Royal Street?'

'It's mine, I play it.'

The customs official placed two beefy hands on the table and leaned forward over the Brash.

'So you play it. Where did you get it?'

He hesitated. He didn't want to say he had found it.

Another bag arrived on the table. The customs official slid the Brash a few feet along the counter and spoke to his colleague. 'See to the other passengers. This might take time.' He palmed Pimple along the counter until they were face to face again.

'So where did you get it?'

'I've had it a long time.'

Chance intervened.

'Excuse me officer, but I can vouch for this person. He's a musician in our band and we are returning from an appearance here in New Orleans. This is the instrument he brought with him from England.'

The customs official flicked his eyes over Chance as if he didn't matter very much, then returned to Pimple.

'Maybe you ain't heard of a Brash before.' he continued. 'Playin' one you wouldn't know I guess - anymore than Stradivarius ain't heard of violins.'

'That's right.' Pimple wasn't sure what he meant.

The customs official pushed his cap back and became less formal.

'Bud, there were ten of these made. The Museum of Musical Heritage traced nine; never did find the tenth, so where did you get this one?'

'I found it.' The question could no longer be avoided.

'Where?'

'On a chimney.'

'Yeah, where else?'Excuse me for being so dumb Bud, an English chimney was it?'

'That's right,' agreed Pimple.

'Fine, just fine…' The customs official pointed to a door marked 'US Customs and Excise'. 'Let's talk trumpets in that little room over there shall we?'

'Just one moment officer.' Chance intervened for a second time. 'I can provide proof that this instrument was in this person's possession before we left London.' Unzipping his cabin bag he produced a copy of 'Back to Earth' and placing it on the counter pointed to the photograph of Pimple holding the Brash. 'Surely this proves that the instrument he is holding is the same as the one you have before you?'

The customs official looked at the CD cover, then at the Brash, then at Pimple.

'OK Brash on an English chimney it is.' He placed the Brash in its case and slid it back to Pimple. 'You know what? Gee I'm tired.' He drew a hand over his eyes. 'I never was too sure about my vocation, maybe I need some career counselling. Have a nice day.'

Pimple thanked Chance for his timely help.

'It was lucky I had some spare copies in my trombone case before donating my trombone to the Heritage Foundation. I wanted something to remind me of the band and all the experiences we have shared.

'It's not going to be much of a band without you,'

'It's generous of you to say so, but I've always held doubts about my position with the New Magnolians. What we saw in the cave simply confirmed my suspicions.'

'It wasn't too bad.'

'Not good enough to convince me. I would feel like an impostor if I remained with the band.'

'Well, I reckon it was a pity we went to the mountains.'

'Perhaps, but we did go. So we can't continue as before.'

They boarded the plane and found their seats. Pimple fastened his safety belt, and once again considered the future. It looked grim. They had gone to America as a band and had come back as a trio. He couldn't even be sure that Dan and Beth wanted to continue. They would be too busy planning their wedding to think of much else, and if Dan moved in with Beth they wouldn't want a lodger. Still, with no band left, he wouldn't be needed in Isby anyway.

A flight attendant offered him a selection of boiled sweets.

'Candy Honey?' She mimicked his gloomy expression. 'But why so sad?' She leaned across to him and smiled. 'Now remember. Everything's going to turn out just fine.' He smiled back. That's exactly what Mirabelle had said, so maybe everything would turn out fine.

The airliner swung onto the runway, and with no more ado the engines went to full bore, and within seconds they were speeding over Lake Pontchartrain. Successful take off music filled the passenger cabin and the reassuring voice of the pilot announced their flight plan.

'Captain Foster welcoming you aboard flight NOR 389. We'll be cruising at an altitude of thirty thousand feet and should be arriving at London Heathrow by twenty hours local time. Say, that's really sumpthin' isn't it? Think about it folks. We'll be travellin' higher than Everest at nearly six hundred miles an hour and you still get there in one piece.'

He wondered what to do when he arrived home.

There was plenty to tell his mum and dad, but Bleak Leigh held no appeal whatsoever, and Crantree was best avoided on weekends. The beer leg in Southness would take care of Sunday, but that wasn't much to look forward to either. After that he could only wait for something to happen.

Adjusting his seat to the full reclining position he listened to 'Mississippi Moan' with strings and tried to cheer himself up. Mr Tranmere might even be waiting for him to record another album with the new trombonist and chubby clarinet player. But the words of the old lady at Isby station once again flitted uncomfortably into his thoughts: *'They never did get it right. Blue Gums and Dorji I mean.'* And after all, she did have a book full of autographs to prove it.

24.<u>Home.</u>

His father closed the lounge window to muffle the rattle of the neighbours' ancient lawn mower.

'It's about time Stan Bones bought a new mower. He's been on shifts since January so he should be able to afford one.'

Having demonstrated some force of character about local events, Mr Pimple returned to his armchair feeling better able to consider the more worldly experiences of his son.

'So one way and another you had a good do son?'

'Yes it was alright, but there won't be much of a band left when I get back to Isby.'

'Tricky things bands. You can't rely on bands for a living. You need something more solid than bands when you settle down.'

'I don't want to settle down.'

'Maybe not now, but it's best to prepare for it. Computers are the things these days. You used a computer when you were at Rilltots didn't you?'

'Yes but that was only for checking up on stocks.'

'It's a start.'

'But I'm not interested in computers.'

His father sank further into the armchair and crossed one leg over the other.

'I wasn't interested in manufacturing at first but I soon got used to it. When I started at Shore & Toop we got seventeen pounds a week for filing the mould marks off castings, and in those days a week meant Saturday mornings as well. Not that filing did me any harm. If everyone knew how use a file there wouldn't be so much dodgy work about. You did filing at the Foundation didn't you?'

'Yes, but I like playing the trumpet dad.'

His mum came in from the kitchen.

'And you play it very well dear.' She put the tea things on the table he had made for his design and technology coursework at Pin Lane High. 'Vi and Rod really enjoyed your CD.'

'Not much good if he hasn't got a band to play with.' His father levelled the tray with a coaster.

'There must be lots of bands who want to play with him.' His mother poured the tea. 'Anyway, Rod said he's good enough to play on his own.'

'A trumpet doesn't sound very good on its own mum.'

'Oh I don't know 'Marine Green' would sound lovely on the trumpet.'

'But they used a string orchestra for that mum.'

'I know that Dear,' said his mother irritably. 'Sometimes you don't listen do you? I only said it would sound nice on a trumpet.'

'You mean a trumpet with a string orchestra mum?'

'Well, that would be up to you wouldn't it?'

He reached for his tea. Like his father he knew the warning signs and decided it would be best not to pursue his mother's reasoning further.

'When will you know about the band then?'

'I'll phone Mr Tranmere on Monday.'

His parents exchanged concerned glances.

'Did you say Tranmere son?'

'Yes, he's my boss.' He sensed something was amiss.

His father shook his head.

'You won't son. Not if he's the Mr Tranmere we read about in the paper.' He reached into the paper rack and passed over the 'Gazette'.

'COMPANY EXECUTIVE FOUND DEAD ON CHIMNEY'

The stark headline jumped out above a recent photograph of Mr Tranmere. The report was brief and to the point:

'A senior Lake & Rilltot executive, D H Tranmere was found dead on the company's central chimney stack in the early hours of Tuesday morning. Night security staff were alerted by a telephone call from Mr Tranmere's wife and immediately carried out a search. Mr Tranmere's body was found beside an astronomical telescope which had been installed on the chimney for use by the L&R Astronomical Society of which he was a founding member.

'Harry' Tranmere, as he was affectionately known to his friends and colleagues, had a distinguished army career and on completion of service joined Lake & Rilltot as a junior production under manager. An early advocate of environmental protection, he pioneered the cold press method of window

*fabrication which reduced production costs and placed Lake &
Rilltot well ahead of their competitors. Well before the present
housing expansion he saw the need for smaller production and
distributive centres away from the parent company.*

*A colourful and sometimes controversial character, his desire
to encourage greater appreciation of music and arts in the
workplace led to the award winning L&R Welding Shop String
Ensemble, and the L&R Dramatic Society.*

*Expressing regret at the loss of such a remarkable executive,
a company spokesperson said that while death appeared to stem
from natural causes, a thorough investigation was being
conducted.*

*Footnote: The L&R Chimney has long been the object of local
debate. Adapted for use in the original smelter plant, it is the
tallest brick structure in Eastern England but was made
obsolescent by the cold forming process introduced by D H
Tranmere. Regarded by some as an eyesore and navigation
hazard, and by others as a distinctive local landmark, it is being
considered for preservation as an industrial monument. The
small observatory and lift to the top was recently commissioned
and financed by DH Tranmere, and the spokesperson said that
the facility would be maintained as a tribute to him.*

Pimple stared numbly at the page until the first shock of the
report subsided.

'Bad news is it son?'

He nodded and stared at the photo. Mr Tranmere smiled
confidently over a full moustache. It was a recent picture.

'Did you know him very well dear?' asked his mum.

'Yes, he was alright.'

He thought back to his meetings with Mr Tranmere. He didn't
always understand what was said, but those meetings made him
feel as if he was important. He would have never played the
trumpet had it not been for Mr Tranmere, and he certainly
wouldn't have had the chance to be a celebrity. Admittedly he
wasn't much of a celebrity now, but Mr Tranmere could hardly
be blamed for that.

He wondered if Dave and the others had received the dreadful
news. Mr Tranmere had made it very clear he didn't want the
directors to know about Chimney Studios, so there would be big
trouble when they found out.

'What are you going to do now son?'

'I'll try to find out what's happening at Isby.'

'Such a shame,' his mother removed the tea things. 'Only last month that nice Mr Davies across the road was taken away before his time.'

'Aye,' his father placed the coaster on the mantle piece with an air of finality. 'But there's not much we can do about it. Nobody is indispensable. So my advice to you son is to start thinking about the future.'

Sunday came, and any lingering hope of fame and fortune was firmly squashed during his phone conversation with Chance.

Chance knew something was amiss when he arrived home to a recorded message from Jack Benson. It seems that three Bentleys' had arrived unannounced at the studios, and after quickly handing over to an assistant, Jack gave himself a few days leave and escaped through the fire doors.

Chance didn't think there was much to worry about, apart from a possibility they might all be charged with conspiring against Rilltots. So just to be sure he had arranged an appointment with his solicitor and would let everyone know the position as soon as possible.

How could things get any worse? Not only had his musical career taken a nosedive, he might even end up in jail.

He wheeled his bike down the garden path and onto the roadway. The waste patch of land at the bottom of the short drive now housed a row of lock up garages, and beyond them on the other side of the junction to Crantree road, yellow construction machinery had gobbled up the copse which once backed onto the playground of the primary school. Piles of topsoil dotted the skimmed land well into the distant outskirts of Crantree, and Haspalls orchard was now a village of portable cabins.

Pedalling up the slow incline from the church and the war memorial, he passed more construction machinery and a vast patchwork of stark concrete foundations confronting the narrow gardens of the old thirties terraces fronting Waterworks Lane.

He dismounted alongside a chain link fence which curved round the site in a huge semi-circle. Crantree Foundation was no more, and further into the valley towards Bleak Leigh, it was clear that Cowgrass Estate had grown vigorously while he was away. Having swallowed up the allotments, it was now creeping over Radcliff's field and behind Godfrey Smiths cottage in a pincer movement to join up with the new site. Constructed with shiny red bricks the new houses glared at their surroundings and proclaimed bellicose privacy to their neighbours over low fences.

It was a depressing scene, and turning his back on it, he pedalled alongside another recent development until the top of Rilltot's chimney rose above a uniform line of new roofs.

He began to have doubts about going to the darts match. For some reason he hadn't fancied a beer since leaving New Orleans, and swallowing pints of 'Belchards' with Red Ears and The Machine Shop Supervisor now held little appeal.

More thoughts bothered him.

It would be even less fun if the Bottom Pincher and her friend were there, besides which, Dave wouldn't be around if he had any sense. By now he must know he was up to his neck in trouble, so he was probably miles away as well.

A uniform line of new terraced houses at the base of Spring Hill displayed equally uniform lines of Vistavacs, so Rilltot was doing good business. It would be a waste of time applying for his old job at Receipt and Despatch though. Even if he did escape the law the directors would make sure he never stepped inside Rilltots again.

He summarized his position. The band had gone, Tranmere had gone, Dave had probably gone, and he was out of a job with a good chance of ending up in jail. Just to make matters worse he didn't fancy drinking beer or playing darts. So what was the point of going any further?

Freewheeling past a new sports centre he gradually came to a halt and gazed abstractedly at the chimney. From the top a faint glimmer spanned the distance between them. It was a reflection from the observatory built by Mr Tranmere, and even from that distance he could see it was a hexagonal construction of eight by four 'Tri-seals' capped with a 'Rilldome'. He recalled what Mr Tranmere had revealed to him during their very first meeting. He had said: *'I will soon have Access to a spot where I can disregard the enormity of human affairs and ponder the majesty of nature.'* He had also said: *'Only my closest acquaintances will know of it, but one day I hope to share it with you.'* ...Well, it was a bit late for that.

He continued to stare at the observatory. Hazy at first, the reflection brightened as the sun broke through and it was soon waxing and waning in giant imitation of the glitter he had first seen on the Isby chimney. It was that glitter which had led him to the 'Brash'. So was it just possible that this chimney was telling him something as well? The sun warmed the back of his neck and the reflection intensified to a sustained sparkle. It would probably lead to nothing but he changed to the lowest gear and headed for Spring Hill and the social centre.

Chaining his bike to a rusting stack of inward openers, he entered an elderly coach parked by the iron walkway where he first heard Dead Loss Blues after his graceless exit from the centre. A few passengers were already on board, and just inside on the front seat, Red Ears was nursing a list and a cash box. He studied Pimple intensely and his list intently.

'You'll be third reserve lad and I'll have five pounds and fifty pence from you now.'

He paid up, and took one of the raised seats straddling the rear wheel arches so he could see in advance who would be entering the coach.

He nodded to the Galvanising Plant Supervisor, and then to the Welding Shop Charge Hand as they went to their seats. Both of them had spent tea breaks in Receipt and Despatch when he was there, but they showed no signs of recognising him. Other familiar faces came onto the coach, and he smiled now and then in the hope that someone would acknowledge him, but no one did. Perhaps his burst of fame had made him too exclusive for them to cope with and they had to make him a stranger in their midst. It was either that, or work and darts excluded all else.

Loud giggling disturbed the air above the coach and he saw with dismay that the Bottom Pincher and her friend were descending the walkway. They entered the coach and looked demandingly at Red Ears.

'We're guests,' announced the Pincher.

'Can't see any guests on this list,' said Red Ears.

'We're special guests,' said the Pinchers friend.

'Then you pay the special guest price. That's five pounds and fifty pence I'll be having from you both.'

'We ain't playin' darts,' said the Pincher.

'You're right enough there,' said Red Ears. 'Not on the beer leg you're not.' He shook the cash box uncompromisingly.

'Say it's a beauty tax Larry!' shouted one of the passengers. 'You'll get double!' He laughed loudly.

The Pincher's friend sneered down the coach.

'He owes you then don't he?'

They paid up, and passing Pimple with pointed looks of non-recognition flopped noisily onto the back seat. Moments later the Machine Shop Supervisor elbowed his way down the aisle to join them.

'I didn't see your name on that seat Len Beggs?' challenged the Pincher.

'Nor did I,' said the Pinchers friend.

'Now now,' chided the Machine Shop Supervisor. 'Uncle Len only wants to be close to his little darlings.'

The Pincher spoke to her friend. 'Hear that Diane? We're his little darlings this morning.'

'We ain't when he's shopping with his missus.'

'You're right there Gloria,' said the Pinchers friend. 'He don't want to know us then do he?'

'No he don't - and I only waved,' said the Pincher.

'Didn't know he could move so fast?' said the Pinchers friend. 'Funny watching him trying to run with the trolley weren't it?'

'Yeah right past the booze rack. His missus didn't half look surprised.'

They laughed raucously.

'Didn't want you to get jealous of the competition,' explained the Machine Shop Supervisor.

'We weren't.' said the Pincher.

Some tinkly buzzing sounds and tuneless humming suggested that earphones were in use. Added to this was the familiar hiss of bottles being un-capped.

'Watch him Gloria!' warned the Pinchers friend. 'He don't treat us to 'Baby Sparkly' for nothing.'

Pimple looked fixedly through the window, but heads had turned and amused faces were looking rearward in anticipation of more drama at the back. His seat shook violently as the Machine Shop Supervisor went into action.

'You Gerr-off Len Beggs!' shrieked the Pincher. 'I'm havin' none of that on a Sunday morning!'

'Now hold you hard Len!' shouted the Welding Shop Chargehand. 'We'll be wantin' some straight arrers from you.'

'Then lets get going before I'm overcome with passion!' roared the Machine Shop Supervisor.

'Gruesome!' said the Pincher. 'He'd burst!'

'Horrible,' agreed her friend, 'just like a boil.'

Red Ears leaned gravely over to the driver, and without Dave Moss or even a mention of him, the coach pulled out of the yard and started down Spring Hill.

It was a harrowing journey. The Machine Shop Supervisor broke into a loud rendition of 'My Way' and mixed with the banter and giggling there had been whispers. Pimple could feel a knee pressing persistently into the back of his seat, and every so often fluttering movements reflected in the window convinced him that fingers were being waggled above his head in imitation of trumpet playing.

He decided to avoid the darts match well before the coach had discharged its rowdy cargo onto the forecourt of the 'Green Queen', and stooping on the pretext that he had to tie a shoelace, waited until they were safely inside before walking to the seafront.

Southness was already making preparations for the holiday season. Shop fronts were being painted and a handful determined swimmers were noisily testing themselves in the North Sea. He stopped before a poster advertising a variety extravaganza at the Pier Pavilion. 'Novelty Quizmaster' Lenny-Le-Strange was grinning frantically beside his 'Finger of Fame' near the bottom of the billing.

'Isby must have done that to him,' thought Pimple. 'But at least he's still surviving, which is more than I am.'

Further along, a banner announced the appearance of Crabapple at the Maharaja's Palace. 'Only a Premier Venue could bring you Britain's Premier Band!' it proclaimed.

Crossing over to a kiosk on the seaward side of the promenade he bought a hot dog and continued past the boating lake. Had he glanced sideways he might have seen the Pinchers friend ducking behind an array of defaced life belts, and had he glanced rearwards he might have seen the Pincher darting furtively ahead to join her friend where they waited until he drew level with the entrance to Funlands.

'I suppose that's where it all started.' he reasoned, and stopping at the entrance arch wondered if Madam Zelda could still be in business. From behind the perimeter wall the shrieks of patrons mingled with blaring music, and just inside the arch the giant rabbit flicked its ears, and for a second time invited him to enter.

'I might as well see if she's still there.' he thought.

Avoiding a party of beer drinking youths, he arrived roughly where his first hot dog had been flattened beneath the sole of an assailant's shoe.

The nightmarish atmosphere of the event returned, and his desire to be isolated from the rest of humankind was re-kindled by a hard faced family chewing open mouthed as they came towards him from the House of Horrors. It was as if he had never quite escaped from a grotesque video game, and having just failed to achieve the winning level was now back to square one as a loser.

A grey sea mist rolled in, making the amusements look grubby and rundown. Flaky paint and some misfiring neon tubes cast doubt over the reliability of the Super Space Destroyer Missile, and just two slowly moving cars could be seen beyond the missing fence panels of the Killer Car race track. He took the track that Madame Zelda had first led him along to: 'Begat patched up.' Plastic wrappers and paper cups still littered the ailing grass behind the windowless bulk of The House of Horrors and the thud - thud of hard rock still mingled with the rumble of generators.

It seemed an unlikely location for a fortune teller to set up shop. But this was the spot, and the short gravel path now led to a brownish circle of weeds where Madame Zelda's tent once stood. In its place a laminated notice displayed a web address and a brief note informing clients that Madame Zelda could only deal with urgent consultations.

Finding room for just one more twinge of disappointment, he spoke to the notice: 'Well, I suppose you got the first bit right, but you're not doing very well now.' Mirabelle hadn't done so well either. *'Remember,'* she'd promised, *'everything will turn out just fine. OK?'*

He jumped.

Her words echoed in his head with such startling clarity that he had to untangle them from the real voice close by.

'Do you still think she's an old fake?' The voice was brushed by a faint American twang, yet it was unmistakable. He didn't have to turn round to know who was beside him.

'Rose!' He grappled with amazement and expectation so soon after despondency. 'How did you get here?'

She pressed a forefinger against his lips then quickly removed it and clasped both hands behind her back. 'Don't say a thing; I just want to look at you for a moment.' She looked, but as she looked, her confidence ebbed away. Averting her gaze downward she said: 'There! I knew I wouldn't be able to face you.'

'Why?' He knew perfectly well why, but had nothing to say in its place - after all what could he say?'

'Because I was horrid to you, really horrid... I'm so ashamed.'

He knew she should be ashamed, and he wanted her to be ashamed, but didn't want to say anything that might cause her to leave.

'There's no need to be.'

'Yes there is! I just went off with Barney without saying a word to you...how mean was that?'

He avoided the question. 'Well, it hurt for a bit.' Then he became angry with himself for not having the words to say how much it hurt, but she gave him the opportunity.

'Did it hurt much?' She asked the question as if it really mattered.

'It did for a bit, but then I started to play the trumpet.'

She seemed somehow to grasp the connection between lost love and trumpet playing. 'I know how you felt. It was just the same with me, except I deserved what I got.' She appeared self-contained in her misfortune.

'What went wrong?'

'Life didn't work out very well for me in America.'

'That's a shame.' He tried to sound sympathetic.

She shrugged and said flatly: 'Barney left me.'

'I'm sorry about that.' He smothered a spark of elation.

'He met a women pilot called Gail and lost interest in me.'

'What was she like?'

'She was clever and knew all about technical things on aeroplanes.' Rose bowed a leg and scraped the ground with the side of a shoe. 'Compared with me she had a lot going for her I suppose.'

'Did he leave you after that?'

'Not straightaway. He told me that he needed Gail to help him with a new idea they were working on. I believed him at first because the company was in trouble.'

'It was an aeroplane company wasn't it?'

'It wasn't much of a company, just Barney and another man making special hinges for airliner seats. It was only a workshop. Anyway, he went away with Gail after telling me they were going to buy some new machinery, and that was that. I never saw him again.'

'What did you do?'

'I couldn't do anything.' She grimaced. 'And then the Rental Agent came round demanding all the rent we owed.'

'It wasn't his house then?'

'It was worse than that. I had to sign all sorts of documents and papers when I arrived and he must have got me to sign something which made me liable for the rent. There was nothing I could do. I just had to pay up.'

'Is that when you came home?'

'No.' She shook her head vigorously. 'I couldn't go home without trying to sort things out for myself. Mum and Dad were horrified when I told them I was marrying Barney. We had terrible rows about it.'

'Did they know about me?'

'Yes, they said how deceitful I had been, and how cowardly I was for not having enough courage to tell you.' She scraped the other shoe on the ground. 'They were quite right, but they kept on and on, and that made me dig my heels in. I hated Bleak Leigh and finding excitement and adventure was more important to me than anything else, so when you said you loved me I didn't know what to do.'

'Did you know Barney then?'

'Yes.' She looked straight at him. 'But I wish I hadn't. I thought I loved him, but that was all wrapped up with the excitement of going to Los Angeles.'

She grinned ironically.

'That was a big let-down as well. Los Angeles goes on for miles in all directions and our place was on a busy freeway between a garage and a warehouse car park.'

'Didn't you have a swimming pool?'

'No one had swimming pools where we were.'

She thought for a moment.

'I suppose Gail gave him the chance of a better life. I was so angry at what he'd done to me, but deep down I didn't miss him that much.'

'Are you still married?'

'No, I found really cheap lodgings and worked in a superstore until I could afford a lawyer. The divorce cost me all the money I had and their lawyer arranged it so that Barney didn't have to pay much at all.'

'Is that when you came home?'

'I couldn't face Mum and Dad. The flight would have cost too much anyway, so I carried on working at the superstore.' Her brow crinkled but she stopped short of crying. 'Los Angeles is a dreadful place when you're lonely with no money. But then a strange thing happened.' She paused to be sure she had gained his attention. 'I heard a scratchy old recording being played over the music system one day. I'd never heard anything like it before and wanted it to go on and on. I just couldn't forget it.'

'That's just what happened to me!'

'I know it did.' She threw him one of her knowing looks. 'Mr Moss told me.'

'Dave Moss! How did you meet Dave Moss?'

'He met me, after I had finished with Buck Milligan's band.'

'But 'Buck Milligan' played in New Orleans!'

'Yes I know - but will you let me finish please?' Some of her old assertiveness returned. '…There wasn't a singer on the recording, but it made me want to sing so much that I just had to try. I listened to recordings of old bands and found I could remember the tunes and words by just hearing them once. I just knew I could sing with any band playing that sort of music. Then I found the Veterans Hall web site at an internet café.

'You went to the Veterans Hall?'

'Yes, the musicians were ancient but they let me join in. I wasn't a bit nervous.

'Was Dave Moss there?'

'I met him later, but a lady told me that Buck Milligan was playing the following night, and he was looking for a singer.'

'I bet it was Mirabelle?'

Rose nodded.

'She introduced me to Buck and I sang 'Bayou Night' with his band before they opened the doors to the public. She was really good to me.'

He wondered aloud. 'That's a difficult tune.'

'Maybe, I just like it'

Rose sang quietly:

Bayou Night, stars so bright, just me here, don't feel right.
Went away yesterday, didn't know what to say,
Feel so blue, feel so bad, only love I ever had.
Wouldn't say what was wrong, took a train - now love's gone
No one here but me alone, bayou night goes on an' on.

The phrasing was perfect and she sang with resignation - exactly as the song demanded. 'Bayou Night' was known to be difficult; not many bands played it. Even he found it hard to hit the right notes with certainty. No doubt about it, Rose could really sing.

Her eyebrows knitted together again and this time she did cry. He moved to praise and console her but she stopped him. 'No I don't deserve it! I really don't! I'll be alright soon.'

The inferred violence of a current re-mix seeped through the walls of the House of Horrors and intruded into the moment:

'OOOh! OOOh! ya Mista fista ya ya ya wishta hitya wista fista!'

She blew her nose loudly.

'We travelled all over the states. It was exciting going from place to place and the money was good, but things started to go wrong. Buck couldn't stop drinking and one night he became so ill that we had to rush him to hospital. We used different trumpet players for a while, but it didn't work out and the band broke up.'

'When did that happen?'

'About a week ago. We were playing in Shreveport when Mirabelle phoned and asked me to fly over to meet someone who wanted me to join a British band.'

'But we were there then?'

'I know, but you'd just gone to the Smoky Mountains for some reason.'

Something occurred to her. 'I wonder how Mirabelle knew I was in Shreveport.'

'Mirabelle's like that.'

'Hmmm.' Rose thought for a moment. 'She was wonderful to me but I wouldn't like to get in her bad books. Anyway, I met Mr Moss who played your CD and asked me to join the New Magnolians.' She looked down again and spoke softly. 'Your playing is awesome.'

He reddened with pleasure.

'Thanks, but how did you get here?'

'I flew over yesterday and took a train from London this morning in time to meet Mr Moss at the Maharaja's Palace.'

'So he's here as well?'

'Yes, otherwise I couldn't have met him could I?' She gave him her 'eyes revolving skywards' look. 'He wants to get the band together quickly to record a tune that would make the world a better place.' She considered this. 'I don't know if I should take Mr Moss seriously or not.'

His mind worked furiously. 'A tune that would make the world a better place'. 'Galactic Rag' was the only tune that could do that.

'What was the tune?'

'He didn't say'

'Who else was there?'

'The band of course, and they're all waiting for you.' She checked her watch and at once became distant. 'So you need to get there - lunch is at one-o-clock.'

'You're going as well aren't you?'

She shook her head. 'I didn't know you were in the band.'

'But you said you liked my playing?'

'Yes, but I didn't know it was you until just now. I can't sing in the same band as you.'

'Why not?'

'You know why not!' She almost shouted it, and the tears came again.

'I want you to be in the band.'

'You know I can't be in the band after what I did!'

Then there were lots of tears. 'Why can't you just be honest? You don't have to pretend anymore!' She snorted, and frantically searched her bag for a tissue.

'I am being honest and I'm not pretending.' He knew he was being quite dishonest and quite pretending.

'No you're not! Her voice filled with rebuke. You should be angry, really angry! Why aren't you angry? I want you to be angry!'

Nose streaming and eyes watering she looked reproachfully at him; trying to prize out some anger. 'Go on be angry - why can't you?'

'I'm not angry that's all!' - He was becoming angry.

'Why?'

'Because I thought everything was finished.'

'What do you mean? I don't understand.' She found a tissue.

He tried to summarize events up to the return from Dorji's cave, but did it badly.

'...So Philip stayed on with Mirabelle, then Chance dropped out because he wasn't on the cave wall. Dan and Beth said they were getting married, and Lutz said he going to back to his girlfriend in Bad Oman, so there wasn't much of a band left. Then I found out Mr Tranmere had died.'

The explanation took long enough for Rose to recover sufficiently to give him her lopsided look.

'It sounds very complicated to me.'

'It is.'

'Is that why you came here?'

'I wondered if Madame Zelda was still in business.'

They gazed at the circle of weeds in silence.

At last Rose said: 'Mr Moss sent me here when I told him I couldn't join the band. He said I should get an answer from the horse's mouth.' She grinned. 'I didn't think you'd be the horse.'

He spoke matter-of-factly but the words floated on hope.

'She said we would get together again.'

'You could never trust me.'

He thought carefully. Maybe he wouldn't be able to trust her but he'd just have to live with that.

'I haven't got much choice.' He squeezed her hand. 'There's no one else.'

A few seconds later she returned his squeeze, and they walked back alongside the 'Killer Car Racetrack' and the 'Super Space Destroyer Missile' towards the arch. A crowd was fanning out from an area near the rifle booths where three youths were shakily dusting themselves down, and headed by Stevie, the Carshalton Brotherhood of Old Rockers sauntered past.

'We're getting too old for this,' said one.

'Yeah, we'll give it a miss next year,' agreed Stevie. 'Better quit while we're ahead.'

All was quiet in the grand saloon of the Maharaja's Palace as everyone stood for one minute in silent remembrance of Mr Tranmere.

'He was a wonderful boss,' declared Mrs Humbleston. 'We owe it to him to succeed.' She clasped her hands together and appealed through closed eyes. 'Please please let this succeed!' Her plea was echoed by all in the room, and after further pause for reflection Dave Moss returned to his vantage point inside the bay window while the others resumed their seats round the large dining table.

Sitting beside Jack Benson and his wife, clarinet player Chubbs Waller resumed his account of how and why he had come to Isby.

It seems that he had heard Dead Loss Blues at the end of a tortured affair with a fellow student at the Grunton Academy of Music and immediately lost the desire to continue training as an orchestral musician. It was the New Magnolians version of Dead Loss Blues that had persuaded him to abandon his studies, and he moved to Isby in the hope that he might get a chance of joining the band as a 'stand in' clarinet player if ever the opportunity arose. He had tracked down the location of Chimney Studios from the 'Back to Earth' CD and after a brief spell as a shrink wrapper with Agriframe introduced himself to Jack Benson who took him on as a temporary studio assistant.

Jack Benson leaned over to Dan. 'The wife thought he needed mothering, so he stayed with us - came in handy for walking the dog.'

His wife glared at him. 'And showing those nice directors round the studios because you were too cowardly to meet them. Just to think of all the upset you caused!' She turned to the others. 'He'd reached Llandudno before we could tell him there was nothing to worry about.'

At the far corner of the table, with no idea what the conversation was about, the new trombonist was unknowingly mimicking his own likeness gazing into the blackness of Dorj's cave thousands of miles away. Unaccustomed to handshakes and friendly faces, he had been welcomed disbelievingly into an opulence he'd never experienced in a lifetime of parental indifference; care homes, and cold pavements.

He was still reflecting on how his tiny store of lucky stars could have crowded together so quickly after booking into a Salvation Army hostel for his quarterly bath and de-lousing. His first lucky star began to twinkle on hearing Dead Loss Blues from the caretaker's radio at just the time when the hostel band was selling off its old instruments. Casting aside all thoughts of Special Brew in the white heat of wanting to play music like that he approached the bandmaster in hope of acquiring a trombone.

Recognising a conversion when he saw it, the Bandmaster decided that this one was spiritual enough to warrant the exchange of an old trombone for some labour in the lavatory block. A few days later a suitably equipped and spruced up Owen Patch was able to venture into the streets with a mission and the means to start afresh.

This was a new beginning. Never again would humiliation and rock bottom self-esteem lead to another legless night in cardboard wrappers. For the first time in his life he could dare to hope for something better. A few days later, another lucky star twinkled above the entrance to Liverpool Street Station when Dave Moss arrived in an airport taxi to catch the train to Southness.

Dave's smart-phone snap of a busker playing 'Stomp On' beside the entrance steps was enough for Chance to confirm that he exactly matched the image in Dorji's Cave, and within minutes a startled Owen Patch had a draft contract and the fare to Southness.

Beside Owen, and also immersed in thought, was a much chastened Lutz.

It seemed that on his return events in Bad Oman had not turned out as he confidently expected. Even with hair and meticulous arrangements for a long and idyllic life together, it was made quite clear that he fell far short of Helga's expectations and was summarily rejected on their first meeting. He had been cruelly ditched, and although his parents sympathised, they said in unison 'We told you Helga was not the girl for you. But you wouldn't listen would you?'

He could have stayed with his parents while he searched for a job in Bad Oman, but it was an alarming prospect. They had made it quite clear that meticulous room cleaning and regular churchgoing would be mandatory conditions for a long stay, and one day of scrupulous tidiness had been more than enough for him to discount this as an option.

He was utterly miserable, but could see that Helga's rejection had removed the only barrier hampering his full commitment to the New Magnolians, and through the muddle of self pity and hurt pride he now understood how much he needed the band. Hands shaking, he phoned Jack Benson then slumped back with relief onto a pristine chaise lounge. Not only was the band intact but his position on banjo was still vacant, so he immediately booked a one way flight to Gatwick.

The flight from Bad Oman to Gatwick was occupied by profound soul searching, then ruthless self examination on the rail journey from Gatwick through to Southness. And so it was a contrite and matured Lutz who entered the Maharaja's Palace that morning to gratefully accept his place back into the band.

At last Dave lowered his binoculars.
'Has it worked?' The Pincher was tense with anticipation.
'Aye.'
'Are they holding hands?' enquired her friend.
'Aye,' he grinned. 'All's well that ends well.'
Everyone crowded to the window as Pimple and Rose walked towards the steps leading into the entrance foyer. Then the room

erupted into noisy celebration. At last, after so much hope; so many ups and downs; so much stargazing; planning and sadness, they now had a full team.

The Pincher and her friend jumped up and down punching the air shouting 'Yes! Yes!' and the Machine Shop Supervisor; Red Ears and Mrs Humbleston danced each other round and round in circles. Then it was tears; hugs; breathlessness and smiles all round. Perhaps now they really did have a chance to make the world a better place. Well… at least for a bit.

Dave walked through the celebrations to the grand staircase, and opening the Fixtures Book drew a double line under the list of players for the next beer leg. That was the last time he would be chasing around for a team. Larry would have to handle the beer legs from now on, and Len would have to take over the Industrial League. Anyway, it was about time they took on the hard graft, starting with that tight fisted landlord in the Freemasons Arms who never put on sandwiches.

No doubt about it, Tranmere had really lumbered him with the big one this time. He thought back to his rushed return trip across the Atlantic to attend the funeral. None of the great and the good had bothered to turn up, and the miserly get together in the pub afterwards had felt more like family relief than grief. But he'd shared plenty of nutty ventures with Tranmere, and more than anyone else owed him success in this one.

'We simply have to make the world a better place.' He had said after a particularly nasty incident had swamped world news. *'…and I am hopeful that with dedication and persistence we will discover the means to achieve it.'*

Dave thought about the world.

Africa was in a bit of a mess and no-one seemed to be having much fun in the Middle East. Come to that, Crantree wasn't exactly a bundle of laughs judging by most faces in the high street.

'Make the world a better place.'

OK…Just like that. He smiled ironically. After all, a good tune and a top lad on the trumpet should sort out the world in no time.

A shaft of coloured sunshine beamed down to him from a decorative skylight high up in the domed ceiling. He looked upwards and whispered: 'No sooner said than done.'

Darts would just have to wait until the world was happy. Anyway, there should be a chance of a few 'arrers' in the club once in a while.

Shaking off a sudden desire to start smoking again, he closed the fixtures book with a sigh of regret and went down to greet Pimple and Rose.

#######

THE AUTHOR

Peter Scott grew up in post war austerity Britain and joined the RAF in his late teens.

His first posting to Kenya sparked an interest in mountaineering and the beauty of the natural world, but it also acquainted him with the cruelty and selfishness of our own species.

Later, as an aircraft maintenance engineer in Africa and the Middle East, he could see how poverty and environmental destruction frequently went hand in hand with rapidly growing human populations.

Now married and settled in Suffolk he dismally concludes that his own precious island will struggle to be a green and pleasant land as it attempts to cater for a population heading towards seventy million and beyond.

Apart from being a general misery, he enjoys playing jazz clarinet and sax; ranting on the BBC, and writing.

Made in the USA
Charleston, SC
07 June 2016